WRITE ME HOME

Crystal Walton

Impact Editions, LLC
Chesapeake, VA

Impact Editions, LLC
www.crystal-walton.com

This is a work of fiction. Names, characters, places, and incidents are a product of the author's imagination. Locales and public names are sometimes used for atmospheric purposes. Any resemblance to actual people, living or dead, or to businesses, companies, events, institutions, or locales is completely coincidental.

Book Layout ©2013 BookDesignTemplates.com

Cover Design ©2016 Victorine Lieske

Author Photo by Charity Mack

Write Me Home/ Crystal Walton

ISBN 978-0-9862882-6-5

Library of Congress Control Number:

Vow

Of all the places to spend one of the last weekends of his senior year, Ethan DeLuca had to be here. The stench alone was enough to drill resentment into his bones.

If Izzy hadn't begged Dad to let her come along on this trip, Ethan would be at home in the mountains instead of circling around the Bronx in their beat-up VW station wagon right now. But someone had to look out for her.

A cabdriver passed them with his hand out the window, shouting something Ethan couldn't hear over the rest of New York City's nightlife. Biting back a response, he gripped the steering wheel and turned onto yet another side street. He might've been able to find his way to his uncle's place if the blocks didn't all look identical.

A group of guys on the corner, passing something between them, stared him down until they faded out of his headlights.

"You could stop and ask for directions, you know," Isabella said.

He cut a glance across the seats. *From the local drug cartel? How 'bout, no.*

The engine grumbled as he let off the clutch. "I've got this."

"Sure you do." Arms crossed, she twisted in the raggedy bucket seat to face him. "We left Broadway like an hour ago. I mean, it's cool with me. The more we get to see, the better." She pointed at the steam rising from an approaching man-hole. "Isn't it the flyest?"

Flyest? Trying not to laugh, Ethan inched the car between the garbage cans lining the narrow street. His ten-year-old sister—a city girl at heart, trapped in a country life. At least she'd finally gotten to see her first Broadway show. As much as he didn't want to admit it, her enthusiasm was contagious.

As usual.

She folded the end of her seatbelt back and forth. "Wish Mom could've come."

The disappointment in her voice weighed on him. If her vivacious love of life hadn't shown Mom and Dad there was more to live for than work, nothing would.

He reached across the console and rubbed the top of her hair. "Someone had to stay behind to keep an eye on Nonna."

She ducked out from under his hand, grabbed it with both of hers, and kept it close. Rather than say what they both knew, she simply held on while staring out the window.

"Thanks for bringing me, Ethan." She turned. "For real. It's been like the best day ever."

Her untamable smile siphoned out every drop of his re-sentment for being here. Until he caught a whiff of an all-too-familiar smell. A white cloud seeped in as he tilted the vent toward his face. "Don't tell me." He turned the air off, but overheated coolant vapors kept pouring in.

The car stalled out, power steering lost. Ethan muscled the wheel far enough to the right to veer the car alongside a brick building before it died completely.

He cranked the ignition. "C'mon, baby. Don't do this to me. Not here."

Isabella pulled the front of her shirt over her nose.

As regularly as the stupid car overheated, they should've both been used to the odor. Then again, they didn't usually have sewer fumes and overflowing trashcans joining the mix.

Ethan stifled the words trekking up his throat and reached behind his seat for the jug of antifreeze they always stashed in the back. Against the force of his pull, the weightless container nearly hit the ceiling. "Are you kidding me?"

"What?" Isabella swiped it from him, unscrewed the lid, and eyed inside it as though expecting to prove him wrong. The empty bottle sank to her lap.

After traveling two and a half hours yesterday, it hadn't crossed Dad's mind to refill the spare coolant? He slammed his palm against the steering wheel, this time letting the words spew out.

Izzy shoved him with the jug. "Hey, there are a few drops left in here. Don't make me pour them over you, hothead."

Her slanted grin almost garnered one out of him. Wasn't like it was the first time they'd been stuck figuring their way out of some mess. Or an *adventure*, as she called them. After as much time as they'd spent together, her optimistic outlook should've worn off on him by now.

She tried to unclip her seatbelt buckle. Brow furrowed, she pushed and tugged. "Little help here."

He squelched a laugh at her expression while shooing her hands away to take over. Man, he had to use brute force to get the blasted thing open.

Freed, she practically climbed into his seat.

"What are you doing?"

She hooked a thumb over her shoulder at the brick wall. "You barricaded me in."

He hadn't exactly planned that, but now that she mentioned it . . . "For your own safety." He waved her back into her own seat and reached for the door handle. "Stay here."

The door didn't budge. Leaning his shoulder into the panel, he rammed it open. Piece of junk car. He swung it closed, turned his back to the wind tunneling between the buildings, and scanned the area. Nothing like breaking down in the middle of a shady alleyway.

Yelling came from the far corner of the street. Through the haze of smoke, he caught enough to see a girl in a dress, waving her arms around at a guy. Probably a date gone bad. The dude turned and lit up a cigarette like he was blowing off whatever she was saying. Creep.

She shoved him, and he grabbed her wrists. Her wince shot up the street, driving straight into Ethan's chest. He had to ground his feet to keep from intervening. Izzy was his only priority. He released his balled-up fists. Getting into a fight with a stranger wasn't going to get Izzy home safely.

She poked her head out the window. "We should help her."

Of course she'd notice. "Not our business."

"What does that matter?" Eyes full of compassion blinked up at him.

She'd always been valiant—naive, maybe, but brave. He ruffled her hair again. "Easy there, Powerpuff Girl. We don't need to get involved in other people's drama right now."

Huffing, she slumped back in the seat.

He rounded the front bumper and forced his attention away from the couple. The second he propped open the hood, a white cloud of hot steam oozed from the engine and blew into his face. He and Dad were definitely gonna have words about this tonight. As soon as he came up with a way to get them out of here.

If they were back in the Catskills, he would've approached one of the apartments and asked to fill up the jug with water. But here? He valued his life too much to dare knocking on one of these rundown doors. No telling who'd answer.

The arguing from down the way turned into a full-on shouting match. If the jerk ended up hitting that girl, so help him. . . .

He left the hood up to block Izzy's view, turned, and stumbled straight into someone. A hunched-over man dropped a metal can to the ground. Gasoline sprayed everywhere, dousing the bottom of Ethan's jeans, along with most of the engine and the pavement alongside them.

Wow. The night just couldn't get any better. At least a gas station must be nearby.

A grimace of stained and missing teeth glared at him. "You gonna pay for that, laddy?" he spouted off in a Scottish accent.

Ahead, a Pit Bull chained to a link fence barked at them.

Ethan wiped off his pant legs. "Excuse me?"

"Me gas. I just filled 'er up." He waved toward a push mower on a tiny patch of grass beside the dog. "How am I supposed to mow?"

He had to be joking. All the dog had to do was pee on that square of grass a total of three times, and the entire "lawn" would be dead anyway.

Cupping his back with one hand, the old man bent over for the can.

Ethan stopped him and picked it up instead. "I'll tell ya what. If you watch my car while I run up to the station, I'll replenish your gas. Deal?"

He eyed the car. "No one's gonna mess with that heap of junk, laddy."

Couldn't argue with him, there. Still, it'd make him feel better.

"Deal or not?"

The man shifted his beret over his white hair as he surveyed the street. "All right, but make it quick. The Mrs. will be wondering where I am."

"Fair enough. Give me a minute." He set the can beside the driver's side and anchored his feet to open the door.

Motioning Isabella back into her seat, he climbed in. "Listen, I need you to stay here while I run to the gas station." He rolled up the window and stretched behind him to make sure the back doors were locked. With the front hood still up, hopefully most people wouldn't notice her inside.

"Why can't I come with you?"

"This isn't the time or place to be parading down the streets. You'll be safer here." He leaned over and buckled her in. Now she definitely wasn't going anywhere.

"Ethan."

"For your own safety, remember?"

Her face turned a shade of red he knew better than to comment on.

"Ten minutes, tops. Promise." He snagged her book bag from the back and set it in her lap. "I want you to put on your headphones, listen to the CD we just bought, and daydream about being on Broadway, okay?"

Still tight-lipped, she glared his way as she unzipped her bag. "Fine. But the only thing I'm daydreaming about is how I'm gonna take you down when you get back."

He rolled his eyes but gave in to a smile. "You wish."

She swung her pack at him.

Catching it in the gut, he laughed and leaned over to kiss her head. "Don't open this door for anyone."

"Like I could even if I wanted to."

True. Maybe the old clunker still had a few perks.

Outside, he gave the door an extra shove for good measure and turned toward the old man again. "Which way is the station?"

He extended a shaky hand behind them. "At the end of the street, make a left. It'll be on your right, just past the subway entrance."

"Got it." Ethan grabbed the gas can from the ground and glanced up ahead. A third person had joined the couple's argument. Great. A hostile love triangle. What was this, a soap opera? If Izzy kept her headphones on, maybe she wouldn't notice. With any luck, she'd end up blocking out this whole night other than the show.

He jogged down the road with the wind at his back. Other than a few wind chimes stirring, the latter half of the street had fallen still. Why wasn't that as comforting as it should've been?

Every strike against the pavement fueled his frustration with Dad. Staying with Uncle Tony in his dump-of-an-apartment might've cut it for most of his business trips, but he could've shelled out the cash for a hotel in a better part of town after agreeing to bring Izzy this time.

Around the corner, the lighted Shell sign beamed like a halo. He ran the rest of the way, paid at the pump to fill the can, and whisked inside for the antifreeze.

With both hands full now, he hustled back as fast as he could. Until he turned the corner.

Flames consuming the end of the street sent a wall of thick smoke pummeling through him. The containers slipped from his grasp. He sprinted for the car. "Izzy!"

The old man groped his way through the haze, wheezing. "Everything was fine a second ago. I . . . I don't know what happened."

A young guy, looking over his shoulder, ran smack into Ethan. Had to be the punk from earlier. Ethan grabbed his shirt, staring him over. Blood seeped from a cut above a busted lip, probably from where the girl had socked him.

The guy's dark eyes latched on to his until an apartment door behind them opened. As soon as Ethan turned, the guy pushed away and darted down the street.

Sparks shot off the engine. Ethan jumped backward with his arm shielding his eyes. His focus rebounded between the car and the guy fading from view. Out of time, he lunged toward the Scotsman instead. It didn't matter how the fire had started. Only that he got them all out of there. He clutched the old man by the wrists and pulled him away from the scene. "Go call 911. Now."

He lifted his collar over his nose and forced his hands to steady long enough to get the right key into the lock. A smoky fog coated the windows, but enough of a view showed Isabella leaning into the door panel, probably passed out from the carbon monoxide. A loud pop sprayed the ground in another round of sparks.

Ethan flinched but didn't back off. The hot metal handle seared into his skin as he heaved. Yelling through the pain, he grounded his heels and pulled harder. Nothing.

He banged his fist into the trim. "C'mon."

Windows in surrounding buildings lit up. A crowd grew along the street corner as approaching sirens blared.

Ethan dashed around, scouring the road for something—anything—to help. He spotted a metal trashcan and bolted to the curb and back. "Hang on, Izzy." He held his breath, prayed the glass wouldn't hurt her, and rammed the can into the window.

Shards splintered in every direction, nicking his face and arms. Smoke billowed from inside and burned his lungs. He chucked the can. Flames roared from the engine but didn't stop him. He shimmied through the window against the jagged glass scraping across his torso until he reached Isabella. Adrenaline surging, he wrenched the seatbelt off her.

"Over here," a firefighter yelled.

Ethan cradled Izzy in his arms and kicked the door with every ounce of strength he had left. The guy prying it open from the other side stumbled backward as it flew open on a busted hinge.

Ethan sprang out of the car and carried Izzy far enough down the road to lay her out of harm's way. Hands shaky, he turned her chin and hunched over to listen for breathing.

A flurry of commotion soared around him. Lights flashing. Hoses unwinding. Voices clashing with sirens. But nothing eclipsed the piercing silence coming from Isabella's nose. How long had she gone without air?

The question quaked through his body.

Time stalled. Overspray from the fire truck soaked into his scorched skin.

He cupped the back of her head. "Iz? Don't do this. You gotta fight for me." Stares from bystanders bore into him, but no one moved. "Please. Somebody help her."

The same fireman from earlier wedged through the crowd and dropped to his knees. He discarded his helmet, removed his mask, and leaned an ear over Isabella's mouth. With one hand laced over the other, he began chest compressions, stopping every few beats to transfer his breath to her.

Ethan wiped his face on his shirtsleeve, leaving behind a stain of blood and soot.

An ambulance pulled up, and two paramedics jogged to their side. The fireman scooted out of their way. "No pulse. Unresponsive," he said as they took over administering CPR.

One lodged a tube down her throat and attached a bag to the end. A third tried to help Ethan to his feet, but he pushed him back. "I'm fine."

"You need to be examined."

"I need to stay with my sister."

The EMT moved in front of him and blocked his view. "The best thing you can do for her right now is to get yourself treated."

Another team of paramedics rushed to the scene. Two EMTs steered him to the ambulance's bumper and flashed lights in his eyes while taking his blood pressure. He peered around them.

One of the others flagged the rest away from Isabella's motionless body. "Clear."

A jolt struck the air and latched on to every nerve ending in Ethan's body. "What's happening? What are they doing?"

"All they can." A female EMT rested a hand on his forearm. Though soothing, her empathetic eyes weren't enough to calm him. Nothing would be until he heard his sister breathe again.

As EMTs and firefighters took control of the scene, he stayed trapped in the ambulance, vowing he'd never be this helpless again.

CHAPTER ONE

Unearthed

Ten Years Later

E than rubbed a hand towel over his face and tossed it on the passenger seat while glancing at the speedometer. Deputy Harris wouldn't pull him over. He knew the reason Ethan was back in this forsaken place. Same as the whole town probably knew. How could he have been the last to get word?

The early morning sun beat against his neck, driving aggravation deeper into his pores. Yeah, he'd been the one to walk out five years ago. That didn't mean Mom could cut him off from family affairs. This was a low blow. Even for her.

The wheels hugged the road above the creek while hints of honeysuckles and mowed grass breezed through his topless Jeep Wrangler. Why did his hometown have to smell this good?

If he hadn't just driven three hours straight from an all-nighter at the fire station, he might've dared to let himself enjoy the ride. Most of upstate New York had a similar feel, but nothing beat summers in the Catskills. Beauty was one thing he couldn't fault Haven's Creek for having.

The single grocery mart within twenty miles passed on his right, followed by the rundown sign for Camp *Misneach* on his left. He kept driving. Past the Morrison farm, past a 1960s version of an Exxon gas station, and down two curvy side roads until his tires crunched over the gravel driveway leading to his grandma's house.

The bits of rock barely outnumbered the memories hitting him dead in the chest. Growing up, this had been a second home for him and Isabella. He braked in front of the house and cut off that train of thought along with the engine. Even after ten years, he still couldn't think about losing her.

He shut the Jeep door behind him, drew in a breath, and stared at the porch his grandpa had made with his own hands. The trouble with trying to construct a new life? You can't unearth the original foundation.

Aside from a single path that stopped halfway across the yard, the grass looked like it hadn't been mowed in weeks. He skipped both steps leading up to the front door where the wooden beams whined under his heavy boots.

"You'll never be able to sneak up on someone, making all that racket," Nonna called from inside.

Well, at least she was feeling like herself.

He let himself in. The trademark aroma of Italian roasted coffee greeted him right before her longhaired dachshund stormed the entryway. Teeth bared, the dog crouched and growled at his boots. Ethan squatted to rub her fluffy ears. "It's okay, Lady. Remember me?"

"She might if you ever came to visit."

As if to accentuate Nonna's point, Lady turned and scurried toward her with her nails clinking against the floor panels. After receiving a quick pat on the head, she curled up on an oval dog bed scrunched inside the bottom of an old hutch in the hall.

Spoiled dog.

Ethan stopped a foot inside the kitchen. "Nonna, what are you doing?"

She turned and brushed her flour-covered hands on her apron. "What does it look like I'm doing? I'm making pasta."

Of course she was. What else would she be doing after just having a heart attack?

She looked him up and down, taking in the full scope of the station gear he hadn't had a chance to change out of yet. He lowered his suspenders to his sides and flicked a glance toward the bathroom. A quick wash-up probably wasn't out of order.

Arms crossed, she continued to stare. Wiry strands of peppered hair strayed from a bun as round as each of her cheeks. Even at only four foot eleven, she could pass for an NFL linebacker when she had that look in her eye. "You can take those boots off, mister. There's no fire to put out here, and you missed the ambulance days ago."

Thanks to Mom not telling him.

Swallowing the retort, he ambled over, curled an arm around her shoulders, and kissed the top of her head. "It's good to see you, too."

She gave his waist a squeeze. "Don't they feed you at that fire station of yours?"

"I get plenty to eat, Nonna."

"Mm hmm. Looks to me like they're short on razors, too."

He ran the backs of his fingers over his cheekbone. He was so used to the stubble, he forgot she probably wouldn't be. He knelt to unlace his boots, lugged them off, and set them alongside the hutch. "Shouldn't you be taking it easy?"

She waved off his concern. "Doctors overreact."

He leaned against the counter and picked a handful of grapes from a fruit bowl beside the set of canisters she'd had since he was a kid. "I hear doctors might know what they're talking about. Kinda goes with the whole decade-of-training thing."

Nonna smoothed the dough with her rolling pin. "A lot of good it did this one. That boy doesn't know what he's talking about. I'm as healthy as an ox."

"An ox with a bad heart?"

She whipped around, rolling pin in hand.

This couldn't be good. Ethan gulped down a grape and backed into the corner by the sink.

She marched right up to him and tapped the pin against his chest. "Don't be using that sass with me, young man. My heart's strong enough to give you a good whipping."

He didn't doubt it. After growing up with her as his second mom, he'd learned never to mess with an Italian grandma. He shoved another grape in his mouth to keep from smiling first.

She tugged him down, released a hearty laugh, and kissed both his cheeks. "Ah, *mio nipote*, I've missed you." She kept her weathered hands on either side of his face. "Thanks for checking on me, but I'm fine, dear."

"Dad said the doc mentioned needing to change your diet." He slanted a glance past her toward the two empty butter wrappers lying beside a mixing bowl.

"Nonsense." She whirled back toward the kitchen island and fluttered a hand at the basement door. "Nothing a little red wine can't cure."

Obviously, the heart attack hadn't affected her stubborn genes.

"Diet. Humph. Next thing you know, they'll be trying to ship me off to one of those retirement homes."

Ethan didn't envy anyone who'd dare to try. This wasn't only a house. It was her heritage. Built by her husband, nurtured with her own hands. She'd make sure she took her last breath here. He was positive of that much.

The knife's blade quivered as she strained to cut a straight line down the dough. She'd aged more than he'd expected. How much time did he have left with her? His throat tightened. She was right. He should've visited more often.

He dusted the flour her rolling pin had left on his shirt, wishing regret were as easy to shake off, and opened the fridge for some milk. Near-empty shelves stared back at him. He settled for a glass of water and joined her at the island. "Has Mom been by?" The least she could've done was bring her own mother groceries.

Nonna scooped up a series of noodles with the flat side of her knife and slid them into a stainless steel pot. "You know she's busy, dear. All that city council stuff."

Was that supposed to be justification? The veins on the top of his hands rose.

She lifted the pot by both handles and almost toppled over.

Ethan rounded the island in time to catch it. "Here. Let me." Whether or not she wanted to admit it, she needed someone here to help her.

Beside him at the counter, she withdrew two mugs from a cabinet and curled both unsteady hands around the coffee pot handle as she poured. He accepted the coffee while swallowing the disappointment that it wasn't her famous espresso instead. But then she'd be drinking it, too, and that was probably the last thing her heart needed.

Speaking of which, he'd better come up with a way to sneak her espresso machine out of here when she wasn't looking.

"You should see your mama while you're here."

His sip of coffee choked halfway down. He held his mug away and turned to cough. "That's . . . not . . . happening," he said between wheezes.

Nonna caught his gaze and didn't let go. "She's *tua madre,* Ethan."

"And you're hers. Apparently, that doesn't mean much in this family."

She clanked her mug against the counter and muttered something in Italian.

Lady flung her head up and barked.

Nonna fanned a dishtowel at her. "Oh, stop your yapping." She fixed a glare on Ethan again. "Neither of you can change the past. Now's all you have. It's time you two settle this rubbish. Enough is enough."

Except that'd require Mom actually speaking to him first.

He led her to one of the bar stools on the other side of the island before her blood pressure skyrocketed. He'd come to help, not tax her heart even more. "Let's not talk about that right now. Why don't you let me pick up some groceries for you? I'll make you a healthy lunch, and we can sit out back and visit awhile. Okay?"

"Don't turn those baby blues on me, young man. You may have your Nonno's eyes, but that doesn't mean I have to fall for them."

He laughed but didn't relent on his hopeful expression.

She crossed her arms above her round belly. "Fine. But don't be coming back here with any of that cardboard stuff."

He kissed her cheek. "Wouldn't dream of it." Though, getting her to cut back on butter and cheese might be a challenge. He swiped his boots from the floor and nodded at the dog. "Guard the house while I'm gone."

Lady stretched her paws off the bed and yawned.

Classic.

Outside, the overgrown grass stole his attention. He caught the door before it closed. "Doesn't the Miller boy mow your grass for you?"

"Stopped last month," she said on her way down the hall. "He's heading off to college."

Already? "Didn't he just start high school?"

"Four years ago." She patted his arm. "The world carried on after you left."

Maybe for some people.

Nonna leaned into the trim while Lady rubbed against her feet. "Camp *Misneach* closed, too. About a year ago, after Colin died."

"I'm sorry to hear that."

"He was a good man." She kept her gaze on the porch, brow furrowed. "I hear his granddaughter's taking over the place."

"Really?" That was quite the undertaking. "She must be sharp."

"I reckon she is."

Or incredibly naive. Either way, not his business. Ethan looked over the yard again. "Is there gas for the mower?"

"Last time I checked."

He paused mid-turn, gaze locked on the path of half-mowed grass. "Wait a sec. Tell me you didn't try to mow on your own."

She shrugged. "I've been taking care of this place since Nonno died."

Which was fine twenty years ago, but now? No wonder she'd had a heart attack. "Nonna—"

"Hurry on, now. We'll be waiting." She prodded Lady back with her foot. "Make sure you bring back *whole* milk, too. None of that watery kind."

Shaking his head, Ethan jogged to his Jeep. Arguing with her had never gotten him anywhere. He tossed his boots into the back, hopped in, and fished around the floorboard behind the seats for a pair of flip-flops until his pinky finger grazed one. He unburied the other and clapped them together over the window. Good ole Hurleys. They'd covered a lot of ground.

He surveyed the jungle-of-a-yard again as he traded his balled-up socks for the flip-flops. Hopefully, they had a little tread left on them. He had a feeling they were going to need it.

Back on the road, he checked the clock—7:30 a.m. With any luck, it was still early enough on a Friday to avoid running into anyone. He slid his sunglasses on and extended an arm into the cool air rolling off the mountainside, but the peacefulness clashed against a gnawing unrest eating at him.

A three-hour commute was too long to check on Nonna every day. But what was he supposed to do? Move back here? The thought sawed into his gut with his seatbelt. He'd cut ties with this town at his first chance. Left memories buried under ashes—where they were supposed to stay.

He flipped on his blinker, turned into Fran's Grocer, and coasted into a parking spot. The Jeep idled, but his brain kicked into overdrive. Could he really move back home? Where would he live? No way Nonna'd let him crash at her place. She'd insist she didn't need a babysitter.

And what about work? The station? He couldn't just drop everything in Auburn and pick things back up here as if he'd never left. There was nothing here for him.

Except Nonna.

The image of her struggling in the kitchen tore into him. He'd expected her stubborn streak. It was in her bones. But her bite didn't compensate for the toll her age was taking on her body. At the very least, she needed time to recuperate from the heart attack.

If she wouldn't follow the doctor's orders on her own, what other choice did she leave him but to step in? Mom could look the other way if she wanted, but he wasn't going to let someone he loved down. Not this time.

Exhaling, he turned the keys in the ignition and glanced up to meet Fran's wide eyes staring at him from behind the cash register inside the mart. The town busy body. Perfect. So much for flying under the radar. If he moved back here, he'd have a whole lot worse than local gossip to face.

He climbed out of the Jeep and slid his sunglasses to his head. "Man up, DeLuca. This isn't your first fire to conquer."

CHAPTER TWO

Adventure

Cassidy McAdams turned off the air conditioning in her Passat and cracked the window instead. She'd forgotten how cool mornings got in the Catskills. Just like she'd forgotten the way these hills made her stomach drop. Her smile faded. After not coming back for ten years, what else did she expect? Would she even still recognize the camp?

Steadying the wheel with her knee, she tugged a band from her wrist and whirled her hair up into a ponytail. The turnoff was around here somewhere. She eased off the gas pedal at the sound of her tires screeching. Whoa, that curve came up fast. Her cat moaned from the back seat.

"Sorry, Jax." Squinting, she scoured the left side of the road for the wooden sign. "There." She braked a car-length in front of it and adjusted the sunglasses that'd slid down her face. With her arm stretched across the back of the passenger seat, she glanced at the cat carrier before reversing. "Guess we found our first repair to make, huh, buddy?"

Her Passat rocked from pothole to pothole up the long, gravel driveway. At the top, she pulled into the parking spot closest to the main building, snagged a clipboard from her briefcase in the floorboard, and jotted down her first notes.

1. Hedge shrubs. 2. Mend welcome sign. 3. Fix potholes.

Something told her one notepad wasn't going to be enough. She clicked her pen in and out against her chin while surveying the old building from behind the windshield.

4. Order a pack of legal pads.

With the clipboard stashed under her arm, she clambered out of the car and into a breeze blowing down the hill. Amazing how the scent of hay could trigger memories she hadn't thought about in ages. Had the place shrunk, or was it just her?

A panoramic glance around the empty basketball court, closed-up canteen, and neglected fields colored over her childhood memories with the stain of loss. It was as if Grandpa had taken the heart of the camp with him when he passed.

Maybe it was better that way.

She pulled out Jax's carrier, stuck a finger through the crate, and rubbed the line drawn down the middle of his face—orange on one side, white on the other. "You ready for this?"

Jax cowered in the back corner.

Cass laughed. "Me neither." She blew a loose curl from her eyes and wrenched her bags' straps up her shoulder. Ready or not, she'd already signed the papers.

She scrambled up the wooden steps and across the deck to the screen door. One touch to the sun-scorched handle sent the door flying open. "Dang it." She caught the screen with her sandal while flapping her hand in the air. Jeez, she needed an oven mitt to touch that thing.

After hopping to resituate her bags, she transferred the clipboard to her teeth and fished for the keys in her purse. With a good push, the front door welcomed her into the mildew-scented hallway. Lovely.

The screen slammed into her ankle and knocked the clipboard to the floor, followed by her bags. She grabbed the banister and bit her knuckle to keep from swearing.

A peek over her shoulder brought a peeled-back, white flap of skin hanging under a stinging gash into view. Just perfect. She glared around the entryway. "Yeah, nice to see you, too," she called out to the empty building.

She set the cat carrier down and squeezed open the latch. Jax bolted out, but she caught his collar and picked him up. "No getting lost. You hear me?" She kissed his head. The second she let him down, he tore off down the hall. "And no eating any vermin, either," she yelled.

Spiders, on the other hand, were fair game. She wiped the dust left from the banister off her hand. One thing was for sure. She had to clean up her ankle before diving into anything.

With her purse and toiletry bag in tow, she limped to the back bedroom. Another train of memories stopped her just inside the doorway. She slid her bags onto the dresser and smiled at the 1970s décor. Grandpa'd refused to upgrade. For posterity, he'd said.

Had he always planned to leave the camp to her? Not that she blamed him for bypassing his own son. The corporate world would always be more important to Dad than anything family related. And yeah, she'd loved coming up two weeks each summer as a kid, but live here? In the mountains? She'd be lost trying to live country life without Grandpa around.

She blinked away the unsolicited rise of emotion. It was a nonissue, anyway. She was here on business, plain and simple. Get the facility up to standard, get the books out of the red, and sell the place. She'd be back to her life in the city in a few months. Her last two consulting jobs should tie her over till then. As long as she made enough profit to pay off Mom's mortgage on the flower shop, it'd be fine. Grandpa had always thought of Mom as his own daughter. He'd want the best for her, wouldn't he?

Her heart sank as she looked around at what he'd entrusted to her. Nice try. It'd crush him to know she planned to sell, but what was she supposed to do? She'd run out of options.

Brushing back the strands refusing to stay in her ponytail, she boxed out the thought. *It's business, Cass. Don't make it personal.*

She winced as soon as she put pressure on her heel. Nothing like pain to keep her focused. At least some things in life never changed.

She rummaged through her bag for a bar of soap and plodded gingerly toward the bathroom in the corner. One foot inside, and she repressed a gag. So much for thinking the well water's rotten egg stench might've diminished with time. And really, when was the last time this place saw a mop? Or better yet, a magic eraser?

Okay, change of plans. First order of business: Disinfect the bathroom.

Gravel rumbled outside the window, along with a series of honks that could only mean one thing. *Ti.* Smiling ear to ear, Cass scurried out as fast as her ankle would let her.

A canary yellow car about the size of a matchbox model glided into the space beside her Passat. Ti had barely pulled the keys from the ignition before jumping out. She flung her arms around Cass's neck, a dozen bracelets clinking together. "Eeee! Girl, I've missed you so much." She bobbed up and down like they were twelve again instead of twenty-seven.

Cass untangled herself from Ti's necklaces. "I can't believe you actually came."

She stepped back, chin cocked. "And miss the chance to refurbish our childhood camp? You kidding me? Where else would I be right now?"

A million answers could've filled in the blank, but Cass wasn't about to give her any ideas. She nodded behind her. "Enterprise is renting out smart cars now?"

Ti turned. "I bought it when I flew into LaGuardia. Got hooked on them in London—the gas mileage is totally worth it." She shrugged. "I'll sell it when I leave."

Which would be in about ten days, knowing Ti. At least she was here now. A lecture on impulsive buying habits could wait for later. Cass lifted a hand to the loose strands of hair dangling from under Ti's edgy newsboy cap. "Brown again?"

Ti's grin slanted. She pulled her hat off, shook out her hair, and ran her fingers all the way down to bright blond tips. "Can't be without *some* blond."

"Of course not."

"Hey, not all of us are blessed with your fiery red curls, chica."

Giving in to her smile, Cass took in the sight of her best friend. It didn't matter what color she dyed her hair. Modeling in Europe for a year seemed to have only fueled her creative beauty. Had it really been that long since she'd seen her last?

A darkish purple mark on her upper arm caught Cass's eye.

Ti flicked a glance at the bruise and covered it with her hand.

Cass choked back the comment she wanted to make. "How's Murray?"

Fiddling with the hem of her sundress, Ti kept her gaze on the gravel. "He's living it up on a photo shoot in Paris."

"You didn't go with him?"

"Wasn't invited." She fit her hat back on and detangled her necklaces.

How many loser boyfriends would it take for Ti to see she deserved better? "Why do you stay with him?"

"Because I'm me."

"Ti—"

"Ooh, we have our own well?" She whirled around, obviously done with this conversation. Same old Ti. Deflecting.

She skipped up the hill and leaned over the stones as if looking for a wish she'd lost inside it. "How did I forgot about this?" She turned, face glistening in the sunlight. "We can plant our own gardens, grow organic produce."

"Don't go getting all Woodstock on me, girl. It's a camp, not a commune." Cass shucked off her jean jacket and lowered her shades to block the sunlight creeping over the treetops.

"But wouldn't it be cool if it were?" Ti bobbed her brows as she sauntered back through the field to the parking lot. "On our own again. The two of us against the world. Like old times." She hooked an arm around Cass's shoulders. "Oh, c'mon. Where's your sense of adventure?"

Adventure? "You do realize where we are, right? In the middle of the mountains. No Starbucks within fifty miles."

One blink. Two. "Okay, that's just tragic." She let go and breathed in. "Guess we'll have to live off fresh air."

"Fresh air and utter silence." Cass set her hands on her hips. "No thrilling city life. What are you going to do for entertainment?"

Ti sprawled her arms to her sides, faced the sky, and twirled. "Fly." At her feet, a dozen dandelion heads released seeds into the air like a hundred wishes she could've added to the well. She stopped mid-spin. "Oh, by the way, do you have a razor I can borrow? After that eight-hour flight from London and then the haul up here, I'm *way* overdue for a bath."

"Um, you might not want to shower before we clean the bathroom."

Already headed to her trunk, Ti looked behind her. "What do you think the creek is for?"

Cass shook her head without a response.

While Ti toted a pink towel down the driveway toward the creek, Cass lugged two crates of cleaning supplies inside and set them beside the bathroom. She slipped off her wedge sandals and tied a folded-up bandana over her cut ankle, careful not to touch it.

With a pair of rubber gloves, a rag, and a can of Scrubbing Bubbles, she got down on her knees to tackle a corner at a time. One of them had to get to work.

The disinfectant fumes joined the sulfur odor assaulting her nose. She pinned her shirt over her face as best she could while scrubbing, but the smell kept penetrating, along with nonstop questions.

Had she made a mistake taking this on? They needed the money from the sale. Mom would lose everything if the flower shop closed. It was her lifeline—past and future. Same way this place had been for Grandpa. If the banks didn't already have liens on both properties, Cass might've had time to find an opportunity with a quicker return on investment so she could pay off the debt. Maybe would've been able to keep both places.

Something stirred from around the corner. She froze, lowered her shirt. "Hello?"

Jax scurried to the bathroom door and meowed.

Cass's pulse slowed. "There you are. Did you de-critter the house for me?"

He rubbed his cheek along the trim, moseyed into the bathroom, and brushed against her knee. He looked up at her with round, expectant eyes as if she hadn't fed him in weeks instead of hours. Well, at least that meant he probably hadn't eaten any mice. She shuddered at the thought. No telling what they'd find in this place.

She scratched his neck. "What do you think, Jax? Am I over my head here?"

He stared at the ceiling behind her. The hair on his back puffed out, his tail twice its normal size. He crouched, backed up, and hissed.

A loud *thud* echoed off the tub and sent adrenaline spiking. Clutching the spray can, she braced herself for whatever was behind them and turned. Something soared straight at her and knocked the can from her hands. Cornered in the tiny bathroom, all she could do was scream.

CHAPTER THREE

Small Towns

Ethan tossed his sweatshirt over the plastic grocery bags in the Jeep's floorboard to keep them from rattling in the wind. Other than a few probing questions, which he'd managed to evade, the run-in with Fran at the mart hadn't been nearly as bad as he'd expected. Maybe Nonna was right about life moving on since he left.

He shifted into third gear and rounded the tree-lined curve. Down the cliff, something bright pink moved by the giant rocks. Was someone bathing in the creek? He faced the road and shook his head. Nah. Couldn't be.

A distant scream shuddered through the trees on his left. In a trained reflex, he jerked the wheel toward the sound and gunned his Jeep up the driveway.

Another series of screams rang from the building. Adrenaline hammering, Ethan darted inside toward rustling in one of the back rooms. He swiped a lamp off the dresser as he blew through the doorway.

A multi-colored cat hissed at him from under a chair right before a girl skittered out of the bathroom, arms flailing around a nest of fiery red hair.

Ethan caught her by the elbow. "Easy, there. You okay?" Still clutching the lamp in one hand, he peered behind her into a bathroom covered in drywall dust, from the looks of it.

She stiffened and peeked through the tangled curls covering her face. "Is he gone?"

"Who?"

"The squirrel."

Mouth tipping, he stifled a laugh. "Let me see." He moved around her to take a closer look inside and set the lamp on the floor. "I think you're safe." He pushed the door back and surveyed the damage to the ceiling. The drywall must've rotted and given the animal easy access to claw his way in. "But you probably want to get that hole patched up pronto." He turned. "At least before the next . . ."

Armed with the lamp-turned-weapon, she blocked the doorway, eyeing him as if he'd been the one to attack her instead of the squirrel.

He raised his palms. ". . . rain."

Though only slightly taller than Nonna, she had her determined stance down pat. Her gaze drifted to a piece of crumbled drywall stuck in her hair and shot right back at him. Eyes as green as her cat's all but dared him to comment on her appearance.

She jutted the lamp at him. "Who are you?"

If it weren't for the pink rubber gloves and that cluster of freckles on her nose, she might've pulled off the intimidation look she was obviously going for.

He lowered his hands but failed to conceal a smile. "Ethan DeLuca. I was driving by and heard you scream, so . . ."

"So, you came running to my rescue?" She looked him over.

His station gear. Right. He squeezed the back of his neck. "Guess you could say that. Though, I'm not technically on duty at the moment."

"Small towns," she mumbled while returning the lamp to the dresser. "Someone yells, and the fire department comes running."

What, was she some big city girl or something? Probably from the Bronx, with that thick accent. "Up here, sweetheart, we call it hospitality." Maybe she could take a few lessons.

She shucked off her gloves. "In Queens, it's called breaking and entering."

He held her unrelenting gaze until he cracked. He couldn't help it. The whole scene had to be a joke.

She pinned her hands on her hips. "Is something funny?"

Fighting another laugh, he gestured toward the bathroom. "Uh, yeah. The whole flying squirrel thing. You, waving that lamp around, giving me the third degree for helping. C'mon, you gotta admit. It's kinda funny."

"Helping?"

"Yeah, I—" He sucked in a breath, turned, and sneezed into the crook of his arm. "Excuse me, it's—" Another sneeze folded him in half.

Her forehead creased. "I haven't had a chance to dust yet."

"No, it's the cat." He pointed at the fur ball still cowering under the chair. "I'm allergic."

She sidestepped toward the wall and scooped the cat into a protective hold as if worried he was going to exterminate it or something. Paranoid much?

The dander bag hissed at him again, and she clutched him tighter. Great. Now he had two pairs of fiercely green eyes staring him down. He wasn't about to gamble on whose claws left a deeper sting.

"You might want to get a watchdog instead."

"Jax is a male calico. You know how special that is? And he knows how to spot trouble just fine." She let him down. He took off, stopped in the doorway long enough to shoot a scathing glance at Ethan, and kept trucking down the hall.

He cocked his chin. "Like I said."

Her gaze marched down to his suspenders. "You a dog lover? Let me guess. You have a Dalmatian."

He arched a brow at her. "You're not into stereotypes or anything, are you?"

"Only if they fit."

What was her problem? She didn't know anything about him. Who was she to size him up like he was second class? "From the way I see things, you're in the position of needing some help around here, so you might want to try being cordial to those offering it."

She stretched her little five-foot-two frame as tall as it would go. "I don't need any help."

"Really?" He dipped his head toward the bathroom. "You gonna patch that hole by yourself?"

"Maybe."

Man, she was as strong-willed as Nonna.

The thought practically slapped him upside the head. The girl obviously needed a worker. He needed a room. The camp was less than a mile from Nonna's. So what if he had to live in the same proximity as Crazy Cat Woman. He could hack it for a month or two. Looking out for Nonna was worth any cost.

He rubbed his chin with the back of his hand. "Or maybe you need a handyman."

"Excuse me?"

"How about you let me work a few days a week in exchange for a room." He motioned to the ceiling. "A place this size . . . There's got to be, what, at least six bedrooms upstairs?"

She blinked. "A room."

He nodded.

"You come running into my house uninvited, and now you're asking to live with me?"

Okay, that might've sounded bad, but this wasn't Queens. "Relax, City Girl. I'm just trying to look out for my grandma. She had a heart attack a few days ago and needs me nearby to check up on her. She lives up the road, so staying here will be perfect." Well, almost.

She didn't lower her guarded stare. "Your grandma."

What was with the two-word reiterations? Exhaling, he strained to prevent his eyes from circling toward the ceiling.

"I'm not talking about anything permanent. Just a month or two until she recuperates." He dipped his head. "C'mon, you could use an extra pair of hands around here. Admit it."

Her scowl gave way to the slightest grin. "So, you're a fireman *and* a handyman. You should have your own theme song. Any other superhero traits I should know about?"

"I make a mean lasagna." He flashed his best disarming smile at her.

Someone came through the front door. "Cassidy? Forget needing Starbucks," a girl called on her way down the hall. "That creek will wake you up in a second. The water's freez—" She stopped two steps inside the room, gaze bouncing from Ethan to her friend and back. A slow smile crept up her face. "Whoa. What calendar did you pull this hunk out of?"

Ethan scratched his cheek, fairly certain it'd turned almost as pink as the towel wrapped around the girl's body. So, he *had* seen someone bathing in the creek.

Sighing, the redhead splayed a hand toward him. "Ti, this is . . . Sorry, forgot your name somewhere between the breaking-and-entering routine and your pitch to live with me."

Better than the tough-as-nails routine she was trying to pull. He extended a hand to the lanky brunette. "Ethan DeLuca. The new handyman," he added without glancing in Ice Queen's direction. Maybe with her friend here, she couldn't say no.

The girl adjusted her towel and slipped a soft hand into his. "Treble Russo. Pleasure."

Russo? He angled his chin. "Italian?"

She curled her long hair over her shoulder. "On my dad's side."

He gave a short bow. *"Piacere di conoscerti."*

"Not *that* Italian." Biting her lip, she inched closer. "But you can talk to me in that accent all day."

A gagging noise erupted from the corner but didn't seem to faze Treble. Her focus drifted from City Girl's tousled appearance to the bathroom and back to Ethan. Her face lit up. "Don't move." Humming, she whirled around and flittered out the way she'd come in.

Ethan rubbed the back of his head. "Well, she seems . . ."

"Eccentric?" Cassidy bent to pick up a rag and a can of cleaner. "You'll have to excuse her. She's a little on the outspoken side."

He laughed. "She can blame her Italian genes for that one. Though, I gotta say, I've never met someone named Treble."

"That's because her real name's Trina." She turned, mumbling something. "Just call her by the first letter of her name. You'll be fine." A handkerchief dangled off her ankle as she struggled to walk without a limp toward the bathroom. She bumped into a chair and dropped the cleaning spray.

He swooped down for it, but she cut him off. "I got it."

Would it kill the girl to lower her guard for half a second?

A flash went off from the doorway. They both turned to meet another camera flash. Still in her towel, Ti leaned against the trim, lowered the lens, and shrugged. "Memories."

"You're a photographer?"

"Some days. Other days I'm a painter. A musician. A writer." She sauntered in. "But always a storyteller, capturing and sharing the memories I find." She tipped the camera at him. "I'll be watching you, Calendar Boy. You've got a story to tell."

He backed up. "Um, wow. I'm not sure if I should be flattered, or if I should call the cops."

"That depends. Are they as cute as you are?"

"Okay." Eyes rolling, Cassidy grabbed Ethan's forearm and directed him into the hall. "Time for you to go. We've gotta get back to work."

"What about our arrangement?"

"How about you start with fixing the ceiling. Then we'll talk."

He stopped her around the corner. "And the room?"

"*After* the ceiling."

So, he'd have to prove himself. Fine. Like he hadn't been doing that his whole life.

She hobbled past him. "I'll have a contract ready on Monday."

Contract? Great. What had he gotten himself into?

"Want me to check on that for you?" He met her at the door and motioned with his eyes toward whatever injury she was hiding under that bandana around her ankle.

"You're a medic, too?"

He grinned. "I have some cross training."

"I bet." She opened the door. "I'm capable of taking care of myself."

Directly in front of her, he matched her arrogant gaze and grinned. "I bet."

The screen banged behind him before he reached the steps.

She shuffled onto the deck after him. "Hey, you know how to fix a broken door?"

So, she *did* know how to ask for help. "There ain't much I can't fix, Red." He jogged down the stairs toward his Jeep before she had the chance to give the nickname a new meaning.

He pulled out, turned up the country music station, and saluted as he drove past her. Halfway down the driveway, he stole a glance in the rearview mirror. Still grinning, he stretched an arm out the window and cranked the music. *Welcome to the mountains, sweetheart.*

Red? Good thing a breeze was blowing in from the woods. Cass's boiling cheeks might've caught fire otherwise.

She barreled back inside, not sure which irritated her more—the fact that she needed his help or the fact that he knew she needed it.

Ti almost stumbled into her at the intersection between the two halls. At least she had clothes on now. In a long, flowy sundress, she twirled around and landed an arm across Cass's shoulders. "Okay, I know I said I could live without Starbucks, but tell me you at least have some form of coffee in this place."

Cass cracked a grin before she could stop herself. If nothing else, Ti'd always be a source of amusement. She prodded her forward. She'd deal with drawing up a contract for Mr. Jack of All Trades later. "No telling what we'll find in the kitchen."

Jax brushed against her legs from behind. She glowered at him. "Oh, so you hear the word kitchen and come running.

Where were you when I was trying to defend you earlier, huh?"

He sat on his back paws, squinted, and meowed. That face got her every time. She rubbed his side with her foot. "Cheater." She looked up at Ti and nodded toward the front door. "Would you run to my car and grab the paper bag behind the driver's seat for me? It has Jax's food and some other groceries in it." She raised a brow. "Including coffee."

"You said the magic word." Ti winked and made a beeline for the deck.

Jax bolted ahead of Cass into the dark room. "Now you decide to be fearless." She flipped on the light switch and pinched her lips to keep from laughing. How was it possible that they never upgraded this place?

Scenes from the weeks she'd worked as a dishwasher flooded in with each section of the kitchen she faced. The walk-in freezer, the breakfast nook with giant steel pots hanging on the wall, the industrial dishwasher beside the three-part sink system with a stack of green crates beneath it.

She ran a hand along the faded-yellow countertop. The longer she took it all in, the more she couldn't picture it looking any different.

Ti whisked in and set the bag on the counter. Jax stretched his front paws up the cabinets and meowed again. She rubbed his head. "I'll feed Jax before he dies from starvation. You find the coffeemaker."

"Deal."

After fishing through two bottom cabinets, Cass pulled out an ancient coffeepot that looked as stained as the dark wood paneling on the walls. "Not sure we want to use this sucker."

Ti examined it. "Hey, if it brews coffee, it's all good."

Hard to argue with that. At least, for the moment. She added the grounds and bottled water, plugged it in, and jumped back. No sparks. That was a good sign. She renumbered the other items on her clipboard and added a line at the top.

1. Pick up a new coffeepot.

Even in the middle of nowhere, a girl has to have her priorities.

Ti hoisted herself onto the counter. "I think I might need to borrow Jax later."

Cass glanced from her grocery list toward her calico, dropping a mouthful of dry food beside his bowl. "Borrow him?"

"If I chase him up a tree, surely McDreamy will come to my aid."

Cass chugged her bottle of water before she gagged. "Leave my cat out of your love life."

She bobbed her brows. "Who said anything about love?"

Oh, brother. They were perfect for each other. Swagger and all.

"Just don't distract him from work." She scoured the top cabinets for a mug. She needed coffee. Fast. Sawdust dumped out of the third cabinet she tried. That couldn't be good. She ran her fingers along the chewed-up shelf. Mice? Nothing her new handyman couldn't fix. No doubt, he was an exterminator on the side.

She wrenched open the last door by the fridge. Mugs. Finally. She pulled one down and washed it twice before grabbing the coffeepot. Why did he have to be so . . . irritating? With his impossible-to-ignore dimples. And those eyes. She spun around. "What kind of Italian has eyes that blue?"

Ti stretched out her crossed ankles and batted her own lovely blues. "The sexy kind."

"You don't count. You're only a quarter Italian." Like that mattered. Cass grew up around enough Italians in Astoria to know any percentage was more than enough to flaunt.

Ti hopped off the counter. "Guess he's just special."

"Is that a synonym for charmer?"

"Oh, c'mon. Give the guy a chance." She flitted around her for a turn at the coffeemaker. "He might just be your saving grace for this place."

She didn't need grace. She needed a worker who could handle following orders. Hopefully, he'd turn out to be half-decent with a hammer. With as much as she had riding on this sale, she couldn't afford for him not to be.

Mug in hand, Ti followed her out of the kitchen toward Grandpa's office beside the front door. "Wow." She bumped into Cass's shoulder. "What happened in here? Someone set off a bomb?"

Cass waded through papers and mail strewn around the floor and sifted through even more piles scattered all over the desk. "No idea." Grandpa wasn't this messy, was he?

"Oh my word." Ti swiped a picture frame from the top mantle, blew the dust off, and cracked up. "Look at us. What were we, like, five there? This had to be primary week." She handed her the faded picture of a group of kids from one of their earliest weeks of camp.

Cass brushed a thumb over the glass. "I don't even remember half these people."

"They probably didn't come back." She elbowed her. "Couldn't hang with the cool kids."

Cass laughed. "Must've been your hot pink slap bracelet that intimidated them."

She snagged the picture back. "Better than the leopard-printed one you were rocking."

"Only 'cause I let you talk me into it."

"Hey, it caught the attention of that boy next to you, didn't it?" Ti returned the frame to the ledge. "Seriously, girl, someone had to give you fashion pointers." She dashed out of the room before Cass could swat her.

"What's wrong? You worried about getting a paper cut?"

Ti poked her head back inside and looked around, face scrunching. "Sorry, hon. You're on your own on this one. You know paperwork and I don't mesh."

Never had. She smiled. "Give me a minute, and then we'll make a grocery run, 'kay?"

"Perfect. I'll be on the deck, soaking up some rays. Holler when you're ready. Oh, and let's check out some paint colors while we're out, too. I've already got a ton of ideas."

Of course she did. Good thing one of them saw possibilities in this place.

The screen shuddered behind her. Still gripping a handful of mail, Cass slumped into Grandpa's old desk chair and surveyed the mess, not sure where to start. She peered up at the old picture again. Why couldn't life be as simple as it seemed back then?

A glimpse of a phone cord peeked out from under some papers. Maybe she should call Dad. Ask his advice. The thought hardened in her stomach. No. She'd do this on her own. Same way she'd been doing everything for the last fifteen years.

She opened a side drawer, unburied a letter opener, and grabbed the first envelope. Had to start somewhere. Her eyes scanned past the city's letterhead but only made it to the middle of the first paragraph before the letter opener clattered to the ground. She rocketed out of the seat. Tell me I'm not reading this right.

CHAPTER FOUR

Gamble

Staying busy for two full days hadn't kept the notice she'd found off Cass's mind. Thirty thousand dollars in penalties? How could Grandpa have gotten that far behind on his property taxes? The question joined the cold morning air searing her lungs. Obviously, a three-mile run hadn't brought her any clarity, either.

Glimpses of daylight crested the trees and cast a glare over the fog while puddles from last night's rain splashed over her Nikes. Halfway up the steep driveway, she braced her hands against her knees, stole a minute to catch her breath, and rotated her ankle. The cut was still tender, but she'd learned long ago to push through pain. Only the strong succeeded.

Straightening, she wiped the sweat from her face with the inside of her shirt and readjusted her ponytail.

A rustling noise drew her gaze toward a squirrel hopping branches above the overgrown path leading to the softball field. Her arms fell to her sides as she stared. Beneath spindly limbs, fractured boards from the footbridge poked out in multiple directions.

What happened to this place? Grandpa'd been a work-horse his whole life. Cared for this property like it was an extension of his character. If it'd gotten too much for him to keep up with on his own, he would've hired someone to pick up the slack. Even if that meant delaying other bills.

She slicked back the strands of hair curling over her forehead from the humidity and left her hands on her head. Was that why he'd gotten behind on taxes? Because some contractor drained him dry? But then why would the camp be this rundown? None of it made any sense.

The questions drove her up the last half of the driveway and straight into the other question she'd put off all weekend. Ethan DeLuca. His black Jeep towered over her Passat. When she'd told him he could start Monday, she hadn't meant at sunrise. Who was this guy?

She took the steps two at a time and jogged across the deck. A mouthwatering coffee aroma greeted her through the screen. Rather than slam behind her, it eased shut. He fixed the door? How long had he been here?

Down the first hall, she peered around the corner toward the back bedroom.

"Coffee?"

She flinched at his voice. Hiding her reaction, she leveled her shoulders and turned.

In jeans and a Mets shirt, of all things, he flashed a smile that was every bit as charming as she remembered and handed her a coffee mug. "Italian roasted. Nothing beats it. I was about to have a second cup, but it looks like you could use it instead."

She stiffened, cringing at what she must've looked like after her run. Wait, what did it matter? This guy was a potential contractor, not a potential date.

He released the mug but not his gaze.

She ran a hand down her ponytail. "What?"

"Sorry. It's just . . ." He rubbed his stubbly jaw. "Your eyes were green when I first saw you, and today, they're blue."

"They're hazel, actually." She pointed to her blue sweatshirt. "They change depending on what color I'm wearing."

"Any other superhero traits I should know about?" His lips slid sideways.

She rolled her eyes. "Yeah, dodging men's witty charm."

He laughed. "And holding nothing back, apparently."

She breathed in the steam from her mug, unable to tame her smile. "One of the benefits of growing up in New York City." Man, she missed home already.

His face fell. He looked away and kneaded the back of his neck.

What was that about? Did her being from the city intimidate him?

The awkward silence swirled around her with a breeze coming through the screen door.

Ethan met her glance, grin back in place. "At least you admitted you think I'm charming."

"Among other things," she mumbled before taking a sip of coffee. One swallow, and she begged her face not to admit it was one of the best things she'd ever tasted. Right. She turned toward the bathroom so he wouldn't see her cave.

"It's already done."

She stopped to look behind her. "What's done?"

He jutted his chin at the room. "The bathroom ceiling."

If his satisfied expression were any indication, he must've thought he could play her. Too bad for him, she'd built her whole life around high standards. No way he'd done a sufficient job that quickly. She'd been gone no more than forty minutes.

She mimicked his overconfident nod and resumed her trek down the hall. If he expected to pass off some shoddy work to get a free room, he'd clearly underestimated her.

Around the doorway, she skidded to a stop. A splash of coffee spilled over her mug, dragging her assumption down with it. He hadn't only patched the ceiling flawlessly. He'd painted and cleaned. She wouldn't have known there'd ever been a hole at all if she hadn't seen it beforehand.

Her back found the wall behind her. She set her mug on the sink and studied the place over. So, maybe he really did have superpowers. Or an ulterior motive. Either way, she couldn't fault him for a lack of quality. And now that she'd have to skim thirty thousand dollars off any profit she made on the sale, she couldn't turn down free labor. Every penny counted.

After chugging the rest of her coffee, she stopped inside Grandpa's office to grab the contract she'd drawn up and headed outside.

"So? Did I pass?" he asked from a yellow Adirondack chair beside the door.

"You certainly have skills. I'm impressed."

"Thanks." Stretching that satisfied grin of his even wider, he flipped the top of a sketchbook over and set a pencil next to his mug on the chair arm.

"Don't tell me. You're an artist, too." Was there anything he didn't do?

He glanced at the book. "I'm not sure it qualifies as art. More like a hobby. But it relaxes me. Helps me clear my head."

Like writing music used to do for her.

He moved the sketchbook to the next chair over and pulled himself up. "Don't worry. No drawing while I'm on the clock."

That was the least of her concerns. "What does your grandma think about you staying here?"

He tugged on his ear. "Said it was about time."

"What does that mean?"

"With Nonna, there's no telling." He laughed.

He'd better not be one of those almost-thirty-year-old bachelors whose family can't wait to hook him up with someone just to get him out of the house. 'Cause she'd hate to have to break some little Italian grandma's heart.

She grasped at one last straw. "What about your allergies?"

He shimmied a white pill bottle with a pink label out of his pocket. "Problem solved."

The guy had a solution for everything, didn't he? Okay, it still kind of bugged her how he'd conveniently shown up here on Friday, eager to offer his help. But he was beyond skilled, punctual, hardworking, and artistic to top it off. She curled the top corner of the contract over her finger, at a loss for any reason not to hand it over.

A vehicle roared up the driveway with a muffler that should've been banned for noise pollution. "Nice pad, DeLuca," a guy called from the passenger window of a pickup truck toting a motorcycle on a trailer.

Cass looked from the two men to Ethan. "What's going on?"

He shrugged. "I can't move in without some of my stuff."

Move in? She hadn't even officially agreed to it yet.

Ti stumbled onto the deck in boxers and a cotton shirt with one side of a wide collar drooped over her shoulder. She parted the hair strewn across her face. "Isn't it a bit early for a party?"

"Sorry for waking you, ma'am." A burly guy wearing the same gear Ethan had on when she'd first met him tipped his hat at Ti as he jogged up the stairs. A younger guy, carrying a duffle bag over each shoulder, followed on his heels.

Ethan clasped hands with the first and leaned in for a hug. "'Sup Briggs. Thought we said three o'clock."

"Yeah, sorry, man." He raised the front of his hat and wiped his brow. "Captain called an all-day drill. So, it was either now or tomorrow."

"No worries. I appreciate you driving out." Ethan squeezed his shoulder. "Ladies, meet Lieutenant Briggs and my buddy Sanders. Guys, this is Cassidy and Treble, my new . . ." He swayed his head. "Employers."

Ti lifted her palms. "That's all Cass."

"Either way, you girls are real brave, taking on this hoodlum." Briggs shook their hands. "Did he warn you he snores?"

Ethan shoved him toward the house. "*Me?* Get outta here." He looked behind him. "Sanders, you hearing this garbage? Help me out."

The guy shook his head. "Sorry, bro. Briggs out bench presses you. I know when to keep my mouth shut."

"Oh, yeah?" Ethan hooked an arm around his neck, tugging his head down. Sanders tossed the bags and crouched to wrestle him.

Ti opened the door. "Anybody else up for some coffee?"

Sanders perked at the offer and gave Ethan a wide-open shot to his ribs. He doubled over, fake moaning. "You're dirty, DeLuca."

Ethan swept a glance at Briggs. "Learned from the best."

"Hey, now. No dragging me into this." He followed Ti inside with Sanders shuffling after them.

Still laughing, Ethan ran his fingers through his hair on his way toward the truck. "See what I have to live with?" he called behind him toward Cass.

Yeah, camaraderie, drills, a life he seemed to love. Why was he leaving that behind to come here? Was this really about his grandma? Something didn't add up.

She met him at the tailgate. "You're pretty sure of yourself, aren't ya? What if I'd turned down your offer?"

"Guess I'm a gambling man."

She clutched the contract while pushing her sweatshirt sleeves up her arms. "I think that's called arrogance."

He grinned. "I like to think of it as hope."

"You learn that from growing up in a small town?"

His brow furrowed. "From someone much braver than me," he almost whispered. Heaving a bag from the truck bed over his shoulder, he dodged her stare. "So, we good?"

What was he hiding? She rolled the sides of the paper in and out while chewing on her lip. Regardless, she'd made a deal. Not to mention she couldn't pass up his quality of work. As long as he respected her as the boss, it'd be fine. She handed over the contract. "I'd like a signed copy before you officially start, please."

He nodded, dimples sinking in. "Yes, ma'am."

She diverted her focus from his smile to the motorcycle. "Is it supposed to smell like that?"

"You don't miss much, do you?" He set his bag on the gravel, stashed the contract in his back pocket, and opened the gate to the trailer. "It has an oil leak. I haven't had time to work on it."

Because he was a mechanic, too. Naturally. She pressed her back into the truck's warm panel and glanced from the bike to his topless Jeep. "You got something against walls being around you when you drive?"

His gaze dropped to his boot, tapping against the tire. "I don't like to be closed in."

There was a surprise.

Ti and the guys strolled up, coffee mugs in hand. She dipped her delicate shoulder into Ethan's ridiculously muscled one. "When are we going for a ride?"

"Not until I make sure she won't break down."

"That takes all the fun out of it." Her smile peeked around the rim of her mug.

Sanders let his gaze roam over her the same way most guys did. Briggs popped him in the chest, handed off his mug, and helped Ethan unload the bike. He checked his watch. "Time to roll." He tipped his hat toward Ti and Cass one more time before loading back into the driver's seat. "Thanks for the coffee. And hey, keep an eye on this stud for me, will ya?"

You better believe it. Cass nodded. A sideways glance caught Ethan smiling as if reading her thoughts. She darted her gaze from his and pulled her sleeves down.

Ti waved as the truck pulled away. Once it rounded the bend, she lowered onto her heels. "For a second there, I thought we actually had some peeps to hang out with." She turned toward Ethan. "Know anyone who actually lives around here?"

He polished a spot on the bike's gas tank with the bottom of his T-shirt. "Unfortunately."

A bark from the tree line drew all their attention up the hill toward the world's shabbiest dog trotting straight for them. Cass skirted behind Ethan without thinking. He squared his broad shoulders, and she had to force herself not to grab on to them.

Not that she needed the protection. The dog went straight for Ti. She squatted and rubbed his scruffy cheeks, squealing as he licked her face. "Is he not the most adorable thing ever? He looks just like the dog from *Annie.*"

More like a twenty-year-old mop that hadn't been cleaned a day in its life.

"Where'd you come from, boy? You hungry?"

Cass slid out from behind her barricade. "Uh-uh. Don't even think about it, Ti."

"Aw, c'mon. Look at him. You can't turn down this face." She pulled his matted fur back with his ears.

Laughing, Cass leaned over and scratched the top of his dirt-stained head. Why did animals have to be so darn cute? He licked her hands, and that was it. She caved. Ti knew as well as she did that she couldn't turn away a stray. "Okay. But he stays outside."

Ti fluttered her fingertips together. "Hear that, Sandy?"

"You're not going to bust out in song, are you?" Cass grinned.

"Very funny." Ti rose to her feet and looked at Ethan, who'd conveniently stayed out of the conversation. "Make sure he doesn't go anywhere. I'll be right back."

Ethan patted his leg, and the dog scurried to him. He ruffled his long ears. "It's probably not a bad idea to keep him around here. I mean, he's not a Dalmatian or anything, but he'll do."

His dimples were almost as maddening as his impish tone.

Ti returned with her camera, shooting pictures on the way. She stopped beside them and scrolled through the frames. "Perfect. We're gonna have so much fun this summer. I can already tell."

"Not if we don't get some major work done first." Something pressed into Cass's back. She looked over her shoulder. "What are you doing?"

"Getting to work." He clicked his pen, shoved it in his pocket, and handed her the signed contract. "Where do we start?"

At least they were on the same page. She motioned behind him. "You can start on the canteen. I haven't been inside it yet, but if it's as bad as the outside, it's gonna need an overhaul. Assess any damage, take measurements, and get started on what you can. Make a list of needed materials, and I'll pick them up on my next trip into town." She peeked at the clock on her cell. "You can take lunch at noon."

He saluted her without saying a word.

"Where do you want me?" Ti asked from behind her.

"You can help me clean the mess hall, but leave Sandy with Ethan." Someone had to watch him. Ti was probably right about Ethan DeLuca having a story to tell. One she couldn't quite figure out. Whatever it was, Cass wasn't about to be the punch line.

He started toward the canteen at the same time she headed for the main building. In the kitchen, she poured a capful of bleach into a bucket of hot water, tossed a rag in, and swiped a pair of rubber gloves off the counter as she hauled it into the mess hall.

Right behind her, Ti set her own bucket onto the bench at the next table over. "You don't have to treat him like the hired help, you know."

"He *is* the hired help." She pulled on the gloves and glanced toward a full-blown scowl staring back at her.

"He's a nice guy, Cass."

"I'm sure he is. That doesn't mean I can trust him. He's a Mets fan, for Pete's sake."

Ti cracked a smile. "Hey, every man has his faults."

"Not sure that one's recoverable." They both laughed. Cass circled her rag across the tabletop. "Seriously, though, he's not my friend. He's a contractor. I've been in business long enough to have learned not to confuse the two."

"Business shmisness. This is about Jesse."

Hunched over the table, Cass froze. Bleach fumes singed her nostrils, the memory of what'd happened with her ex-boyfriend burning deeper. It was bad enough she couldn't get away from him while home. His name was off limits here. Ti knew that. She balled the rag under her fingers and scrubbed the grime off the table. Why couldn't all ties to him be as easy to erase?

"I'm just sayin'. This isn't Astoria."

Cass snorted. "I hate to break it to you, but the world works the same way regardless of where you are."

Ti washed the opposite end of her table. "Well, I hate to break it to *you*, but I think Ethan's gonna prove you wrong."

"Just because you're all cozy with lover boy doesn't mean he's different from any other guy."

"Not every guy's a scumbag, Cass. And don't worry. He's not my type."

Cass dropped the rag. *Seriously?* She pushed her hair back with her arm. "So, you're just making passes for sport?"

Ti rounded the front of the table. "A girl's gotta have some entertainment around here, remember?" Head tipped, she sighed. "Kidding. I was just trying to feel the guy out. It's obvious he's a keeper. You know I only go for ones with commitment issues."

"Ti—"

"We've known each other since we were two. We're a little past the saving face game." She shrugged. "Things are the way they are."

Cass leaned a knee on the bench, her heart hitting the floor. "That doesn't mean they have to stay that way."

"Look who's talking." Wringing out her rag, Ti winked at her. "Besides, the only male I plan to snuggle up with is Jax."

Cass arched a brow at her. "What about Sandy? Thought it was love at first sight."

"He's adorable." Ti scrunched her nose. "But the smell kind of overrides the cuteness factor."

"Oh, c'mon. He just needs a bath."

"Or twenty." A ring from her cell phone clipped into her laugh. She withdrew it from her pocket and grimaced. "Speaking of losers . . ." She swiped the screen and wandered toward the other end of the room near the fireplace. "Hey, Murray."

Only two sentences in, and they were already arguing, from the sounds of it. Cass washed the corners of the table closest to the window. Peering toward the canteen, she slumped into the concrete wall. Some changes were too costly to hope for.

CHAPTER FIVE

Walking Flames

Ethan jotted down numbers on a pad and released the notch on the measuring tape. In front of the canteen, Sandy popped his head up as the tape zipped back in with a *clink*.

"Sorry, boy." Ethan grabbed the corners of his T-shirt, pulled it over his head, and wiped off the sweat dripping down his temple. Even with the giant wooden shutters propped open, it had to be a thousand degrees in this little snack shack.

Bracing his palms against the counter, he jumped over the ledge and landed beside the dog. Sandy wobbled up to his feet, shook fur everywhere, and panted expectantly. He was definitely the scruffiest Otterhound he'd ever seen.

Ethan knelt to detangle the dreadlocks blocking his eyes. "Trust me. You don't want anything from in there. That candy's got to be at least a year old."

A *thud* rippled from the mess hall and drew both their glances toward the unopened door. "I don't think they want us in there, either." At least, Red didn't. He gave the dog's shaggy ears one more rub and pushed up on his thighs to stand. "She sure knows how to put you in your place, doesn't she?"

Sandy closed his mouth and tilted his head.

Ethan laughed. "Don't worry. You can kick it with me. We boys gotta watch each other's backs."

The dog lolled on the cement again and sank his chin over his paws.

"I feel ya, bro." Ethan loosened his neck. He hadn't done this much construction work in a long time. The ache in his muscles felt good, though. Like the burn after a hard workout.

Sanders's comment from earlier wrangled another laugh out of him. Briggs out bench-pressing him? He shook his head. Not if Miss Drill Sergeant turned his summer into a giant CrossFit training. He stretched the tape measure up to the ceiling above the counter. Maybe missing drills at the station wouldn't set him back, after all.

Ti's laugh rebounded off the hill. Ethan set his pencil on the notepad and peered over his shoulder. They must've opened one of the back doors. Another laugh rang from inside. This time, Cassidy's. Huh. The girl knew how to laugh. Imagine that.

He backed up to get a good view of the canteen's roof. The water stain on the ceiling's back corner didn't bode well. His gaze traveled up the pine tree beside the shack. What were the chances he'd fall through rotten plywood if he climbed on top to check it out?

A moment's hesitation faded into a shrug. Only one way to find out. He jumped to reach the nearest branch and walked up the trunk until he had enough momentum to set his knee on the branch.

How did a girl like Red end up being friends with someone like Treble . . . or Trina . . . or whatever her real name was? Okay, so she was a little out there, but she seemed like she knew how to have fun—something that obviously wasn't in Cassidy's vocabulary. And what was with her small town digs? He'd earned the right to call Haven's Creek that if he wanted. Being from Queens didn't make her high and mighty.

He steadied his feet on a branch level with the roof. Rubbing the sap on his hands, he leaned against the trunk and tried to assess the extent of damage from this view. His cell rang right as he inched out. He grabbed the branch above him for balance and swiped the screen. *Nonna.* His pulse jumped. "Everything all right?"

"Fine, dear. Just checking how your first day's going. Don't have a coronary just because you see my name flash on that fancy phone of yours."

He grinned. "So, you're making heart jokes, now?"

"You don't get to be my age without having a sense of humor." She laughed. "I've learned a lot in my thirty-five years."

Ethan pressed his tongue to the side of his cheek. "Thirty-five, huh?"

She huffed. "Okay, fine. Give or take forty years, you big downer. You know, it's a good thing you're sticking around this summer. We've got major work to do. Starting with brushing up on your flattery skills."

A lot of good that'd do him here.

An echo of the mess hall's screen door closing shuddered toward him. Cassidy's fiery red hair blazed from the patio. "Nonna, if you're sure you're all right, I gotta run before Ice Queen docks me for slacking on the job."

"Ethan James." She rattled off a whole lecture in Italian, probably repeating the same scolding she'd given him on Friday after he'd first told her about Crazy Cat Woman.

Squatting on the branch, he circled his eyes skyward. "Yeah, I know. Give her a chance." It'd be nice if that worked both ways. "Listen, I'll come by later tonight, okay?"

"Only if you're gonna let me have an espresso."

Persistence at its finest. "Love you, Nonna. See you soon. *Ciao.*" He maneuvered down the branches. Sandy flanked his side as soon as his boots hit the pavement. "You're gonna be a buffer if I need it, right?"

But rather than approach, Cassidy stayed on the patio, sweeping the concrete squares, one section at a time. The girl didn't do anything without precision, did she?

Ethan grabbed his T-shirt off the counter, slung it over his shoulder, and headed toward walking flames he had no clue how to tame. With the sun directly overhead, the day's heat bore into his chest. Or maybe it was something about being around her. He stopped along the edge of the patio and clicked his boots together to knock the dirt off.

She flicked a glance toward him and cast it right back to the ground, cheeks pink. "Do you always work half-naked?"

His gaze ricocheted off her to his bare stomach. "Sorry." He snagged his shirt from his shoulder and tugged it on but couldn't lose his grin. "I'm used to working with a bunch of guys."

Was it just him, or was she sweeping hard enough to snap those bristles in half?

Sandy pushed his wet snout up under his hand. Ethan rubbed his head while peering behind him at the shack. "It's pretty bad."

Cassidy leaned on the broom handle and finally looked at him head-on. "What is?"

"The canteen." He crossed the cement and handed her his list. "But nothing that can't be mended."

A hint of dejection touched her eyes as she read over the page. "Let's hope the same can be said about the rest of the place." Keeping her head down, she tucked the page into her pocket. "Thanks for this." She set the broom against the wall and walked inside without saying anything else.

He looked at Sandy and mirrored his curious expression. "Stay."

The dog trotted after him.

Ethan turned, hand lifted. "Okay, we'll have to work on that one. But take it from me. You don't want to go in there."

Inside, a gust of bleach-scented fumes almost backed him through the door. At the opposite end, Ti struggled to push one of the collapsible tables against the wall. He jogged over to help. Folded in half, it butted into the cinder blocks with a *thud*. That must've been what he'd heard earlier. The concrete walls and low hanging ceiling made the perfect sound system for shooting the echo all the way out to the canteen.

"Thanks." Ti flexed her hands. "My arms are starting to get a little shaky."

For good reason. They'd cleared the entire mess hall, propping a table between each window. Those babies weren't light.

"We're about to scrub the floor."

"Actually, can you do that?" Cassidy grabbed a bucket on her way past them. "I'm going to start on the shower hall instead."

"Sure you don't wanna break for a quick breakfast first?"

Red whisked the screen open. "Not hungry." The door fanned behind her.

Ethan turned to Ti. "Why do I get the feeling she left because I came in?"

She offered him an empathetic smile. "Give her time. She'll warm up to you." She hauled another bucket off the ground. "Trust issues."

There was the understatement of the year.

She headed toward the kitchen, bucket swinging. "Want some coffee?"

"A bottle of water, if you have any." He had to have sweated out a gallon while in the canteen. The place probably hadn't been aired out in a solid year.

"Sure. Cass picked some up Fri—"

The same scream he'd heard three days ago rang up the hill. His gaze met Ti's right before they both sprinted outside.

"Cass?" she yelled.

Red bolted from the standalone bathhouse, doing the same flailing dance she had when he'd first met her. Squirming, she wiped off her clothes from every angle.

Ti reached for her. "What's going on?"

"Roaches," she eked out. "Like, *hundreds* of them." She shuddered again.

Ethan crept around the open-walled entryway, nudged the screen door with his foot, and jumped back against the cinder block. She wasn't lying. Only a few patches of the dingy white walls peeked through a solid covering of roaches.

Ti whirled around the corner, but he caught her at the waist and shook his head. "Trust me." He redirected her to the side of the building.

Cassidy tapped her forehead against the chipped stucco-coated wall. "They weren't here yesterday. Where'd they all come from?" Spinning around, she caught his gaze. She blinked away but not before a twinge of helplessness in her eyes hit him in the chest.

Who could blame her? He'd never seen an infestation this bad. Maybe if he fixed it, she'd be less stressed. Exhaling, he rolled a pinecone back and forth under his boot. "I can call an old friend, if you want. Jenni's dad owns a pest control business."

The moment's softness hardened over her face again. Unfolding her arms, she trudged up the hill past him. "I can take care of it myself."

No one said she couldn't. Ethan arced a brow at Ti. "Trust issues, huh?"

Ti raised her shoulders. "Just a tad." She set a hand on his forearm, her voice as gentle as her touch. "She has a reason, Ethan. But that doesn't mean you can't prove her wrong." With that, she flitted up the hill toward some measure of hope he couldn't see himself.

He swiped the pinecone from the ground, tossed it in his hand, and chucked it across the field into the woods. He probably should be glad she didn't want his help on this one. The thought of calling Jenni sent shivers down his spine worse than any roaches would have. He raked his fingers through his hair. What was he doing back in this town?

"She has a reason." Ti's words pummeled through him. If Izzy were here, she'd tell him to stick with it. Always the valiant one. If he made it through this summer, maybe he'd finally live up to her level of bravery.

His fire pager beeped. Dispatch announced a call nearby, and Ethan released a sigh of relief. At least there were still *some* fires he knew how to put out.

Cass shed her sweatshirt, tossed it in the passenger seat, and yanked the door to her Passat behind her. Why did Ethan have to be so quick to intervene? Did he think she was incapable of running the place? After the way she'd almost lost it back there, what else would he think? Worst part was, he was probably right. She reversed from her parking spot.

Ti flagged her down. "Where are you going?"

"Into town." Somewhere she could think clearly.

Rather than argue, Ti simply leaned against the deck, smile in place. As always. If Cass could live free of responsibilities, maybe she could smile like that, too.

Ti drifted out of view in the mirror, but guilt for thinking about her best friend like that dug into Cass's gut all the way to the bottom of the driveway. She shouldn't take her frustrations out on Ti. With the way things were going, her free spirit might be the only source of levity around this place.

Idling at the crossroad, Cass looked both ways, unsure where she was heading. Maybe it didn't matter. She turned left, set her arm on the door panel, and waited for the sun-soaked breeze to carry her stress into the mountainside.

A sign grabbed her attention several miles down the road. Without thinking, she pulled into the lot as if a homing device steered the car instead of her. A bell above the flower shop's door joined the sweet fragrance of gardenias ushering her into one place up here that finally felt like home.

Surrounded by the familiarity of flowers, she almost curled into a ball in the middle of the floor, just so she could soak it all in. The colors, aroma, tranquility. All those years of managing Mom's shop had caused their share of heartache. But through everything, the beauty had always anchored her. Like one small constant ray of light.

She smoothed out her tank top and shoved the lump in her throat back down. She couldn't break under pressure. All the work she'd put in to proving to Dad she could hack it in business wasn't about to end now.

"Can I help you?" A short, round woman in an embroidered apron strolled out from behind the counter, carrying a spray bottle. Her gentle voice and soft expression drained the tension out of Cass's shoulders.

She let out a breath. "If it's all right, I'd just like to browse the flowers for a while."

"Of course. Take your time." She cupped her hand under the leaves of a peach dahlia plant and misted the petals. "Don't you love early summer?"

"My favorite time of year." Cass drifted around the arrangements. Freesia, pansies, hyacinths. Pinks and oranges burst from each shelf. In the far corner, she slowed by a hutch filled with bouquets made of wild flowers.

The bell above the door chimed again. A clean-cut guy about her age, wearing a light gray dress shirt and textured tie, approached the counter. "Do you have any Daphne plants in?"

"Wrong season." Cass darted her head toward the flowers in front of her and bit her lip. Nobody'd asked her. "Sorry." She ducked behind a back display, moved on to a simple plant that most people probably overlooked, and leaned over to smell it.

"They're stunning in yellow, aren't they?"

She peered at the guy from the counter, standing right beside her now. "Excuse me?"

He motioned to the flowers. "Anemones. I rarely see them in that color."

If she could get her eyelids to move, maybe her jaw would follow. A guy like him knew about flowers?

A perfect smile sloped up his closely-shaven cheek. Evidently, some guys in Haven's Creek owned a razor.

"Didn't mean to intrude." Dipping his head, he turned.

"You just caught me off guard." She ran her hand along the flower's stalk and kept her gaze on the petals.

He laughed softly. "You're not from around here, are you?"

She could've asked him the same thing. He certainly didn't fit the rugged mold she expected for this area. Not like Ethan did—all muscles and scruff, solid work hands that smelled like the earth. Why did he have to be so . . . ? Her stomach plummeted at the realization.

The guy leaned in front of her. "Are you okay?"

Aside from apparently being attracted to someone she shouldn't be? She cringed. No wonder she was so edgy around him. What was wrong with her? She was supposed to learn from her mistakes, not repeat them.

The ceiling vent poured cool air onto her bare shoulders, somehow bypassing her hot cheeks altogether. "Yeah, fine." She cleared her throat. "I'm from Queens. You?"

"Bona fide Haven's Creek native."

Her head flashed up toward a sultry grin.

"Let me guess. Caught you off guard again?"

She fumbled her purse strap, words floundering even more.

"In all fairness, I'm technically from the city. Moved here when I was five. My uncle took me in after my parents died in a car wreck."

Her hand flew to her chest. "I'm so sorry."

He shook his head. "Don't be. It was a long time ago. And this town isn't a complete dead end. As long as you know the right people." He rubbed a knuckle across his eyebrow. "I never could get into the farming business, though. Guess my city roots had a stronger pull. I work in Manhattan a few days a week. Telecommute from here the rest."

"Ah." Made sense now. She swept past him to the next display. "Wall Street?"

"Maybe one day." He slid his cuff above an oversized watch. "Speaking of business, I need to run. Pleasure to meet you . . ."

"Cassidy."

"Nick Ashton." His smile hitched up his cheek again. "Hope your time in Haven's Creek isn't boring."

Not if Ethan DeLuca had anything to do with it.

Nick slipped by her into an open section of the floor. He stood for a moment before turning and handing her a torn-off piece of paper with his number on it. "In case you happen to get too bored and need a night out."

With all the work she had to do, that wasn't likely. "I'll keep that in mind."

"Please do." With another dip of his chin, he strode through the rows toward the exit.

Nick Ashton, huh? She would've filed him away with every other power-suit guy in Manhattan if it weren't for his knowledge of flowers. Either way, she already had enough distractions to worry about.

Images of the roaches shuddered over her again. But same as it had in the moment, the genuine concern in Ethan's eyes shook her even more. She turned the paper around in her hands and sighed. She might end up needing the distraction of a night out more than she wanted to admit.

CHAPTER SIX

Priceless

The exterminator van's taillights faded around the bend of the driveway the next morning. In the canteen, Ethan pried a piece of plywood off with the back of his hammer. Cassidy had taken care of it. Just like she'd said she would. Not that he was surprised. The woman was more than capable of handling things and obviously had something to prove.

In a pair of rolled-up jeans and a fitted gray T-shirt with a butterfly on it, she rounded the back of the main building and strolled toward him.

At least it wasn't as hot in here as it had been yesterday. Maybe the place wouldn't go up in flames from whatever fireballs she decided to throw at him today. He steeled himself as she approached, but the sunlight caught soft features instead of her usual hard lines.

Sandy rose from his retired position in front of the counter and scratched his ear with his hind leg, hair flying everywhere. She stopped to pet him. "Almost twenty-four hours later, and I still feel like I have things crawling on me."

He slid the hammer's claw under another rusted nail and jimmied it out. "I don't blame you. I'm pretty sure those roaches showed up in my dreams last night."

Was that an *actual* smile he'd gotten out of her? Unable to look away, he couldn't help returning it.

She folded her arms on the counter. Her gaze roamed around the inside of the canteen until it landed on the shelves behind him. "Are there any Swedish Fish back there?"

He peeked over his shoulder at the supply of outdated candy. She couldn't be serious. "Yeah. You have a loose tooth you're looking to pull out?"

The side door opened, and she headed straight for the yellow box. "I haven't had these in forever." She tore into the package and tapped a handful of red gummy fish onto her palm. Her face lit up like she was a preteen camper, ready to live off a sugar rush for the next week.

He kept his mouth shut, but his laughter tumbled out anyway.

Long curls brushed over her cheeks. "What? You don't like candy?"

"Oh, no, I do. Just not usually the expired kind."

She tossed two fish in her mouth. "Your loss."

Who was this girl? *Don't tell me she has split personalities.*

The box hit the floor as she flailed her arms around her hair. "Something just landed on me."

Ethan dropped the hammer and steadied her by the shoulders before she ended up knocking over the shelves.

Head down, she grabbed his sleeve. "If it's a spider, I'm gonna scream."

With her color-changing eyes hidden from him, he didn't bother hiding his grin. She looked as cute as she had during the squirrel episode the other day. This close to her, scents of vanilla overrode the smell of sawdust and lured him even closer.

"Do you see it?"

He cleared his throat, refocused, and searched her hair until he found the culprit. "Let's try to make it one full day without any screams." He swept the ladybug into his hand and held it out for her to see.

Straightening, she looked from the bug to him and made a face that wrinkled her freckled nose. "It felt heavier when it landed."

"Common mistake," he said with a wink.

She stopped him before he flicked it. "Don't kill him." She uncurled his fingers and scooped up the tiny bug.

"They might seem harmless, but if they breed here, you'll end up having to call that exterminator back."

While pulling her lip to the side, she nudged the ladybug onto the counter and waved him off like she was trying to set him free. "Guess we better hope he finds a new home, then."

A fierce taskmaster who beamed over eating candy and saving innocent bugs' lives. She wasn't as tough as she tried to let on.

A hint of sadness creased her face when she met his glance. She blinked it away and nabbed the box of fish from the ground. "So, I'm curious how you're able to drop everything in your life to move here."

Back to business. He scratched his cheek and reached for his hammer. "Guess you could say I don't set down many roots. I room with Briggs and Sanders. Between the three of us, my share of the rent isn't much."

He squatted, lifted a two-by-four he'd taken down earlier, and eyed it from several angles to check if it was too warped to salvage. "I have more than enough in savings to cover it while I'm gone."

"What about your job?" Cassidy propped her foot against the wall behind her.

"I took a leave of absence. Transferred to Haven's Creek's volunteer squad for now." Using the wood for balance, he pushed up to his feet and adjusted the pager on his belt. "The station will still be there when I get back."

"Sounds like a bold move."

Smiling, he flicked his chin at her. "Look who's talking."

Rather than retaliate, she dodged his stare. "Where'd you learn construction?"

Why was she evading? And what was with the twenty questions? He spun the board on its corner. "I worked with Habitat for Humanity for about a year. Got out of this town for a while." He wiped his face on his sleeve. "I learned a lot. Helped out where I could."

"And never stopped?"

He looked over, but she didn't unlock her focus from the box in her hands.

Ti swung around the opening in a hat twice the size of her head and some kind of crazy fringed shirt. Face scrunched, she peered inside. "Cass?"

Cassidy pushed off the wall and stashed the candy behind her back like she'd been caught with drugs. "What's wrong?"

Ti lowered a pair of police-style sunglasses down her nose. "Um . . . you might want to see for yourself. It's the cabins."

Cassidy looked from her to Ethan, dread already shadowing her eyes.

He stowed the hammer through his belt loop and nodded at Ti. "We'll be there in a sec."

She disappeared around the corner, and Ethan inched toward Cass. "You good?"

A series of blinks brought her gaze to his. "Yeah, sorry. Fine."

Doubtful. She was probably worried something could top the roach infestation from yesterday. He dipped his head at the fish behind her back. "I'm sure it's nothing a little expired candy can't cure." He leaned in to whisper. "And don't worry. Your secret's safe with me."

The corner of her mouth slanted to the left. "Better be. 'Cause if Ti finds out we broke into the candy, we're both gonna be stuck eating nothing but nuts and berries all summer."

Laughing, he followed her through the door. "Is that why the fridge is so empty?"

"You don't miss much," she said in the same teasing tone he'd used on her yesterday.

But once outside, business mode kicked in. On a mission, she charged up the hill so fast, he had to jog to keep up with her. Sandy ran ahead of them, probably thinking they were getting ready to play. Ethan met him at the stairs to the first cabin and held him back. "Not right now, boy."

He skipped both steps, wheeled through the door, and stumbled straight into Cassidy's back. She stayed glued in place, hand clamped over her mouth.

Ti weaved through their shoulders. Halfway across the foam and feather-covered floor, she turned. "I came to scope out what needed to be painted and found it like this. What do you think happened?"

Cassidy finally moved then. She drifted from bunk to bunk, tracing her hand down gaping tears in the mattresses. He might not've known her well enough to read all her expressions yet, but that glossed-over look wasn't good. The stress lines crinkling her face left his insides almost as gutted as the mattresses.

She clutched a gashed pillow against her torso. "How did they get in here?"

Ethan met Ti's same confused stare. "Who's they?"

"Whoever did this. Kids. Gangs. I don't know." The pillow and its contents landed on the floor. She cupped her forehead.

Ti moved to her side and reached for her hand. "We're not in Astoria. I kinda doubt kids from the sticks walk around with knives, vandalizing people's property for kicks."

Cass withdrew her hand. "Then how else do you explain this? Wild animals?"

Ti shrugged. "Makes more sense."

Both girls turned toward Ethan, as if just remembering he was in the room with them. Cassidy splayed a hand toward the mess. "What do you think? Animals or vandals?"

Both sets of eyes searched his for an answer he didn't have. What was he supposed to say? Do? He couldn't fix this. At least, not without time and money. No wonder she was stressing. She probably felt short on both.

If nothing else, at least he could defuse the tension. He snagged one of the pillows on his way toward them. "Well, there's really only one way to tell for sure." Without giving Cass a second to prepare, he swatted her in the face with the pillow. Feathers spewed everywhere, dousing her and the floor in white and gray layers of softness.

The wooden bunk beds had nothing on how stiff her face turned. Priceless.

"Yep." He picked a ball of fuzz out of her hair. "I'd say it was animals. See the way the tear marks release the feathers like that? Definitely animal work here."

Ti sidestepped away from them. "You're bold, my friend."

"So, I've been told." He looked at Cass, straining to keep the corners of his mouth straight.

She advanced. "You find this amusing, don't you?"

He backed into a bedpost. "Would it make you feel better if I said no?"

"No, but this might." She clobbered him with two pillows at once. "How's that for amusing?"

A series of camera flashes followed a trail of giggles. They both snapped their heads toward Ti. She set the camera down and ran, but Cassidy was too fast. An all-out pillow fight took over the middle of the cabin.

Ethan slinked off the battleground toward the camera. Five pictures later, he lowered the camera, a smile freeze-framed on his face while the two friends wiped off feathers matted to their cheeks in laugh-induced tears. So, Cassidy McAdams knew how to have fun after all.

She turned, as if hearing his thoughts. "What are you smiling about? You know you're cleaning this up, right?"

Joining forces, both girls chased him out of the cabin all the way down the field with a train of feathers floating behind them.

They obviously had a ton of work to do, but he couldn't let the moment end. Not yet. He spun and continued speed walking backward. "You know what you need?"

Cassidy motioned for him to go on, probably patronizing him, but he'd take the chance.

"You need to let your hair down. Pretend you're an eighth grader again."

Her arms came undone. "What?"

The main building passed on his left. "Think about it. You're going to be running a camp for kids. It might be helpful to see things from their perspective."

There were those fierce hazel eyes again. Was he digging his own grave?

He swung his arms out. "Take a look around you. This place is full of memories, right? Why not relive them? Be a kid again."

She stopped under the pine trees behind the building. "I'm not a child, Ethan."

He retraced the steps he'd taken and edged so close, her soft inhale almost drew him even closer. "Maybe it's time you remember how to be one." A current he hadn't expected held him in place, her face right beneath his. Did she have any idea how gripping those hazel eyes were?

Ti coughed, and he stepped back before he risked losing his room. Staring at the roots by his feet, he kneaded his shoulder blade and cleared his throat. "What are some of your favorite memories from here?"

"Climbing trees," Ti answered for her.

Ethan looked up. "Really?"

"She was the fastest climber at camp. Even beat the boys."

He smirked. This he had to see.

Ti swung around the trunk beside them and pointed up. "Her initials are carved at the top of this one."

Shielding his eyes, he craned his neck beneath the massive pine.

Cassidy blew it off. "That was over a decade ago."

Obviously not long enough to lose the pride in her tone. "So, you're saying you can't beat me to the top right now?" She made taunting her too easy.

Her lashes fluttered off the bait. "We have work to do."

"Oh, c'mon. I'll even give you a head start."

She cocked her head. "What are we, like twelve?"

He rubbed his hands together. "One . . ."

"Ethan, we don't have time to play around all day."

"Two . . ."

She stood her ground. "I'm not racing you."

"Thre—" A solid shove to his chest sent him stumbling backward down the hill. By the time he caught his balance, she'd already scaled at least five branches.

Ti stood against the trunk, laughing. "You *did* offer a head start."

Shaking his head, he hustled up to the base and leaped for the closest branch. "So, that's how you won all those times?" he called up to her. "Cheater."

Pine needles falling into his face were her only response. He stretched and climbed. Wind picked up the higher he went. He might've had strength, but she definitely had speed. And experience.

Above him, she dangled her legs off a branch, claiming her throne on top of the world. "Guess it hasn't been *that* long since I've been up here."

"I knew you had it in you." He ducked around a series of smaller branches and pulled himself up to one beside her.

She returned his smile but kept her focus on the bark while running her fingers over the carvings. "I didn't expect to see these ever again."

"You mean scaling to the top of a pine tree wasn't in your plans?"

She plucked a pinecone and flicked it at him. "Nothing you make me do is in my plans."

He caught the cone and laughed. "Oh, *make* you do, huh? I'm pretty sure your fist hit my chest all on its own down there."

"Well, you instigated."

No denying that. But he'd do it all over again. In a heartbeat, if it meant getting to see her up here, red curls blowing in the breeze, face alive in the sunlight. Where was the camera when he needed it most?

He rubbed the patches of sap glued to his skin and turned his palms toward her. "Penance?"

She brushed her thumb over his hand. An unguarded smile blazed back at him with almost more intensity than the sensation of her touch.

"I know a secret for getting that off, but I'm not sure you've earned it."

Scowling, he extended his scratched-up arms. "Do these count?"

"Baby." She smirked while brandishing her own battle scars.

Pain taken in stride. If those scratches stung anywhere near as much as his did, she hid it well. Was that what she'd been doing this whole time? Hiding? He slipped a hand under her arm and brought it toward him. "Looks pretty bad."

"I hear there's a medic on the grounds." She laughed. Genuinely.

The sound curled around him. "That's nice."

"What?"

"Hearing you laugh. You should try it more often."

She drew her arm to her lap and locked her eyes on it as if her gaze would bring supernatural healing.

"Relax, boss. I'm just an employee making an observation." He lowered his head under hers until he met her gaze. "Or a friend."

She lifted her chin but looked out across the top of the tree line. Away from him. The pressure she carried on her shoulders was all but crushing her. He'd seen it since day one. Why couldn't she see he was trying to help?

"Cassidy, renovating the camp is a big undertaking."

Her back stiffened. Even covered in sap and feathers, she upheld a level of dignity like no one he'd ever met.

"I'm not saying you're incapable."

Her chin drooped. "And what exactly are you saying?"

Nothing right, apparently. He scooted forward on the branch and straightened his jeans. After finding a small opening in her armor today, he didn't want it close again. "It's easy to get so driven by a goal that we lose ourselves in the process. Forget why we even started." He ran his fingers down the bark. "Sometimes, we have to take a step back from it all and just *be*, you know?"

Vulnerability practically bled through her soft eyes. "What if we lost who we were a long time ago?"

He swallowed, fighting the need to pull her into his arms and heal whatever hurts she carried. "Then we find someone who can remind us."

She flinched as gravel crunched under tires rolling up the driveway. They both peered down. One glimpse of a blue Saab approaching was enough to turn Ethan's blood cold.

What was *he* doing here? Ethan balled his fists, about to climb down and use them. Except that'd mean ending a moment with Cass he wasn't ready to let go of yet. Not that he had a choice. The look on her face made it clear it was already gone.

CHAPTER SEVEN

Slammed

Nick Ashton. Just the thought of his name made Ethan cringe. What did he think he was doing, showing up here?

Cassidy strode toward the car, plucking feathers off as she went. Behind her, Ethan didn't bother with his. As soon as Nick's face came into view, the feathers would probably burn off his skin on their own.

Nick stepped out from the driver's side as Cassidy approached. "Well, don't you look . . . ?"

"Ridiculous?" She tried to shake a stubborn feather from her fingers.

He steadied her wrist and pulled it off. "I was going to say adorable."

Eyes rolling, Ethan barely choked back a few words he wanted to say himself. He was already gagging on the guy's cologne. Jeez, did he take a bath in it or something? He could've gotten a secondhand buzz standing five feet away from the guy. What he'd do for a fire hose right now. . .

Cass rubbed a thumb over her palm. "How'd you know where to find me?"

Nick shrugged. "Small town."

They shared a laugh. "Speaking of which." He ducked into the car and withdrew a bouquet of yellow flowers. "Only seemed fair for one windflower to be among others."

Windflower? *Please tell me she's not buying into whatever load of crap this loser's dishing out.* And how did they even know each other?

Nick removed another feather from her curls.

Okay, that was enough. Ethan circled the hood and took up post beside her.

Nick lowered his arm and gave him a curt nod. "Ethan."

"What are you doing here?"

Cassidy looked between them. "You two know each other?"

Unfortunately. "I'm from here, remember? I think the question fits you better." He cringed at how that came out. What was with the jealous boyfriend routine? They weren't dating. Heck, they were hardly friends. But this wasn't about them. It was about Nick.

Enough heat radiated off her to burn a hole through the overcast skyline. "Excuse me?"

With his fists still clenched, he didn't back down. He'd probably pay for his insubordination later, but he didn't care. Not while Flower Boy looked at her like a petal he could hold in the palm of his hand.

Nick fiddled with his keys. "Well, I'm sure you both have a lot to do. I'm actually on my way to check on some work myself. Just stopped by to remind you of my offer."

"What offer?" Ethan hadn't meant to say that out loud.

Like it mattered. They both ignored him.

Nick leaned against the frame above his door. "Still got that number?"

She nodded.

He smiled while climbing into his Saab. "Guess I'll see you around, then." He reversed and revved his engine on the way out.

All these years, and he was still overcompensating.

Ethan coughed and waved away the exhaust. Though, he had a feeling whatever reprimand was about to leave Cassidy's mouth might be harder to swallow. Instead, she trotted up the stairs and through the door with the flowers in hand.

Ti flittered onto the scene. How much had she seen?

She grinned. "Bold."

"Is that what you call it?" He stretched out his neck. "I was thinking more along the lines of a glutton for punishment."

"That, too."

Behind them, Cassidy pushed through the screen door on her way back out. He squared his feet, bracing for impact.

Ti wedged between them and averted the imminent collision. "You guys gotta see these pics." She scrolled through the takes on her camera. "Aren't they classic?" She elbowed Cassidy. "Reminds me of that pillow war between cabin two and three in eighth grade. Remember? Well, minus the feathers." She laughed, and remarkably, so did Cassidy.

"I whipped you then, too," Cass said, shoulders relaxing.

"Wha?" Ti shoved her with the lens. "You wish, girl."

Ethan mouthed "Thank you" to Ti from behind Cassidy. He'd take the diversion. However temporary it might be. He slipped into the mess hall and kept his hand on the door until it retracted into its frame without a sound.

Inside the empty hall, his stomach growled on cue. He kicked himself for not remembering to pick up groceries when he'd checked on Nonna last night. He'd have to scrounge. It wasn't much different from living with Sanders and Briggs. Empty fridges meant getting creative, and he could certainly use any kind of distraction right about now.

He swung around the open doorway, hopped up the step leading into the kitchen, and stopped short. Nick's flowers garnished the center of the table. He almost checked for a card but traipsed toward the fridge instead. Wasn't his business.

Yet even across the room, the fragrance still gagged him. He stood in front of the refrigerator's cool draft, waiting for it to knock his body temperature down at least a notch.

Pointless. He swiped a can of Coke from inside the door and dragged it across his forehead.

The cat scampered in and stopped at the sight of him, back arched.

"Perfect timing, bro." What was one more thing to set him off today?

The fur ball rubbed his cheek against the corner of the wall. He had a thing for marking his territory, didn't he? Maybe he wasn't the only one. Jax meandered closer, curious eyes scoping out the counter. Ethan raised his empty hands. Glaring at him, the cat rolled backward and proceeded to lick his rear.

Ethan laughed. "The feeling's mutual, buddy. I assure you."

He loaded his arms with the ingredients for a sandwich and skimmed the countertop for a place to set them down. No paper towels? He dumped the food onto the gritty surface. A little dirt never hurt anyone. Assuming it was dirt and not something worse. He waved it off. Ignorance was bliss.

He hooked a finger around a drawer handle and tugged it open. Empty. Same as the next two. No silverware either? He glanced at the unscrewed mayo jar, rolled a piece of bread into a cylinder, and dipped it in. Creative.

While leaning back on one elbow, he stopped mid-bite and pulled a feather out of the sandwich. The scene from earlier replayed in his mind. The carefree look on Cassidy's face. Her genuine laugher. The glimpse of vulnerability she'd shared . . . until Jerkwad showed up.

She'd been here less than a week, and Nick already found a way to sink his claws into her. Looking back, he wasn't surprised that Nick had duped Jenni. But Cassidy? She was too smart to fall for his charm. He'd warn her if she'd actually trust him. The thought ended in a snort. *That* obviously wasn't happening.

He tore off a bite of his sandwich and glowered at the flowers again. If pastrami didn't mask their scent, nothing would. He needed to get out of this kitchen and back to the canteen, where he could swing a hammer. He returned the food to the fridge and strode to the door with his sandwich. Maybe outside, he could stomach it.

With the girls still out front, he backed up, left through the opposite exit, and plodded to the garage. He wasn't a coward. Okay, maybe he was. But Cassidy didn't exactly exude self-control right now, and he was on the fringes of losing his own. He kicked through a pile of pine needles. Besides, he was just the handyman.

Ti adjusted her giant sunhat. "What's up with the suit?"

Cass rolled her eyes. "He has a name."

"I bet he does. Let me guess. Chump Somebody."

"What's with the attitude?" Cass toyed with a strip of paint peeling off the deck's railing. "He's just a guy I met at the florist's yesterday."

Ti angled her head. "So, then he brings you a bouquet the next day?"

She didn't expect her to get it. "He appreciates flowers, too. It's not a big deal."

"It's kind of creepy. That's what it is. Unlike what Ethan did for you today, which was thoughtful."

"You mean tampering with evidence and creating a huge mess that's going to pull him away from the real work I need him to be doing?" She climbed the steps. "Real thoughtful."

"Okay, first of all, I took pictures when I first found it. Evidence saved." Ti matched Cass's strides. "And second of all, he was trying to lighten your stress level. Help you laugh."

Cass turned. "I don't need to laugh, Ti. I need to get a camp up to code ASAP."

"You don't know what you need." She huffed back down the stairs.

"Where are you going?"

"Into town." Ti spun in the gravel and walked backward toward her smart car. "Off to meet my prince in a flower shop."

Why did everything with her have to be so dramatic?

From around the corner of the building, Ethan trekked toward the canteen with some tools over his shoulder. Back to the work Cass had assigned him.

Her earlier remarks stung with regret. Images of the pillow fight and tree climbing replayed over the ones in front of her. He'd stirred up memories today. Awakened things she'd forgotten how to feel.

The mixed emotions of it all slammed into her doubts about being here. She shoved them down and hustled toward the other set of cabins on the far side of the grounds. If they were damaged, too, she just might lose it. Now that she had to pay off those taxes, she barely had the money to cover basic maintenance repairs. Forget major renovations. She couldn't handle anything else going wrong.

At the door, she drew in a breath, turned the key, and pushed it open. An undisturbed view bounced back to her. Thank God. It wasn't only an issue of money or time. This cabin used to feel like home for her. A place where she'd found escape.

She drifted across the wooden floor, dragging her hand along the bunks until she came to one in the middle. Please let the same acceptance she'd found here as a kid meet her now.

She slipped out of her sandals and curled her legs onto the flimsy mattress.

Thoughts churned against the stillness. Maybe Ti was right. Ethan—a stranger without any connection to the place—seemed better suited to inherit the camp. It was more than his skills. It was like this vivacious love of life anchored him no matter where he landed. And the way he'd talked about running the camp from a child's perspective . . . It'd be effortless for him. The way Grandpa would've wanted it.

Ethan had no idea she planned to sell. Would he think less of her if he did? Would Grandpa? After today, part of her wanted to keep it, but how could she abandon Mom when she was counting on her? Dad had done a sufficient job of that already. She couldn't turn on her, too.

Staring at the bottom of the top bunk, she brushed her fingers across names carved into the wood. Someone had to keep the camp's legacy going. It just couldn't be her.

She reached beneath the bed, pulled out the guitar she'd stashed there the night she first arrived, and drew it into her lap. And as softly as she could, she strummed until the music hedged back the tears she couldn't afford to shed.

CHAPTER EIGHT

Empty

Ethan held a beam to the canteen wall and steadied a level against it. Windflower? Who called a girl a windflower? He wiped his eyes on his sleeve and refocused on the level.

Sweating for the last two hours hadn't drained his irritation. He shouldn't be letting Nick get to him. He'd written the guy off almost nine years ago. The loser could do whatever he wanted with whomever he wanted. It wasn't Ethan's concern anymore.

He traded the level for his nail gun. Two *pops* shuddered throughout the shack and pounded against his already-throbbing temples. He squatted and shot another two rounds in the base. Cassidy never asked for his input. If she wanted to walk into the lion's den, fine. Her call. He was here for Nonna. Nothing else.

Cassidy's Passat slowed around the curve and pulled into her parking spot. Ethan used the front of his T-shirt to dry his face. She'd left not long after Nick had. Where'd she been for two hours? The possibility soured in his stomach. He shouldn't care. But as soon as those hazel eyes found his, logic fell to the ground alongside the discarded nails.

All cleaned up from the feathers, she heaved two gallons of paint out from the trunk.

He was at her side before she reached the stairs. "Here, let me."

"I got it." She kept walking, face as determined as ever.

Was she still upset over how rude he'd been to her and Nick, or was she stressing over the cabins? "Cassidy, about earlier . . ."

"I already ordered new mattresses. The sheriff said he'd come check it out. If it ends up being vandalism, hopefully my insurance will cover some of the cost."

Across the deck, he grabbed the door for her before she set the cans down. She could raise her chin all she wanted. Her eyes were like windows whether she wanted them to be or not. It wasn't easy to hide being overwhelmed. He rested a hand on her arm. "It'll all work out."

Nodding, she blinked away the moisture in her eyes. "Ti's testing out paint colors in the cabins, and I'm going to start on the bedrooms upstairs. If you can stay in the canteen, that's where I need you."

Business as usual. So much for finding a hole in her armor this morning.

Curls drifted over her shoulder as she adjusted her hold on the cans. "I'll be making another run into town tomorrow. Is there anything you need?"

A do-over? He backed up and shook his head. "Nothing at all."

"Okay, then." She disappeared inside, and he returned to his post.

Ti met him on the lawn, swinging a water bottle. She'd traded her crazy hat and hippie-looking skirt for an oversized pair of sunglasses and cutoffs. She might've looked halfway normal if it weren't for the flower power rain boots she was rocking.

"Going to the creek?"

Her glance bounced from her boots to the sky and landed on him. "It's gonna rain. You don't feel that? A storm's blowing in."

A photographer *and* a meteorologist. He hid a smile and opened the side door to the canteen. "Hope you're right. This place could use some cooling off."

From outside, she leaned onto the counter. "It's a defense mechanism."

He lugged his nail gun up from the dusty floor. "What is?"

"Cass's shell." She set her water bottle down and rubbed paint off her fingertips. "Underneath it, she still has some of that kid left in her."

Ethan slanted a brow.

"No, really." Laughing, she withdrew some kind of hemp wallet thing out of her pocket, flipped to a picture, and held it out. "Here. See?"

He hunched over a faded photo of the girls in the main building's kitchen, from the looks of it. Covered in suds, they each held half of a broken plate up to the other.

"We were twelve. Not a care in the world." She stared past him as though reliving the memory. "You should've seen the head cook's face when we dropped that plate. We knew we were in for it, but we kept our cool. And a token." She ran a thumb over the photo. "Best friends forever."

He steadied her wrist for a closer look at the picture. Cassidy's hair was shorter, her legs lankier, but that smile . . . one like he'd never seen from her.

Ti must've read his expression. "Yep. That's pure, bona fide joy right there, my friend. Captured in a photo as proof."

"She looks so full of life." Young, open, carefree. Everything he wished she'd let herself remember how to be.

"She was." Skin wrinkled around her eyes as she returned the wallet to her pocket.

The screen door on the deck creaked open. Cassidy strode toward her trunk, probably for more paint.

Ti glanced backward and wound a straw wrapper around her index finger. "She's six months younger than me, but she's always filled the big sister role. Always the responsible one." She let the wrapper unfurl. "Guess we all deal with pain differently."

He knew that as well as anyone. He unhooked the hose from the gun and coiled it into a circle. "Sounds like you guys have been through a lot together."

"After twenty-seven years, you could say that. Don't know what I'd do without her." She turned, leaned back on her forearms, and lowered her sunglasses over her eyes. "I couldn't talk her into moving to London with me, though."

London? "You live in England?"

She angled toward him. "At the moment, I live here."

"So, you came back just for her?" He set the rolled-up hose on the counter beside a daddy-longlegs making his way to the corner.

"And for me." She peered across the grounds. "You can travel the world, chasing after something that's missing. But sometimes it takes coming home to remember who you are."

The door swung behind Cassidy as she toted the paint inside. Off to work on her own. Would she ever find that joy again? "What happened to her?"

Ti stirred the straw in her water bottle. "Same thing that happens to all of us. Life." Smile sagging, she tapped the ledge and pushed off it. "Not all stories are mine to tell."

He stretched forward. "What if she won't tell me?"

"Wrong question, Ethan." She looked over her shoulder. "The one that matters is what you do when she does."

She'd crossed the full length of the lawn leading to the cabins before he finally moved. But even then, her words kept every muscle in his body locked in a grip he couldn't explain or release. "*Sometimes it takes coming home to remember who you are.*" What if there was no home to come back to?

A white sedan with a city logo on the panel rolled up the driveway. Ethan's already-taut muscles clenched so hard they could've snapped. He pressed his back against the wall in the shadows and peeked through the window. Was Mom sending someone to check up on him?

Cassidy met the city worker at the bottom of the deck. All business, the guy handed her some type of letter. Ethan couldn't hear the conversation from this far away. But if that glimpse of vulnerability flashing across her face meant anything, it couldn't be good. What now?

Shoulders rigid, she uttered a response, nodded, and backed up two stairs. She didn't so much as blink until the city vehicle disappeared from view. Alone, she gripped the rail and closed her eyes.

The strain in her movement propelled Ethan toward her. He didn't slow until three feet away from the steps.

Her eyes flashed open toward the sound of his boots over the gravel. She shoved the paper into her back pocket while he stood there, rubbing the sap left on his hands. Everything he wanted to say stayed buried under his ribcage, but it didn't matter. His face must've said enough.

She stared at the steps. "You can't fix everything."

"What's that supposed to mean?"

"You see me upset and run over here like . . ."

"Like what?" He jogged up the stairs toward her. "Like I might care about what's going on with you?"

She backed into the post. With her face just below his, she inhaled and blinked away from his gaze. Her voice caved to a whisper. "Like you feel sorry for me."

What? "Cass—"

"I need you to fix the camp, Ethan. Not me." She slipped past him, still dodging his eyes, and hurried toward the door.

It took less than a second for the knot in his chest to burn. Fix everything? Couldn't she see he was genuinely concerned about her? Temples pounding, he got in his Jeep and took off. Let her worry about her own problems if she wanted to make everything about work.

At the bottom of the driveway, Deputy Harris's cruiser waited to turn in. Their gazes locked as they passed, but Ethan kept driving. He didn't let up on the gas until a sign for an old friend's café beamed with the remedy he needed.

Coffee.

He parked on the side of the building, stared at the creek behind it, and stalled a minute before killing the engine. If as many people hung out here as in the past, he'd need a lot more than a caffeine-fix to tame his headache. He tapped the dashboard, debating. It had to be better than sitting here, fuming over Cassidy.

A light sprinkle dotted the windshield and garnered a grin out of him. Ti had more instinct than he gave her credit for. He unrolled the Jeep's soft-top header, secured it in place, and hustled inside the shop.

A dozen heads turned as he strode across the black and white tiled floor toward a bar with low hanging lights. In front of the multi-colored chairs, he smiled while perusing an overhead menu written in fluorescent chalk. Same old, eccentric Amy.

On cue, she came out from the back and stopped with two plates balanced on her arm. "Ethan DeLuca. Well, aren't you a sight for sore eyes."

He sat down. "Love the new look."

"Thanks." She blew a strand of spiky, bottle-red hair from her dark-lined eyes and fiddled with a half-inch gauge in her lobe. "It's a work in progress."

Grinning, he lowered his gaze to the bar. "I meant the shop."

"Oh, right. That too. It's a far cry from the hole-in-the-wall place I started with, isn't it? We're even serving food now."

"Perfect. Give me your favorite." He'd burned off that pastrami sandwich hours ago.

Her lips pulled to the side as her gaze traveled over him. "You got it." She whirled around the counter to deliver the plates to a couple in the corner.

Whispers swept across the room with about as much subtlety as the blatant stares pointed his way. Keeping his head down, he dragged a silver napkin holder over from the spot beside him and toyed with the dispenser.

"Jenni know you're here?" Amy glided past him to the register.

He glared around the room full of busybodies. "No. But I have a feeling she will now."

Amy set a glass of water in front of him. "Ham, egg, and cheese croissant okay?"

"As long as it comes with the largest coffee you got."

She laughed. "It's good to have you back, man. Most of these guys can't stomach the kind of coffee we're used to. They only want the frou-frou kind."

He shook his head. "Amateurs."

Another laugh led her through the swinging door into the kitchen at the same time a bell above the front door chimed.

Deputy Harris planted himself on the next chair over. That was fast. He probably spent a whole whopping five minutes inspecting the cabins.

"Ever plan on telling anyone you were back in town?"

Without facing him, Ethan lifted his glass and swirled the ice cubes around. "Figured my mom would have that covered. Haven't her scouts filled you in by now?"

"There ain't nothing wrong with a council woman taking an interest in her city."

Ethan snickered. "You're telling me I've gotten it wrong this whole time? I just have to move back into her jurisdiction for her to care about me. Good to know."

Amy whisked in with his coffee.

Harris nodded at her. "The usual." He pivoted toward Ethan and adjusted his belt buckle. "I see you haven't lost that attitude of yours during your time away. And here, I thought you might be able to set an example for that big city girl you're working for."

Ethan clanked his glass onto the counter. Stares shot toward them from around the room. "You know, Cassidy says we're small town people. Can't imagine where she gets that idea from." He shoved away from the bar and dug out his billfold. "Sorry, Amy. I'll take mine to go." He never should've come in here.

The over-the-door bell rang again. "So, it's true. The cowboy has returned."

Ethan dropped two bills on the counter and froze, gripped by the voice that had broken his heart too many times. Finding his breath again, he inched around and tipped his chin. "Jenni."

Outside light filtered through the windowed door and set off her blond hair. She stood with her thumbs hooked in her jeans pockets, looking as unfairly gorgeous as she always had. She nodded behind her toward the door.

Inhaling, he followed her out. Probably better that way. Whatever showdown she expected, he wasn't about to let it happen in front of an audience.

Clouds filled the sky, but the sprinkle hadn't turned into a full-on rain yet. Shame. He needed that cool-down more than ever. Couldn't his pager go off with a reason to leave? At least he had the excuse to go back and get his sandwich if she tried to drag this on.

She smiled. "Oh, c'mon, Sour Puss. Give me a hug." Rather than wait for a response, she curled her arms around his neck. Her curves pressed against him, feeling way too familiar.

He rolled his eyes, forced in a breath, and pushed her back by the waist. "I'm on the clock, so I should probably run."

Like it'd be that easy. She dragged him down the hill toward the creek. "We haven't seen each other in ages. I think you can spare a few minutes for a friend."

Except they weren't friends. Not anymore. And their old stomping grounds were the last place he wanted to be right now. Not that going back to the camp would be much better.

Alongside the creek bed, she pressed her shoulder into his. "You wanna talk about it?"

"About what?" He knelt and rifled through the rocks for a smooth one.

"Whatever's got your face creased like that?"

She shouldn't still be able to read him like an open book. The connection tore at the edges of the nine-year-old scars she'd given him as a parting gift when they broke up.

Shadows darkened overhead. He flipped a stone around in his hand and skimmed it across the water.

Hands in her back pockets, she swayed from side to side. "O-kay." The dragged-out word ended in the same laugh that used to set everything in his life in balance. "Guess some things haven't changed."

He rose to his feet and met her stare. "Guess not."

She tilted her head. "Ethan . . ."

Without giving them a chance to take cover, the drizzle merged into a downpour. Cold beads pelted his skin through his clothes. She squealed, grabbed his hand, and ran up the hill to his Jeep. They both jumped in and swung the doors shut. Good thing he'd put the top on earlier.

Laughing, she shook the rain off her bare arms, but her soaked clothes stayed glued to her body. He kept his gaze neck up as she scooted toward him and shivered. "Summer rains. Gotta love 'em. Brings back a few memories, doesn't it?"

Regrettably.

He reached in the back seat for his station sweatshirt and handed it to her. Taking it slowly, she grinned wider than necessary. He jerked his focus to the steering wheel, hating the effect she still had on him. "Where's your car?"

She pulled the shirt over her head. "I walked."

Great.

They could go back inside the café, wait out the rain. Except that'd mean instigating even more gossip. His sandwich wasn't worth it. Blowing out a breath, he started the Jeep. At least she didn't live that far away. This interaction had already lasted long enough.

Rain whirled off the windshield as they drove. The silence might've been nice if Jenni's stare from across the seats weren't burning into him like a heat lamp. He snapped on the air, bumped the wipers up another notch, and massaged his forehead. What he wouldn't do for that coffee right about now.

"You're really not going to talk about it, are you?"

He flicked his blinker on. "What's there to talk about?"

"Us."

In front of her house, he lined the Jeep beside the curb but didn't face her. "There's no *us*. You ended that conversation a long time ago."

"We were kids, Ethan. What did you want from me?"

"Oh, I don't know. Commitment, maybe. That little thing you promised when you agreed to marry me." He jabbed his seatbelt buckle and wrenched if off.

"I tried."

He sneered. "I've heard that copout one too many times." They weren't rehashing the past. It was over.

"That's not fair." She twisted in her seat. "You avoided me for years, refusing to give me a chance to make things right. Then you just up and moved away without a word. You have any idea how many times I wanted to come find you?"

"Figured you had your hands full with Nick."

She stretched out her seatbelt. "You knew that wasn't gonna last."

"What, did all those years sharing his bed get a little boring for you? Or let me guess, it got too crowded?" He flipped the unlock button. "Actually, don't answer that. It doesn't even matter."

"He proposed," she almost whispered.

"And you bailed." He shook his head. "At least the next guy down the line has a fair warning of your MO—"

"Nick's not you, Ethan. That's why I said no, okay?" She lowered her chin and her voice. "I should've realized sooner."

The door handle dug into his fingers. "You made your choice." He shoved the door open, stalked into the rain, and pushed his wet hair out of his face.

Her door slammed right afterward. "You want to blame me? Fine. But you're the one who pushed me away. It's because of this." She barreled around the bumper and waved a hand up and down him. "This hurt inside you. It consumes you, Ethan. It has ever since the fire. You ran off with Habitat, then off to some fire station, thinking if you rescue everyone, the pain will go away. But it won't. You can't bring Isabella back."

She faced the sky and swiped the wet hair off her forehead. "After all this time, I thought you might've realized that and finally been ready to let someone in."

He turned and banged his hand against the top of his door. "Enough." He couldn't hear the truth. Not from her.

Rain cut right through him and pounded the pavement as if he were nothing but empty space.

Jenni set her hand on his shoulder. "Ethan—"

"Don't bother." He got in the Jeep, tore down the road, and didn't look back.

Trouble was, even in the rain, some fires still raged.

CHAPTER NINE

Embers

His fight with Jenni still smoldered in Ethan's stomach as he coasted into Nonna's driveway. He'd lost track of how long he'd been driving. Hours, maybe. Not that it'd made any difference. His anger might've faded, but all it left was emptiness.

He gave the door a quick rap before letting himself in. Lady's yapping rivaled an entire alarm system. Man, some days he'd love to stuff that dog inside a fire hydrant.

"If you didn't bring my espresso maker with you, you can stay outside," Nonna called.

Through anything, he could always count on her to make him smile. He shooed Lady back from the door and toed his boots off in the entryway. "I think your espresso days are over, Nonna."

She waved a wooden spoon at him as soon as he rounded the kitchen corner. "We'll see whose days are about to be over if you don't bring that machine back."

Laughing, he crossed the linoleum to kiss her. "I'm twice your size, and you still kinda scare me."

She patted his cheeks. "That's because you're a smart boy." Her gaze paraded down his damp clothes. "Get caught in the rain?"

"Something like that." He opened the fridge, stared blankly inside, and shut it. What was he even looking for? Comfort food? After going all day on just one sandwich, he was past the point of being hungry, anyway. His stomach was numb. Same as the rest of him. He turned and practically tripped over Lady.

"Leaky roofs at the camp?" Nonna asked.

"Among other things." He plopped onto the nearest chair and caught her knowing glance. "What?"

"You tell me."

He blew out a breath. "Nothing to tell."

"Mm hmm." She turned on the burner under a teapot and withdrew a mug and a jar of honey from the cabinet. "You need a cup of hot lemon water before you catch a cold."

Wasn't he supposed to be the one taking care of her? He rose from the chair, but she held a hand up behind her. "Don't even think about it."

"Wouldn't dream of it." Shaking his head, he sat down again and rubbed his feet over Lady's back. Maybe he should forget the camp and talk Nonna into letting him stay here instead. He picked at a loose thread on the embroidered placemat in front of him. "Ever wonder if what you're doing is pointless?"

"All assignments feel like that at some point along the way." She squeezed the lemon and stirred a spoonful of honey into the mug, releasing hints of citrus and intuition into the air.

"Assignment?"

She tossed the lemon into the trashcan, shuffled over, and handed him the mug. "You don't think you're at that camp for no reason, do you?"

He blinked. "I'm sorry, are you trying to say I'm *meant* to be there?"

She tapped his face again. "Like I said. Smart boy."

She couldn't be serious. "If you mean some sort of retribution, then you might be right."

Easing onto the seat across from him, she laughed. "Quite the contrary, dear. I mean restoration."

"Of the grounds?"

She clinked her spoon against the top of her own mug and set it on a napkin. "And perhaps more."

He breathed in the lemon-scented vapors as he took a sip. Her tonic soothed as intended, but her words left him unsettled. "It's kind of hard to restore something that wants to stay broken."

Another telling gaze found his. "You don't say."

This wasn't about him. "You haven't met Cassidy. She doesn't want or need my help. Trust me."

"Oh, I doubt that." She wobbled to her feet.

Ethan rose, caught her elbow, and helped her around the chair.

She made her way to a canister near the microwave and came right back with two pieces of homemade biscotti. "Even if that were true, helping isn't about receiving as much as giving. You know that."

After as many times as she'd drilled that adage into his head growing up, he'd better know it. Wasn't as easy to live, though. He dunked the biscotti and munched into it.

"God has a reason for you to be there, Ethan. You hold on to that, if nothing else."

He tried not to snort. "Yeah, well, if putting up with Cassidy McAdams is my reward, then God has a real sense of humor."

She patted her leg. "The best I've ever known."

Her warm laughter made it hard not to join her. But even the distraction and comfort of being with her couldn't put out the embers Jenni had stoked today.

What about his assignment to protect Izzy? How could God entrust him with anything else after that failure?

The weight pressed on his shoulders and pulled his head down. "I miss Izzy, Nonna." So much that the pain of losing her burned through the dull ache of remorse until he had nothing left to numb it with.

"Me too, sweetheart." She circled the table and held him tight. "Me too."

His sister wasn't the only one he'd lost that night. Ten years of saving other people's lives, and he still hadn't saved his own.

Nonna stroked his back. Held in the closest thing he knew to a mother's embrace, the little boy inside him almost came undone.

She lifted her cheek from his head and patted the weathered skin under her eyes. "Now then, about that espresso maker."

He cracked a grin. "Nonna."

"Okay, okay. But promise me you'll at least bring me a gelato next time."

He squeezed her hand on his way up. "I'll see what I can do."

Lady trotted behind them down the hall. Ethan gave her ears a good scratch and opened the door to nightfall. He must've been out longer than he'd thought. He snapped on the porch light. "*Ti amo*, Nonna."

"*Ti amo*." She kissed his cheeks. "Be careful driving home."

Home. He'd be lucky if he still had one after running off all day without a word. He started his Jeep and tightened his fingers around the gearshift. Only one way to find out.

A mile down the road, he cranked the heat. The earlier rain had brought in a cold front behind it. His headlights tunneled through the steam rising off the pavement. The storm had passed, but he had a feeling a certain redheaded one was waiting to strike next.

At the camp, he crept into his usual parking spot, closed his door as quietly as possible, and peered up at the dark windows in the main building. Maybe he'd luck out and get to sneak inside. His clothes might've dried a while ago, but a hot shower was calling him.

Wind ripped down the mountain with a blustery exclamation point and shook water from the trees onto his head. Rubbing his arms, he turned and caught a glimpse of a light flickering through the mess hall's windows. Cassidy was probably using the fireplace. On a night this chilly, he didn't blame her. It'd almost be as good as a hot shower if it didn't come along with having to face her reprimand.

He glanced back at the deck, his body pulling him in one direction, his thoughts in another. He let out a gruff exhale. "Fine." No use putting it off. He opened the side door and peeked into the quiet room.

The cat flinched in the middle of the floor. Ears flattened, he released a low growl as Ethan started toward him.

"Shh. Don't tell me you're gonna start acting like a watch-dog now."

Jax darted under a chair and stared him down with glow-in-the-dark eyes. Better than getting a death stare from the *other* pair of piercing green eyes in this place. Was it crazy that he wished they were hers instead?

At the end of the room, an almost-burned-out fire waved in front of a loveseat she must've dragged in from another room. The flames cast a glow over Cassidy, curled up with a plush blanket drooping off her shoulder and a book pitched over her stomach. *Redeeming Love.* Grinning, he shook his head. Her tough girl routine was crumbling by the second.

The cat jumped up to the couch arm. Ethan steeled himself for an incoming hiss. Instead, Jax purred and looked up at him as though waiting for Ethan to pet him. Seriously? He extended an arm and rubbed Jax's head with the very tip of his pointer finger. Jax kneaded his paws back and forth against the couch arm. "There ya go. Nice kitty," he whispered. "No waking Cassidy."

A stinging sensation climbed up his chest and throat. He spun, buried his face in his elbow, and held in a sneeze as best he could. Turning, he glared at the cat. "Yeah. That's from you, big guy."

At least he hadn't woken Cass. Talk about a sound sleeper. What else did she keep hidden under that shell of hers? Would she ever let him get close enough to find out?

He covered her shoulder with the blanket and lifted the book. A letter slipped out to the floor. His gaze rebounded from it to Cassidy, but she still didn't move. The city's logo stood out as he picked it up. This must've been what that worker had dropped off today. He glanced at Cass again. Would she want him to know?

Curiosity getting the better of him, he opened the flap and scanned the three-part letter. An inspection? No way they'd pass yet. They needed more time. This better not be Mom's way of taking an *interest*, as Deputy Harris had called it.

The veins on top of his hands throbbed. He shoved the notice back in the book and set it on the couch before he hurled it into the fire. No wonder Cassidy was on edge. The girl couldn't catch a break. He cringed at how he'd reacted earlier. Like she didn't have enough to deal with already without his storming off like an immature teenager this afternoon. He shouldn't take things so personally.

Yeah, right. When had he ever not made things personal? All or nothing. React first, think later. Maybe that was the real reason he'd driven Jenni to choose someone else.

Burying his frustration, he knelt beside Cass and brushed a loose curl as soft as the blanket off her cheek. Relaxed and peaceful. No tension lines. What he'd give to see her this at ease all the time.

His conversation with Nonna burrowed into him and drove him back on his heels. Was this what she'd meant about an assignment? Getting Cassidy to let her guard down?

He rose, backed away. Nonna didn't know what that'd mean. He couldn't open Cass's heart while keeping his closed.

Thoughts churned as he stoked the kindling and added three logs to the fire. A shadow flickered outside the window. He jerked around toward a rustling noise echoing from the deck.

His gaze flew to Cassidy, pulse jacking. He might not be able to protect her heart, but he'd protect her home. Shoulders squared, he swiped the fire poker and slinked out front.

Sandy's bark jolted Cass up from the loveseat. She gripped the top edge, pulled herself up, and waited for the empty hall to come into focus. Ti was still out when she'd fallen asleep. She'd probably just gotten in. Yawning, Cass folded the blanket over the end of the couch and rubbed her arms. The fire crackled and invited her closer to its warmth.

Something zipped past the window. She whirled around. "Ti?"

No answer.

She clutched her elbows and froze, all senses heightened. The fire popped again. Heat spread up her body. Outside, something clawed against the shingled siding. Backing into the stone fireplace, she groped around for the fire poker, grabbed the shovel instead, and brought it to her chest. "Ti?" she whispered this time.

The clawing intensified, closing in all around her. Heart pounding, she dropped the shovel and sprinted to the kitchen, where she fumbled around for the flashlight hanging above the counter. She pushed the button. Once. Twice. "Come on." She hit it against her palm.

A crash rang from the deck. She opened drawer after drawer. With all her lists, how did she forget to pick up batteries? And where was Ethan?

She shoved the last drawer in, spun away from the counter, and calmed herself. It didn't matter that Ethan was gone. If someone were on her property, she'd take care of it. It was time people knew this wasn't an abandoned camp to vandalize for kicks.

She marched down the hall, still gripping the flashlight. At least it'd work as a weapon if she needed it. Sandy's barks grew louder. She crept across the last few feet leading to the door and flipped on the outside light, but the deck stayed dark. Drawing in a breath, she nudged the screen open and almost stepped onto a pile of broken glass in front of it.

Sandy chased two animals into the woods along the edge of the field. Footsteps closed in from behind her. Her pulse skipped. She raised the flashlight and whirled around.

Someone grabbed her arms. "Whoa. It's okay."

She flailed against him, trying to break free.

His hold tightened. "Cassidy, calm down. It's just me. Sandy and I ran off the raccoons. No one's gonna hurt you."

Ethan's reassuring voice rushed over her, but panic kept surging. "What are you doing out here? You left." She winced at how much hurt came through those two words.

"I'm sorry." He let go. "When I got back, I heard a noise on the roof and climbed the fire escape to check it out. Looks like someone dumped garbage up there. The raccoons were having a field day."

"Garbage?"

He nodded. "They'll be back if we don't clear it, but there's nothing we can do about it now. I'll get up there in the morning."

Garbage on the roof to draw raccoons. That seemed a little farfetched. Did the kids around here think this was some kind of joke? They had no idea what was at stake, what this was costing her. "Who's doing this, Ethan?"

"I don't know." He rested a hand to her cheek. "But we're going to stop them."

The fear still tearing across her muscles dwindled at his touch. She rested a palm to the front of his shirt, wanting to draw near, wanting him to be right. "What if we can't?"

He curved an arm around her back and pulled her close. "I won't let that happen."

Enclosed in a promise she wished more than anything she could trust, she closed her eyes and pressed tighter. His whiskers rubbed against her hair as she nestled her face beneath his neck. The scent of the mountain clung to him. Strength, hard work, passion. It all wrapped around her in layers of yearning she thought she'd forgotten how to feel—desires she knew better than to give a hold.

What was she doing?

She pushed away. "It's, um . . . It's going to be an early morning." She backed up toward the door, tucking her hair behind her ears. "We should both get to bed."

He blinked but didn't move. His confused expression launched her inside and down the hall. In the safety of her bedroom, she hunched against the door and craned her neck to the ceiling. *Get a grip, Cass.* She tapped her head behind her. *Business. Just. Business.* If someone really was attacking the camp, how could she be thinking of anything else?

CHAPTER TEN

Brooding

What little sleep Cassidy had gotten last night made facing today even more exhausting. How could she expect Ethan to respect her as his boss after practically melting in his arms last night?

She banged her chisel against a stubborn strip of paint on the deck's railing slat. Working alongside him all morning in silence had only exacerbated the problem. At least, for her. He was probably avoiding it because he sensed she'd felt something.

She grabbed the strip of paint and yanked it off with her hands. She shouldn't have let him see her that vulnerable. The frustration of it all grumbled with her empty stomach.

From the driveway, Sandy alternated between jumping and crouching as he followed Ethan's movement back and forth across the deck. He might've been a good watchdog last night, but he was gonna get a muzzle today if he didn't stop barking louder than the sander.

She tossed her fleece pullover into the corner and exhaled as a breeze ran over her damp skin. It was crazy how much the temperature swung in a matter of hours. By afternoon, Ti's bath of choice was always more than a little tempting. Especially today. Maybe the freezing creek water would shock some sense into her. Lord knew she needed to get a grip. They had an inspection to prep for.

Ethan turned off the sander and rearranged the Adirondack chairs before starting on the next section. Sweat beaded on his temples and soaked through his navy blue T-shirt.

He had to be exhausted. After clearing the garbage off the roof first thing and checking for any damage, he'd been slaving away on the deck nonstop.

Sandy darted a glance toward the tree line. Ears and tail raised, he sniffed the air and took off, probably to chase some innocent squirrel.

Ti blew through the screen door, pinching a pair of rubber gloves off. "If I never see the inside of an oven again, I won't mind."

Cass lifted a hand to shield her eyes from the sun. "Might as well make it a first and last experience all at once."

"Like you can talk." She shook the wet gloves over Cass's head while sauntering across the deck. "Not sure all that scrubbing did much good. You should just buy a new one."

If only it were that easy. Cass twisted her hair off her neck. "Unfortunately, the oven has to stay. A new range is all I can afford right now."

"Well, maybe we can . . . Eww. What's that smell?"

Ethan walked over and whiffed. "Skunk." He took one look at Ti's scrunched nose and laughed. "Welcome to life in the mountains."

She tossed her head back. "Don't remind me." She leaned her elbows beside an empty planter on the rail. "Please tell me they at least have some good coffee joints in the mountains."

Cass wouldn't mind a latte herself right now. Especially if it came with a chocolate muffin. Or twenty.

"We've got a few." He strolled back over to the sander. "Even ones with real life baristas."

Ti grabbed a paint stick off the rail and flicked it at him. "Hey, a town without a Starbucks is a little shady. I'm just sayin'."

"Well, small town America might just introduce you to this thing called mom-and-pop shops." Grinning, he wiped his face across his sleeve. "You should check out my friend's café down off Jamison Street. Amy's sort of . . . eccentric. I think you'll like her."

Cass wedged the chisel under another piece of splintered wood. Amy. Jenni. How many girlfriends did he have around this place?

Ti's face lit up as if he'd spoken the magic password into her world. "Like, artsy eccentric?"

His dimples curved. "You could say that."

"We're going." She looped her bracelet-covered arm around his. "C'mon."

Cass dropped her tool. "Excuse me? Ethan's on the clock." She winced at how that came out. He'd earned more respect than that. And why was she referring to him like he wasn't standing there?

She rose, adjusted her jeans, and forced herself to face him head-on for the first time today. Bad move. Regret hit her in the gut the second the transparency in his eyes showed her response had hurt him. Again.

"It's noon, Cass. The guy deserves a lunch break."

Ti had her, there. Ethan worked as hard as she did. Harder. And for what? A subpar room in a rundown camp? Of course he deserved a break. More, if she could give it to him.

"Sorry, right. I lost track of time." She lowered her defenses along with her arms.

Ti didn't miss it. "Why don't you come with us? You obviously need a caffeine break yourself."

And be the third wheel? Or the fifth, or however many wheels the guy had going? Ti was the better choice for a good time. Cass tightened her ponytail. "I should stay and work." *And keep boundaries where they belong.*

"Always the responsible one." Ti glanced up at Ethan, as though sharing an inside joke.

His forehead pinched, and Cass looked away. She'd already shown him enough weakness. Her knees hit the deck as she resumed the only thing she needed to focus on right now.

"Fine, Party Pooper. We'll bring you back something." Ti tugged Ethan down the stairs toward his Jeep.

Cass chucked the chisel across the deck the minute the gravel settled behind them. *Get it together, already.* She strode inside, flushed her face with water, and backed against the wall in the bathroom that Ethan had patched flawlessly.

They were both here to work. Plain and simple. Anything else was simply a distraction. Yesterday's visit from the city had made that much clear.

The letter weighed against every thought. It wasn't like she didn't know an inspection would be in order before selling. She just anticipated having more time to prepare.

Okay, so it'd been a full year since Grandpa had died, but she couldn't get here any sooner. She had responsibilities. Had to make arrangements. Surely, they could understand that.

Was this more about the taxes owed? She'd settle up if they'd give her the chance. It'd be in the city's interest for her to sell the place and pay off the balance instead of shutting it down and carrying the bad debt even longer. Did these people know anything about business?

She released her tight fists. Fuming over it wasn't getting the work done. If she only had a month, she'd have to push even harder. On her way out, she stopped just past the bedroom door, retraced her steps, and picked up a slip of paper lying on the dresser. An extra pair of hands definitely wouldn't hurt.

Before over-thinking it, she dialed Nick's number and returned to the deck. He worked a few days in the city. He probably wasn't even around right now. She ran a finger along a crack in the empty planter while the phone rang.

"Nick Ashton."

She hopped back from the rail. "Oh, hi. Sorry. I, uh, sort of didn't expect you to answer. This is Cassidy." The girl who usually didn't ramble.

"I was starting to think you weren't going to call."

She picked at the planter again. "It's been kind of busy. Actually, that's why I'm calling. You wouldn't happen to be in town, would you? I'm a little under the gun to get some renovations done and could use the help."

"Wish I could. My mongrel boss has me cooped up in the city most of this week, negotiating a big deal. Can I take a rain check for next week?"

"Yeah. Yeah, of course." Her shoulders slumped. "You know what? Don't even worry about it." What was she thinking, asking him to come to begin with? He and Ethan obviously didn't get along.

"You sure you're okay? DeLuca's not slacking on the job, is he?"

She almost laughed. "Not at all."

"Okay. But do me a favor and be careful around him."

"What are you talking about?"

He paused as if debating whether to fill her in. "The guy's kind of a loose cannon. He almost put me in the hospital when he found out his fiancée chose me over him."

Fiancée? She stiffened. "Wait, you guys fought over the same girl?" That explained why Ethan was so uptight when Nick came by the other day.

"It wasn't like that. He drove Jenni away. She shouldn't still be—" He stopped himself and released a gruff breath. "He's got a history of letting people down, Cassidy. I'm glad he's there to help, but don't put too much faith in him, or you'll end up disappointed."

She glanced at the sander, lying on the deck where Ethan'd left it after busting his tail all morning for free. Would he end up walking out on a job half-finished? The image didn't jive with what she'd seen of him so far. But either way, Nick had nothing to worry about. She'd stopped putting faith in people years ago.

Someone called him in the background. "Listen, I gotta run. We'll catch up next week, okay?"

"Okay." She hung up, but his warning kept festering. She shouldn't have called.

An SUV with a canoe strapped to the top soared around the corner and parked in front of the deck.

She had just enough time to shake off the effects of the call before a gorgeous blonde glided up the steps. Cass stood a little taller. "Can I help you?"

She peered around her. "Yeah, I'm looking for Ethan DeLuca."

"And you are?"

The girl's attention drifted to her then. A swaggering grin touched her face. "An old friend." She extended a hand. "Jenni Weiss."

She was his ex-fiancée? Begging her face not to flinch, she shook Jenni's hand. "Cassidy McAdams. Ethan's not here."

"But he works here, right?" Blondie scoped out the camp in one panoramic sweep. "Don't even worry about answering that. A fixer upper like this has Ethan's name all over it." Her scrutinizing gaze trailed down Cass's profile. "A lost cause is his specialty."

This chick was about two seconds away from being strangled by her salon-perfect hair.

"Would you return this for me?" She held out a sweatshirt. "Tell him I said thanks."

Was that where he was last night? Sharing his clothes with an old "friend"? It took a moment for Cass to find her voice again. "Did you, um, hang out with him recently?" What was she doing? It wasn't her business.

Jenni stopped at the bottom of the stairs with her back toward her. "If you can call it that." She peered over her shoulder. "From one girl to another, stay away from that one. He's a heartbreaker."

Sounded to Cass like it was more the other way around.

Jenni strolled to the car, curvy hips swaying with each strut.

If there weren't spiders under the deck, Cass might've crawled under it until enough time passed for Ethan to forget the way she'd held on to him last night. As if it couldn't get any more embarrassing, now she had the firsthand image of who he was used to having in his arms. She closed her eyes and massaged her temples.

Something wet brushed her elbow. Head cocked, Sandy looked up at her with sympathetic eyes.

"Do I look that bad?" She squatted and rubbed both sides of his mud-crusted face. "Look who's talking, buddy. I think it's past time for a bath. What do you say? Good idea?" If she were lucky, it'd wash away the stress she couldn't get a handle on. At least, until Ethan got back.

In front of the turn to the driveway, Ethan waited for a string of cars to pass from the opposite direction.

Was Cassidy going to ignore him all day? He hadn't meant to pull her into his arms last night, but the helplessness on her face had just about crumbled him. She was scared. And for good reason. If some punks were trying to trash the place, they could end up putting her and Ti in danger.

Maybe they should get a security system. Except that'd mean an extra expense she probably wouldn't want to pay for. And who would they get to install it? Wood and a hammer he could handle. But techy stuff, he had no clue.

At the very least, he could stay on the property more. She could do the cold shoulder thing if she wanted to. Keeping his heart off the table would make it easier to stay on track, anyway. But they needed someone around to keep an eye out.

He gassed the Jeep up the driveway, suspension squeaking. Was it really so bad for him to want to protect her?

Ti grabbed his forearm. "Slow down, Speed Racer. I know this thing has four-wheel drive and all, but I'd rather not toss my lunch getting seasick from these potholes."

"Sorry." He let off the gas pedal. "Wasn't paying attention."

She transferred her hold from his arm to her seatbelt. "Brooding will do that to ya."

"I'm not brooding." He circled the wheel and pulled into the spot beside her smart car.

"Yeah, just like you weren't brooding for the last hour. Which we happened to have spent visiting Amy at the coffee shop, in case you missed that part while lost in your own head. Good thing I was there. She would've been talking to a wall."

He gaped at her. "Were you guys off getting pedicures the day they were handing out filters or something?"

She laughed. "Glad you're finally catching on."

He clambered out of the Jeep, shut the door, and stared over the hood. In jean shorts, a tank, and Ti's rain boots, Cassidy danced around the basketball court, trying to get Sandy to stay still while she sprayed him with the hose.

She must not have noticed they'd come back. Covered in suds, she laughed and played with the dingy dog she'd had too much compassion to turn away.

Ethan's foot slipped off his Jeep's rock rails, his heart falling after it.

Ti looked between the two of them, grinned, and waved the coffee she'd brought back for her. "Yo, Cass. Coffee time."

Cassidy sprayed off her hands and jogged over with Sandy galloping behind her. "Thanks." She practically inhaled the drink.

Ti rubbed the top of Sandy's wet head with a single finger. "Thought you had work to do."

"This *was* work. Trust me. That dog had at least ten years' worth of junk on him."

He wasn't the only one.

Hands in his pockets, Ethan shuffled around the front bumper and forced his gaze to stay on Cass's face instead of her wet clothes. Not that it made things much easier. He couldn't take his eyes off her. Damp curls matted around her cheeks. A streak of mud smeared across her freckles. Short enough without her heels to fit into his arms perfectly.

If he didn't come up with a reason to excuse himself fast, he was gonna be in trouble.

Sandy shook from head to tail, showering both girls in dirt-tinted water.

Ethan called him over and kept him still. Wet dog smell clashed with hints of some kind of Hawaiian fragrance. He smiled. She'd washed him with dish detergent.

Cassidy took one look over herself and cracked up.

Ti, not so much. She wiped the dirty residue off her arms. "It's a good thing we have to get cleaned up tonight, anyway."

"For what?" Cassidy lifted the wet tips of her hair off her shirt.

"Ethan's taking us out to a club tonight."

He rose and almost tripped over the dog.

"What?" he and Cassidy said at the same time.

"His friend Amy was telling me about this cool joint where they used to hang out. It's only like three blocks from here, if you can believe it. Bar'll be open from six on, but dancing starts at eight. Ethan agreed to take us. Well, his side of the conversation was more like grunts and nods in between brooding over you, but whatever. We're going."

Wow. Just when he thought her no-filter issue couldn't get any worse. He scratched his warm cheek. But if Cass caught anything other than the we're-going-out part, she didn't show it.

"Ti, I'm not here to go dancing."

She grabbed Cass's arm and led her toward the deck. "Yeah, you're here to work. I know. You have a full eight hours to work to your heart's content. Then, we're having fun."

They disappeared through the door, leaving him and Sandy outside. "Got a doghouse we can go hang out in?"

Sandy rolled on the gravel and squirmed back and forth with his paws in the air. So much for staying clean. He sat up and yawned.

Ethan laughed. "I'd love a nap after a shower, too, buddy. But it's gonna be a long afternoon." And night. He'd stayed away from that bar the last eight years for a reason. Just the thought of bringing Cass there made his stomach turn.

He looked back at the soap-covered basketball court. Images of her laughing with Sandy balled his heart in a knot. And he was supposed to keep his distance from her? Like that was happening. Especially not tonight.

CHAPTER ELEVEN

Invincible

Eight hours might as well have been eight minutes. Working like a madman the rest of the day hadn't kept Ethan's mind off the club. He glared at his silent pager, willing it to go off on command so he could cancel.

He finished brushing his teeth, trimmed his "scruff," as Nonna called it, and ran his hands through his toweled hair. One glance at his antsy reflection in the mirror sent him hustling downstairs and into the night's cool air.

At least the stars were perfect. Probably the only thing about tonight that would be. Ti and Cassidy were about to be handed the small town weekly special—gift-wrapped in beer bellies, greasy beards, and even slimier hands. Two gorgeous girls from out of town walk in, and those country star wannabes will be all over them in a second.

He gripped the rail, stomach tensing. Last time he'd stepped foot into Corbit's club was the night he gave up drinking for good. But if "getting cleaned up" meant Cassidy would look even half as attractive as she did in jeans and a ponytail, his eight-year streak of no bar fights might be over.

Ti bounced through the door, looking chic as usual, but his attention gravitated straight to Cassidy's long red curls swaying over her shoulders. She stepped out in heeled sandals, fitted jeans, and a flowy shirt that complemented her petite frame in all the right ways.

The lump in his throat plummeted past the pit of his stomach and bottomed out on the nerve ending controlling his ability to move.

Ti patted him on the shoulder as she passed. "Ready?"

Not if being ready required breathing.

Cass kept her gaze on the deck. "Why are you looking at me like that?"

The fact that she didn't know made her even more attractive. He waited for her to meet his eyes. "Because you're beautiful, Cass." All sense of logic lost, he edged closer and raised her chin. "Don't ever doubt that."

Her lashes closed and lifted slowly, sending his pulse thundering under his skin.

Ti snapped a picture from the Jeep. "You two are adorable, but save it for the dance floor."

Backing up, he rubbed his neck. Cass hurried past him and climbed into the passenger side. Ethan joined them, never so thankful for his topless ride. The cool wind was bound to save him.

If only it would've lasted. The crowded inside of Corbit's bar cranked his temperature up in two seconds flat. And when some young thing in boots and a low-cut dress brushed by him while pulling a cherry between her teeth, his dinner almost came back up, too.

How did he ever stand that nauseating stench of beer?

At the bar, Joe Schmoes One and Two gawked at Ti and Cass as if they'd locked their John Deere headlights on them.

Ethan tried to block the girls behind him, but Ti bubbled around his shoulder. "Excuse me. A hard lemonade's calling my name."

"How about you let me get that for you." He intercepted her and steered them both toward a table by a window. "Cass, you want something?"

"Whatever you're having." She caught his wrist before he left. "Actually, just a Coke is fine."

An exhale of relief oozed out of him as he turned. Having to watch her get tipsy in a place like this might've sent him over the edge. He made his way to the bar and nodded at a girl in all black behind the counter. "One Mike's Hard Lemonade and two Cokes, please."

A hunched-over guy on the stool beside him waved a beer bottle in his direction. "Well, I'll be damned. Hey, Corbit," he yelled toward the guy behind the bar. "Look who decided to show his pretty face in these parts again."

At the register, Corbit wobbled his oversized self around. "If it ain't Ethan DeLuca. Knew you was talking trash when you said you wasn't coming back."

God help him. As if merely being here weren't enough of an embarrassing reminder of how he used to get wasted to dull the pain of missing Izzy. He slapped two bills on the counter. "I'd love to take a trip down memory lane with you guys. But since you've got a packed house, you probably want to keep those customers happy."

He turned before they got another word in and weaved through the crowd. Four feet in front of the table, he almost fumbled the drinks. Some lumberjack dude was escorting Cass onto the dance floor, and all Ethan could do was stand there. Staring.

Ti snagged his sleeve and pulled him to the corner. "She has trouble saying no."

He deadpanned her. "That girl has never had trouble telling me exactly how it is."

"You're different." She swiped her lemonade from his arms. "That's business."

"Thanks for reminding me." He set the cups down and sank onto the chair. Fresh air breezed through the half-open window, but everything about the stuffy room still choked him. People yelling over the music, sweat and cologne warring for dominance, girls eating up every lame come-on thrown at them. His past had never looked more repulsive.

Without releasing Lumberjack from his sight, he tapped a straw on the table to unwrap it and plunked it into his glass. Cassidy could dance with whomever she wanted. She'd made it clear where he stood in her eyes. He sucked down his Coke, the sting harder to swallow.

The slimeball's hands drifted down her back. Clutching his glass, Ethan forced himself to lower it slowly. The dude slipped his hands past her belt, and Ethan sprang up.

Ti swung an arm in front of him. "Easy, tiger. It's too early to start a bar fight."

If she only knew. Not that Cassidy needed him to intervene. She twisted the guy's wrist in some kind of self-defense move that had him moaning and stalked off the floor to the table.

"You okay?" Ethan's voice was about as smooth as the chair still teetering behind him.

She shrugged. "Fine."

Not if her eyes had anything to say about it.

Ti threw back a swig and glided around the table. "Why don't you two go out back for some air? Chill by the creek for a while."

Cass raised a brow. "Doesn't that defeat the purpose of being here?"

"Depends on whose purpose we're talking about." Grinning, Ti whisked into the crowd.

Cassidy curled her hair to one side, looking in about every direction but his. All she had to do was say the word, and he'd get her out of here in a second. Take her anywhere she wanted to go. Except out by the creek. The inside held enough regrettable memories of its own.

She smiled faintly. "It *is* kind of loud in here."

Resigning, he nodded at the door and led her out.

Under the porch light, she fiddled with the hem of her shirt. "Sorry. I'm not very good at the letting loose thing."

Was she seriously apologizing for that? "No one said you had to be."

She scoffed but turned instead of saying anything and moseyed toward the back of the building. Taking a breath, Ethan followed her down the firefly-lit path. At least the stars had held up their role for the night.

Moonlight covered the creek running downstream over rocks and gullies. They must've gotten a lot of rain this spring. He couldn't remember seeing the current this strong.

Cass leaned against a tree trunk and closed her eyes. "I forgot how peaceful the Catskills are. Probably sounds funny, but I think that's one of the things that fascinated me most as a kid. No rumbling from the subway. No yelling matches coming through apartment walls. Just quiet." She laughed. "Well, other than that twangy country music."

With the way she stole his focus, he'd tuned out the bar's noise completely. Lightning bugs stirred around her, probably drawn to her as much as he was. He shouldn't have thought twice about coming out here with her. As familiar as it was, she made it new. "Cass, I—"

The back door swung open. Of all people, Jenni stumbled out with a glass splashing all around. Her moment's surprise at seeing them transitioned into amusement.

She staggered forward and latched on to the garbage can for balance. "Look at you, Ethan, sharing like a good boy. And here I thought these woods would always be ours."

She slipped off her heels and almost tottered over. "Canoeing, bridge jumping, camping in the same sleeping bag. We had fun, didn't we?" She stumbled toward them and waved her glass toward the woods. "Don't worry . . . Cassidy, is it? Ethan knows how to show a girl a good time."

"That's enough, Jenni."

Cassidy didn't move a muscle in response. She didn't have to. Her eyes said enough. And what could he possibly say in return?

"Aw, sweetie, I didn't mean to . . ." Gripping the nearest tree trunk, Jenni hunched over and hurled.

Perfect. He steadied her by the waist.

Jenni slid a hand to the back of his hair. "Same old Ethan. Always coming to a girl's rescue."

Jaw clenched, he helped her toward the door. "I think it's about time you headed home."

Cassidy hugged her arms to her chest and stared out toward the creek.

His heart sank at her guarded pose. No telling how much damage Jenni had just caused.

"Let me call her a cab. I'll be right out."

Cass turned then, face wiped of any emotion. "You can take her home. I'm gonna walk back."

"What?"

She pushed off the tree. "We're only a few blocks away. And I didn't get my run in this morning. It's fine."

"You're not walking alone in the dark. Just . . ." He sighed. "Give me a sec to get her settled and grab Ti, okay?"

She nodded, and he swept open the door. A flood of everything from his old life that he'd tried to put behind him rushed out from inside the crowded room again. He should've gone with his instincts and stayed home.

He set Jenni in a chair, pulled out his cell, and made the call.

She clutched his sleeve and pulled herself up into his arms. "This is right, you know. The two of us. Tell me you don't still have feelings for me."

"We've been through this." He unwound her arms from his neck and lowered them to her sides.

She looked up with blue eyes that had finally lost their hold over him. "People change."

"Exactly." Smiling sadly, he curved a strand of hair around her ear. He didn't want to hurt her, but she had to accept they were done.

"It's been nine years, Ethan." She grabbed his hand as he turned. "I thought you would've forgiven me by now."

His chin drifted to his chest with an exhale. "I have. But forgiveness doesn't erase consequences." He knew that better than anyone.

He released her hand and wedged through the people on the dance floor. A quick backward glance caught Nick approaching Jenni. Where'd he come from? Ethan faced forward. Not his business. He pried Ti away from some hipster-looking dude. "Time to roll."

Her gaze veered toward the overhead clock. "Not even close."

"Cassidy's ready to go."

"Good job, Columbo." She patted his back and winked. "Now's the part where you drive her home by yourself."

He jutted his chin. "And what about you?"

A telling grin peeked over the top of her bottle. "I'll figure it out."

And he was supposed to be okay with that? His shoulders dropped. "Let me see your phone."

She handed it over, and he plugged in his cell number. "If I don't hear from you by midnight, I'm coming back."

She saluted. "Yes, sir. Now, hurry up. The girl you really want to protect is waiting."

And probably ready to put him in his place after Jenni dredged up his past.

Turning, he caught another glimpse of Jenni and Nick, arguing from the looks of it. Thank God, his days with that were over.

At least, he hoped. He steeled himself on his way out the back door again, but Cass was gone. He jogged around to the parking lot. Empty. Pulse picking up, he made a beeline to his Jeep and gunned out. Gravel sputtered under his wheels and tumbled across the road behind him.

Cass came into view around the bend. He rolled up beside her. "I told you to wait."

"The driveway's right there. I'm fine."

He swerved the Jeep in front of her and opened the door. "Get in the car."

Huffing, she climbed in.

He sped up the drive, the potholes nowhere near as volatile as his emotions. "You don't just go walking the streets at night by yourself."

"This isn't the city." She folded her arms and stared out the window.

He barreled into the parking spot. "I don't care where you are, Cass. You're not invincible."

She glared at him, lips tight. Whatever she held in practically burned through her cheeks. She stormed out of the car and toward the deck.

He cut her off at the stairs. "Will you stop running already?"

She grabbed a sweatshirt from the top step and shoved it into his stomach. "Jenni dropped this off earlier."

A tendon on his neck hardened. "Jenni and I are ancient history."

"History tends to repeat itself." She turned. "I'm not another of your girlfriends who needs to be saved, all right?"

He caught her hand. This wasn't just about Jenni. "You can give up the tough girl act. I don't buy it."

She snatched her arm away and crossed it over her chest, hair blazing in the wind.

He didn't care if he lost his room over this. He was done watching her hide behind a mask. "Who are you trying to be? You care for stray dogs, set ladybugs free, read romance novels. You're not as hard as you pretend to be, Cass. You're . . ." Everything he'd seen in her—the strength, compassion, determination—pounded inside him and drew him toward her.

She backed into the rail. "Don't look at me like that."

"Like what?"

"Like you want to kiss me."

She had no idea. "Would that be such a bad thing?"

Head lowered, she looked away. "You might be disappointed."

Was that what she was afraid of? He edged closer. The transparency in her voice just about depleted the strength enabling him to wait until she met his eyes again.

He smoothed his thumb across her warm cheek and cupped the back of her neck. A breath at a time, he leaned in until his lips nearly brushed hers. "Or I might fall for you even more than I already have."

Her breath touched his skin and brought his lips to hers. His fingers slipped into her curls. Soft and unassuming, she moved with such gentleness, it drew him in even tighter.

She glided her palms up his chest to his neck and broke the last barrier holding back his reservation. His kiss deepened until something wet collided with his hand on her cheek. He pulled away.

Tears streamed down her face.

He searched her eyes. Did he push too far? "I'm sorry."

Without looking at him, she withdrew up the stairs and stopped at the top. Her shoulders rose and fell with the same intensity moving his. He jogged up to her, lost for words. *Please tell me I haven't just ruined everything.*

She turned, slid her fingers behind his ears, and kissed him on her own. She held on, pulse beating against his skin.

He drew her hands down to his chest as she lowered back to her heels. "Cass . . ."

"Please don't say anything," she whispered before letting go and slipping away. As always.

He almost went after her into the house but sensed he shouldn't. He caved against the wall, heart still pounding. And with the tingling of her kiss still on his lips, he faced a sky that had just fallen into second place.

He hadn't planned on kissing her tonight. Or at all. Not that he hadn't wanted to a dozen times, but she'd been so closed off, so determined to keep her walls up. Was it all a defense mechanism because she was afraid to admit how she felt? But the way she kissed him back . . . that had to be real. Then why had she cried?

A knot of unease coiled itself around his insides until it smothered the intoxicating feeling left from having her in his arms. He was scared, too. More afraid of what would happen tomorrow.

CHAPTER TWELVE

Deflection

Cass backed up and eyed the sparkling new gas range from the hundredth angle. The installers left hours ago, but she hadn't managed to drag herself out of the room since first thing this morning.

She tightened the bandana under her hair and pulled her gloves off. One thing was for sure. An inspector would have to admit the kitchen was spotless, at least.

Too bad her thoughts weren't.

Ethan had given her space all day. Hadn't approached her, even once. But she didn't have to see him to feel his lips against hers. The tender strength in his hold, his stubble under her palms. She'd relived it a thousand times since last night, always torn between wishing she'd stopped him and relieved she hadn't.

She should've been stronger. Not let him see how scared she was to feel anything for him. Or to feel, period. Now that he had, how could she redraw professional boundaries?

Jax weaved between her legs.

She crouched and rubbed the line running down his nose. "How do you wear a split face so beautifully, huh?"

He propped his front paws on her knee and nuzzled his face under her chin. She scooped him up and savored his purr against her chest. The perfect massage therapy. If only it could keep the tension from claiming the rest of her body.

"Ahem," Ti said from the doorway. Gaining Cass's full attention, she sashayed into the room, donning a pair of dark brown, square-shaped glasses and a tan trilby hat.

"Who are you supposed to be, Johnny Depp?"

Ti ran her fingers across the brim. "You don't like my style?"

"Which one? It changes every day."

"Ahh . . . the brilliance of variety."

"Or deflection." Cass set Jax down, rose, and pulled her apron over her head.

"From what?"

"You tell me."

Avoiding the comment, Ti whisked the fridge open. "I'm going to a show tonight. I need some inspiration for the art pieces I want to make for the mess hall."

Case in point. "What, like off-Broadway or something?"

She withdrew a bottle of water. "More like impromptu backstage stuff. This guy at the club last night was telling me about it."

"How do you find these people?"

Ti twirled her beaded necklaces into a spiral. "Kindred spirits call to each other."

Must be why Cass didn't have many friends. "Well, be careful with these *kindred spirits.*"

Ti waved off her concern. As usual. "Is Ethan back from his call?"

"What call?"

After guzzling half her water, Ti set it on the counter. "I don't know. He got a page and left in his gear." A grin hiked up her cheek. "Speaking of which. Don't you wonder how easy his suspenders are to get off?"

All Cass could do was shake her head.

Some pop song ringtone blared from Ti's cell. She tipped it out of her hemp purse, made a face, and ignored the call.

Cass polished the new backsplash with the balled-up apron. "Still fighting with Murray?"

"I'm *always* fighting with Murray." She adjusted her purse strap. "Whatever. If he can run off to Paris with a bunch of models and call that work, then I should be free to have my own fun without him."

"As long as you don't go back to him again. The guy's a jerk, Ti."

"No worse than Jesse."

Cass wrung the apron and stifled the reaction her ex's name always brought. "He didn't start out that way."

"Yeah, because he was playing you. Then he had the nerve to freak out when you ditched him, acting like you belong to him or something." Eyes rolling, she huffed. "Creep. And seriously, you'd think after this long, he'd get a clue."

"You never liked him, did you?"

Ti tilted her chin. "Before or after he pulverized my best friend's heart?"

Cass swiped a handful of silverware from the drain rack and opened the drawer they went in. "That's a bit dramatic."

"Not as I recall."

Cass straightened the stack of spoons, trying to even out her voice. "I'm the only one responsible for my heart."

"Oh, c'mon, already. Will you stop trying to be so responsible all the time?"

Cass shoved the drawer closed. "One of us has to be." The words singed with regret before she'd finished them. Ti's face only made it worse. "I'm sorry. I didn't mean—"

"Don't worry about it. Other people don't affect our hearts, right?" She blew out the side door, leaving it propped open.

Cass knew her well enough to let her go. They'd work it out later.

Outside, Ethan hauled one of the new mattresses up the hill to the cabin. He must've returned from his call and gone straight back to work. Maybe they were all overstressed. And for what? Would any of this be worthwhile?

A glance around the kitchen and mess hall sent her yearning for the days she'd played across these floors instead of falling apart on them. She grabbed a sweater from the rack behind the door and headed outside. With the sun setting, the temperature was already dropping.

Across the broken footbridge, she meandered onto the overgrown softball field and sat on the rock wall lining the edge. The flat stones warmed her skin while a flood of childhood memories paraded across the yard.

What she'd give to slip into the parts of her past when things had felt safe. Carefree. Would letting go of the camp mean she'd lose those memories for good?

"I thought I saw you over here." Ethan looked across the field while strolling toward her. "Envisioning building plans?"

She smiled. "Not a chance. We used to play softball out here."

In a long-sleeved T-shirt, he rubbed his cuff over his forehead. "You could have a maze. You know, kinda like a corn maze, except with grass."

"Not funny."

He settled beside her. "Kidding. I saw a mower in the garage. Not sure how long it's been sitting in there. So, I might need to change the carburetor first, but I think we can get the field softball-ready in a few days."

"Because you're a mechanic, right? I'm starting to lose track of all your superpowers."

He laughed. "Believe it or not, you can learn a thing or two without growing up on the streets. I know, shocking."

Before she could dish out a comeback, a shrill, scream-like bark echoed from the tree line. She latched on to Ethan's arms and scoured the field until her gaze circled up to his slanted grin. She unlocked her arms from his and scooted back.

"It's just a fox."

"And don't tell me, you're a fox hunter, too?"

The corners of his lips reached for his dimples. "If I need to be."

She resituated her shirt and tried so hard not to gape at the suspenders hanging at his sides. "What does that mean?"

"Means I do what I have to."

Story of her life. "Sure you didn't grow up in Astoria?"

He stared at her as if she'd spoken in another language.

"You've at least heard of Queens, right?" Wasn't he supposed to be a native New Yorker? She shoved his shoulder. "And don't look at me like you're searching for a gang tattoo or something. You're the Italian. You don't see me looking for mafia tattoos."

"I seem to remember *you* being the one into stereotypes." His dimples quirked. "Or did you forget the whole fireman Dalmatian crack?"

Her mouth opened, but nothing came out. She headed toward the swing off in the corner instead. "Anyone ever tell you you're exasperating, Ethan DeLuca?"

His laugh rippled over the quiet field. "A few."

She spun and walked backward. "They weren't lying."

Exasperating and way too attractive for his own good. Why did his station gear have to include blue shirts that made his eyes that captivating? Those babies had to top all his superpowers combined.

She dusted off the wooden seat, mounted the swing, and ran her hands along the rugged ropes. The elm's branches shook overhead but held her weight and even more memories. It didn't make sense for the few she'd shared with Ethan to outshine the rest.

Even now, when things should've been awkward, he made it so natural to be around him. No way she'd be able to keep things just business unless she hid in the kitchen nonstop like she had today. Not that it'd made much difference.

Maybe she should give up already. But how could she risk getting hurt again? Jenni was probably right. She was a lost cause if she expected this situation between them to work.

Ethan strolled over to the swing. She didn't have any idea how cute she was, did she? Hair swept back with a bandana, jeans rolled up, bare ankles in the air.

Thank God, she was talking to him again. He wouldn't have been able to go much longer, wondering if he'd ruined everything between them last night. Though, being near her now wasn't much easier. He'd given her space today. But man, how was he supposed to keep that up when all he wanted to do was relive their kiss?

Think about something else. He leaned against the base of the tree and breathed in the fragrance blowing off the gully behind them. "Nothing beats honeysuckles."

"Actually, I think that's jasmine."

"Excuse me, *Windflower.*" Or whatever lame pet name Nick had called her. Ethan almost choked on the guy's cheap cologne just thinking about it.

Cheeks red, she grabbed a stick from the ground and tossed it at him.

He dodged it and laughed. "Either way, I'm just saying we should slow down more and enjoy it, you know?" Something flew up his nose right as he exaggerated an inhale. Flailing, he turned and tried to blow it out.

"You all right over there?"

"I think I just snorted a mosquito." He blew his nose a dozen more times until he could breathe normally again. Wow, that was classy. He stood upright and chuckled. "So much for being smooth."

She doubled over with laughter.

He gave the ropes a good spin. She wouldn't think it was funny if he told her about the grasshopper five inches up from her hands. So tempting. He knocked it off instead. He'd rather hear her laugh than scream. He wasn't about to ruin the moment now that she was finally at ease with him again. Maybe she hadn't shut him out completely after last night.

He reclined against the tree trunk. "You know, I remember playing on this field as a kid."

Her feet dragged along the dirt until she stopped, mouth slack. "What?"

"I came to camp one summer when we first moved here from the Bronx. I was like four or five, maybe."

"Why'd you stop?"

He shrugged. "My mom said we didn't belong here."

Her hands slid down the ropes and fell to her lap. "Why?"

"Who knows?" He propped his foot behind him. "The woman has a serious chip on her shoulder."

She twisted the swing toward him. "You got some kind of beef with her?"

"You could say that." He picked at a callous on his palm. "Both my parents are workaholics. They left my sister and me to fend for ourselves most of the time."

"I didn't know you have a sister."

"Had." His boot dragged down the bark. "She died when I was seventeen."

Her hand soared to her chest.

He pushed off the trunk and faced the gully, not ready to go there yet. "Mom never paid me a lot of attention. But after that, I pretty much became nonexistent. Everyone did. She divorced my dad, buried herself in work, and became Ms. City Council Woman of the Year."

Cass eased over to him and rested her slender shoulder against his. "I'm so sorry. I had no idea."

"It's not something I really talk about." He exhaled. "Can't change the past."

"Only the future. I know what you mean. Doesn't stop you from wishing you could." Her chin sagged to her sweater, and he had to restrain himself from lifting it and begging her to feel safe enough to open up to him.

She drifted a little closer to the gully, separated the vines stretched across two saplings, and peered inside. "I used to belly-crawl in here. Scale the boulders. Pretend I was . . . *invincible*." A sigh trailed a sad laugh. "Guess I never stopped."

The desire to hold her picked up with his heart rate, but he dug his boots deeper into the grass to keep from moving. After the way she'd responded last night, he promised himself he wouldn't kiss her again unless she initiated. Getting too close to her would make that impossible.

"What happened?"

She ran her fingers over the tiny white flowers covering the vines. "My dad walked out on us when I was thirteen— classic secretary scandal. It sent my mom into a tailspin of depression and me into running her flower shop for her just to put food on the table."

"At thirteen?"

She shrugged. "Can't beat on-the-job experience."

No wonder she was all business. She'd hardly known anything else.

"Between being a kid *and* a girl, it wasn't exactly easy to earn respect from our employees." She plucked off one of the flowers and brought it to her nose. "I had to learn a lot of hard lessons, but pain makes you stronger, right?"

She wandered farther down the edge of the ravine. "I stayed on a year after high school, then went to NYU, got a business degree, and started my own consulting company."

And she called *him* a superhero. "With all the experience, why go to school?"

Another sad smile tugged at her lips. "Honestly? I thought it'd impress my dad." She tossed the flower into the trees. "Stupid, I know."

The hurt in her voice overrode the willpower binding his feet in place. At her side, he curled his fingertips under hers. "It's not stupid, Cass. Your mom's not the only one he hurt by breaking his vows."

She turned her hazel eyes on him, and he almost broke his own promise. Her lashes swept down. "I thought vows meant forever."

"They're supposed to." A deep inhale steered his gaze out to the field.

She set a tender hand on his forearm. "Nick told me what happened with Jenni."

His eyes jerked back to her. Every muscle in his body hardened. "I bet he did. How'd he spin it this time? Second thought, spare me." Hearing Nick's side of the story once was more than enough. He strode into the grass, threaded his fingers through his hair, and released a long breath. It didn't matter anymore.

"I'm sorry, Ethan." She inched up behind him.

"There's nothing to be sorry for. He saved me from making a huge mistake."

"From marrying her?"

"From losing myself." He turned. "Things were shaky between us the year after my sister died. I left with Habitat when I found out she cheated on me. And when I came back, I knew it was time to start over. It took me a few more years to get out of here for good, but I did. No looking back." He shook his head. "None of it matters now, anyway. We were just kids."

"That doesn't mean it can't still hurt." This time, her fingers found his. Soft, comforting.

Meeting her eyes, he swallowed. "Cass . . ." He ached to kiss her again. To let her know he'd moved on from Jenni. That coming home was reopening old wounds, but it was healing them, too. And being with her played a part in it, even if he couldn't explain how.

He brushed back her curls and studied her face. He couldn't fault her for wanting to keep lines between them. But did she really think they could? His mouth turned dry, strength fading faster than the words that wouldn't come.

Her forehead creased as she withdrew.

His chest sank. Did he push too far again? What was she thinking right now?

She rubbed her arms. "We should probably go before any more foxes come out."

They couldn't end the night yet. Not like this. He slipped his hands into his jeans pockets. "Would you take a ride with me? I have somewhere I want to take you."

Head angled, she scrunched her lips to the side.

He tossed an arm over her shoulders and nudged her forward. "A little adventure's a good thing." Not to mention a nice distraction. If she wanted him to pretend that kiss didn't happen last night, he'd need every ounce of help he could get.

They stopped by the garage, and he handed her a full-face helmet.

"What's this?"

He slipped it over her head, patted the top, and motioned to his bike. "We're going for a ride."

She raised the tinted shield covering her eyes. "I thought it had an oil leak."

He straddled the seat and lifted the kickstand. "I fixed it last night." He turned, grinning. "I had a little trouble falling asleep."

A shade of pink dusted her freckled cheeks. He pulled on his helmet before his smile got any wider, walked the bike backward, and tapped the seat behind him. "Hop on."

She stared at the ground with her hands in her back pockets. "I think you want Ti for this one. She's better at the adventurous stuff."

Was she serious? He twisted and lifted his face shield to meet her gaze. "I don't want anyone else, Cass." He held out a hand. "Trust me. I'll keep you safe."

Using him for balance, she climbed on. "Where do I hold?"

Forget it. Trying to control his grin was pointless. He circled her arms around his waist and released the clutch before she changed her mind.

CHAPTER THIRTEEN

Brave

Ethan lowered the bike's kickstand in front of Gregorio's parlor and slid his helmet over the handle.

Cassidy climbed off the back of the motorcycle and waddled ahead of him like she'd just dismounted a horse. She couldn't get any cuter if she tried. "Are my legs still supposed to be vibrating like this?"

"You get used to it."

"Not sure I want to." She shook her curls out from the under the helmet. "I think that wind noise might be worse than the subway. You got a thing for speed?"

He laughed. "More like a thing for freedom. Space. Just you and the wind. Nothing like it." Well, almost nothing.

Her cheeks blushed the way they always did when he couldn't look away from her. She shifted her glance toward the parlor's sign. "Gelato, huh?"

"Best in the area."

She tucked the helmet under her arm. "Probably more like the *only* one in the area."

He fought a laugh, not about to let her know she was right. At the counter, Ethan tapped the bell. "Hey, Mikey, give me two cups of *gianduja* and one *caffée espresso* to go." Nonna would get a kick out of that. Or give him a good kick in the rear. Either way, the look on her face would be worth it.

Cass squinted to read the overhead menu. "*Giandjua?*"

"Chocolate hazelnut. This stuff will melt in your mouth." He intercepted one of the cups before Mikey put it inside the to-go bag, stuck a spoon under the lid, and handed it to her. "Try it."

She scooped a spoonful into her mouth and pulled her lips together, clearly trying to resist a smile. "Almost as good as the ones you can get in the city."

He forced his inward flinch not to show. Anytime she mentioned the city, his stomach clenched without warning. He shouldn't still be having these reactions. Izzy died ten years ago. Enough time had passed for him to stop reliving that night.

Trying to shake it off, he added her cup to the plastic bag, tied the handles together, and handed it to her. "Tough critic."

She followed him across the lot. "We're not staying?"

He straddled the bike and helped her climb on. "One more stop." Good thing, too. The drive would give him a chance to get it together. He was supposed to be helping her keep her guard down around him, not raising his own.

The open road absorbed all his thoughts. With Cassidy's arms around his waist and the wind rushing over him, his failures were easier to forget.

Too bad they couldn't ride all night. The bike rumbled up Nonna's driveway.

"Is this your grandma's place?" Cass asked while dismounting.

She never missed much. "I owe her a treat." On the porch, he went to open the door and almost smacked into it. When did she ever lock the door? He rapped a knuckle against it. "Nonna?"

Lady skidded down the entryway and stuck her snout around the curtain, teeth baring. Nice try. Like she used those suckers for anything other than gnawing on a milk bone.

Cass smiled. "Charming."

The porch light flicked on right before Nonna cracked the door open. A sliver of the hallway peered through behind her. "Ethan. What are you doing here?"

"What do you mean what am I doing here? I came to visit. What's wrong?"

"Nothing." She stood tall as if her four-foot-eleven frame could block his view inside.

He moved closer and whiffed. "Is that . . .?" Gripping the trim, he fixed one of her own notorious glares on her. "Nonna."

"It's nothing. You two run along. I'm sure you kids have better things to do."

He nudged the door open, circled around her, and marched straight into the aroma of her legendary espressos. A brand new machine topped the kitchen counter. "You didn't."

She whisked down the hall with her hands moving about as fast as her lips. He couldn't make out her Italian at that speed. Something about not taking away her last pleasures in life.

She hovered in front of the machine like a mama bear protecting her cub. "Now, you listen to me, young man, I didn't get to be this age only to have someone else start running my life. I make my own decisions."

He cracked a grin and kissed her cheeks. "You're one stubborn woman."

She patted his chest and dished his grin right back. "Runs in the genes."

Cass giggled from the doorway and covered her mouth when they both looked at her. "Sorry. Couldn't help it."

Nonna's aged eyes glistened. "Sweet child, you have your grandpa's smile."

Wide-eyed, Cass looked from her to Ethan and back. "You were friends?"

"Oh, yes." She fumbled with a mug on the counter and blinked as though drawing herself back to the present. "You don't live in these parts without getting to know everyone."

"Small town," Ethan mouthed from behind her.

Cass bit her lip. Her smile turned his insides softer than the gelato. Did she have any idea how hard it was to wait for her to make the next move? What if she never did? Exhaling, he stretched his neck. *Focus on Nonna.*

He set the plastic bag on the counter, handed Cass her gelato, and withdrew Nonna's. "Since you bought an espresso maker, I guess you won't be needing this *caffée espresso* I picked up for you." He took a bite, dramatizing how good it was. "Yeah, you definitely don't need this. I'll take care of it for you." He jumped back the second she reached for it.

Glaring, she grabbed a wooden spoon from the drawer and brandished her weapon at him. "Don't make me chase you."

"Now, now. No getting that heart rate going." He backed up, bumping into the island and the kitchen chairs until she finally cornered him. They might not have any ties to the mafia in their blood, but Nonna could've fooled him. Surrendering, he handed over the gelato.

She tapped his cheek. "Wise man."

Off by the counter, Cassidy was already scraping the bottom of her cup.

He raised a brow. "Thought it wasn't as good as the kind you're used to."

She circled her spoon around and rolled her eyes. "I couldn't let you waste your money."

"Mm hmm." He strutted over to her, leaned in close enough to smell the hazelnut on her lips, and reached behind her for his own dish. "That's very considerate of you."

Eyes locked on his, she let out a small breath.

Nonna swatted him from behind. "Stop making the poor girl blush." She filled two espresso cups. "I'll make you a deal. If you turn down my espresso right now, I'll return the machine." She waved the cup in front him, scents latching on to him like hooks.

Cheater.

He swiped the cup and leaned against the island while she handed the other to Cassidy.

"So small." Cass held the tiny cup with her pinky sticking out like she was about to have a spot of tea.

She was seriously trying to cripple his willpower. He laughed. "Trust me. That's all you need."

After one sip, her perked expression agreed.

Nonna picked Lady up and prodded Ethan back to the door. "You two go on, now. Lady and I have a date with Cary Grant."

On the porch, she kissed both Ethan's cheeks. Watching her do the same to Cassidy sent warmth spreading across his chest.

The feeling of contentment stayed with him on the ride home and hedged back the night's dropping temperatures. And as soon as they moseyed up the stairs to the same spot where they'd kissed the night before, the warmth stretched through every muscle.

She looked across the still yard. "Where's your watchdog?"

Off somewhere, hopefully having way more self-control than Ethan was at the moment.

He tugged on his ear. "Hey, you have to admit, he came through with chasing off those raccoons."

She swayed her head. "Okay, true. But Jax would've gotten 'em if they'd come inside."

"Sure he would've."

Her smile drifted into a pensive stare across the field. "I can't believe you were here as a camper. You really don't remember it?"

"Come to think of it." He rubbed his jaw. "I do recall this one feisty redhead who smoked all the boys in tree climbing."

Lips pursed, she shoved him.

"Kidding." He laughed. "It was just one week when I was five. I don't remember much." Yet he still felt connected to the camp—to her—more than he could explain. Longing inside him grew as he took in the sight of her beneath the deck light's soft glow.

She rubbed her arms.

"Cold?"

"A little."

He edged closer. If she wouldn't pull away again, he'd close her in his arms right now. Keep her warm, safe.

She dodged his eyes and fidgeted with the buttons on her sweater.

Blowing out a breath, he faced the stars and then nodded across the deck. "Let's get inside. I'll make you a fire."

At the door, she jerked her hand away from the handle. "Sorry. It's wet."

He cupped her wrist and held her hand under the light.

Her face paled. "Is that blood?"

His pulse hammered. He scooted her behind him and opened the door. Sandy galloped down the hall toward them. What was he doing inside?

Something crashed in the bathroom, followed by a shriek.

"Ti." Cassidy shoved around him and sprinted toward the sound.

"Cass, wait." He ran after her.

They both whipped around the bathroom doorway. In her pajamas, Ti sat on her hands and knees while picking up shards of a broken wine bottle.

Cassidy flew to her side. "Are you okay? What's going on?"

"Nothing. Go away."

Ethan scoured the halls to check for any indication that someone else was there. Finding no one, he jogged back to the bathroom.

"Dang it." Ti dropped a piece of glass and drew her finger to her mouth, careful not to touch a gash on her lip.

"Leave it." Cass brushed back the hair matted in the blood on Ti's cheek that matched a red stain on her hand from where she must've smeared it. "Talk to me. What happened?"

She pushed away. "The same thing that always happens in my non-responsible life." She rose and stormed past Ethan through the doorway.

He shot an anxious glance at Cassidy.

Compassion took over her eyes. With a gentle touch to his shoulder, she passed him on her way after her friend. "Ti."

Maybe this was a girl moment, but he wasn't ready to leave their sides. He leaned against the trim to Ti's bedroom, heart finally slowing. Beside him, Sandy panted and licked his hands. "Good boy," he whispered. At least he had some back-up to guard the house if he needed it.

Ti buried a pillow in her arms. "I don't need to hear any I-told-you-so speeches right now."

Cass settled alongside her on the bed. "How about the you're-not-alone speech?" She stroked Ti's hair. "C'mon. Don't make me sing it."

Hiding a smile, Ti rested her cheek on Cassidy's leg. "We're not twelve anymore, Cass."

She curved Ti's hair around her ear. "Good thing our song's for life." Humming at first, she drew circles over Ti's back with her fingertips. Notes slowly turned into lyrics. "When the lights turn dark and the shadows deep, close your eyes and drift to sleep. To the place of dreams that sweep us away, together we run. Best friends, always."

Ti's tear-coated voice joined Cassidy's as they sang together.

Ethan slipped out of the doorway and backed against the wall while the tender song washed over him. Could he fall for this girl any harder?

The song gradually waned. Ti sniffled. "Everything was fine until they wanted to shoot up," she said. "I couldn't, Cass. Hitting me wasn't gonna change that."

Ethan's jaw twitched. Any man who hit a woman deserved ten times worse.

"You're the brave one." The same level of compassion in Cassidy's eyes earlier filled her words. "You know that, right?"

"I'm pretty sure that's you."

Silence stretched. Ethan didn't move, afraid to interrupt.

Ti sighed. "Why do the things we long for so much leave us this empty?"

A squeak from the mattress springs filled the pause.

"Maybe we're looking in the wrong places," Cass whispered back.

Sandy broke free from his grasp and trotted into the room. Ethan turned the corner, flashing them a look of apology.

Ti ruffled the dog's ears. "Sorry about letting him in. I didn't want to be alone."

"It's fine." Cass kissed the top of her head.

Ethan backed up and strode for the kitchen. He hadn't meant to stand there the whole time, eavesdropping. But the way Cass cared for her . . . He couldn't pull himself away.

In the kitchen, he went straight for the coffeemaker. As much as Ti loved coffee, maybe that was one way he could help. He'd poured two cups by the time Cass strolled in.

She slid him a smile. "That espresso wasn't enough caffeine for ya?"

"It's decaf. I made some for Ti." He handed her the mug. "Would you mind?"

Nodding, she took the mug and then disappeared back down the hall.

Ethan fixed one more cup in case she wanted one, too. Several minutes later, she flitted back in on a path leading to the coffeemaker. He arched a brow. "That espresso wasn't enough for ya?"

She shrugged. "It's like comfort food."

Couldn't argue with that. He set his spoon down. "You're an amazing friend, you know."

"I've always kind of played the big sister role, I guess." She sat on the counter overlooking the mess hall, something unspoken visibly weighing on her.

"What is it?"

She let out a breath. "Ti wants you to know about her past, but . . . it's not pretty."

He shifted on the counter beside her, as if there were some position that'd make hearing whatever it was easier to handle.

Cass cupped her hands around the mug and took a sip. "She stayed over at my house a lot. Her parents were total meth heads. It got to where they'd sell anything for crystal. Even themselves." She ran her nail over a stain on the rim of the mug. "And whenever her mom got too sick to turn tricks . . ."

The implication turned Ethan's blood cold.

"No kid should have to go through the things she has." Years of sorrow turned her eyes glassy. "The worst part is, when you're used for so long, you start to believe that's all you're worth."

The tremor in her voice shook with such empathy, he had a feeling she was speaking from experience. He almost crushed his mug at the thought.

"When you can't escape reality, you learn to make your own." She set her coffee down and gripped the counter. "She unofficially changed her name from Trina to Treble to spite her parents. But then it became part of her identity, a place to hide. Music spread into photography, writing, anything beautiful enough to paint over the darkness."

Pieces of Ti's story fused together, making so much sense it hurt. And the fact that, yet again, Cassidy's life had forced her to grow up much sooner than she ever should have carved an ache into his chest he didn't know how to stop.

"I'm so sorry, Cass. Thank God for the grace that carried you both through all that."

"Grace?" Her eyes hardened. "Where was grace when Ti's parents left her in a back room with some drug dealer?"

Didn't she see? He moved closer and took her hands. "Here. In a friend who was there when she needed someone to help her feel safe and believed in." Like she was doing for him? His stomach tightened at the realization.

"I wish I could've been enough for her." With a pained smile, she slid off the counter. "I think I'm going to go bunk with her tonight. As long as Sandy left me some room." She stopped in the doorway and looked behind her. "Thanks for earlier, Ethan. I had a good time."

He dipped his head, and she drifted out, taking the undone pieces of his heart with her. He didn't move. The clock's second hand ticked into the silence on its way to morning, but he wasn't anywhere near ready for sleep.

He wandered out to the deck. Fog coated the quiet field and obscured the line of pine trees, his thoughts just as hazy.

Ti's experience burned him. Both of theirs did. He'd rewrite Cassidy's past in a second if he could, undo the scars it killed him to know she had. At least he could be here for her now.

He ran his hand over a damaged section of the stucco siding. Maybe Nonna was right about being here for a reason. He might not get to pick his assignments. Or fully understand them. But if some small part of this one included Cass, he'd choose it again and again. Even if it meant he'd end up with scars of his own.

CHAPTER FOURTEEN

Alone

Half-awake, Ethan trudged downstairs toward the smell of coffee. A staccato tapping noise coming from behind the office door stopped him short as he rounded the banister. What was she doing in there, banging on a typewriter?

He tucked his sketchbook under his arm and rubbed his temples. It wasn't her fault he woke up this morning with a headache. He was the one who'd stayed up half the night working. Good thing he knew the cure. The vision of sitting on the deck with his coffee and sketchpad drove his feet toward the kitchen.

Ti handed him a mug as soon as he passed through the doorway. "Returning the favor."

"Thanks." He breathed in the steam, took a sip, and nodded. "Not bad."

Ti laced her hands around her own mug and curled up on a chair at the breakfast table. The bruise on her cheek made his stomach churn again, but she simply smiled as though nothing had happened.

Cassidy's comment from last night hit him square in the chest. *"When you can't escape reality, you learn to make your own."* Ti had pretty much said it herself the other day. Everyone dealt with pain differently. But that didn't make it easy to watch.

"Jax, get off the keyboard already," Cass yelled from the office.

The cat bounded down the hall and skidded into the kitchen, claws scratching across the tiles. With huge green eyes, he wandered up to Ethan and meowed.

"Sorry, dude. I know better than to be a coconspirator."

"Come here, Jax. I'll love on you." Ti scooted her chair back and swept him into her lap. He circled around twice before nestling up to her stomach.

The typewriter noise echoed down the hall.

"What's she doing in there?"

Ti munched on her cereal. "Crunching numbers. She's been plunking away on that adding machine for the last hour."

An adding machine? That couldn't be good. Maybe some breakfast would help. He left his sketchbook on the table and got to work at the stove.

Cass shuffled in right as he flipped the second omelet. Beside him, she opened two cabinets and pulled out a bowl and a box of Cheerios.

He stretched a hand over the bowl while nodding at the pan of eggs. "Hold that thought."

"Okaaay." She flashed him a curious expression, returned the cereal, and plopped onto the chair across from Ti. The second she sat down, Jax abandoned one lap for the other. He obviously hadn't been *that* put out earlier. The cat was loyal to her. Ethan would give him that.

He slid the omelet off the pan onto Cass's plate and motioned to Ti. "Want one?"

"I'm good." She carried her cereal bowl to the sink. "I'm gonna get a head start on staining the deck." The side door closed behind her and whisked in a cool morning breeze.

Maybe work would keep her mind off things. It usually did for him.

Ethan joined Cass at the table and set a cup of coffee in front of her. She bit into her omelet, lashes fluttering. He tried not to laugh. He really needed to show these girls how to cook before the summer ended. "Good?"

"Mm hmm." She nudged a piece of ham off her lip. "You have no idea."

And she had no idea how attractive she was. He diverted his gaze from her lips to his omelet.

"So, what's with the drawings?" She reached for his sketchbook.

He hurried down a swallow. "Nothing. Just something I got into as a kid."

She flipped through the pages and eyed him like she'd caught him in a lie. "That's not nothing, Ethan. That's talent."

Between her compliment and his hot coffee, heat climbed up his neck to his ears. He folded his napkin back and forth. "I don't usually show people my sketches."

"Why? They're incredible."

He moved his hands to his lap. His napkin-turned-accordion sprawled open, his insides even more undone. "After working with Habitat, I got interested in architecture for a while. Thought I might've had the skill for it. But, I don't know, I . . ."

She froze with her fork halfway to her mouth.

Did he say something wrong? "Never mind. It's stupid." He waved it off. "Daydream stuff."

"It's not stupid." She dragged the last piece of her omelet around her plate with her fork and waited a minute before looking up again. "Why haven't you pursued it?"

"I have a job." He slumped against the back of his chair.

Her intuitive gaze peeled him apart a layer at a time. He couldn't hide anything from her.

He scratched his jaw, the cat dander getting to him. "I almost applied to Cornell once, but my life took a different direction." He shrugged. "No looking back, remember?"

Elbows on the table, she angled her head. "You can still change the future."

"That ship sailed a long time ago, Cass." He rose and headed to the sink. He'd made his choices in life. For better or worse.

She scooched her chair back, sending Jax off her lap and down the hall. Beside Ethan, she turned on the faucet and swirled her fingers over the plate while staring at the backsplash. Her forehead pinched. What was she thinking about?

"You okay?"

"Hmm?" She blinked toward him. "Yeah, fine. Lost in thought."

Clearly. She'd been off since she came out of the office. He hated seeing her stressed. Especially when she wouldn't talk to him about it.

He leaned against the counter. "Why don't we take the day off?"

A deadpan stare answered that one.

"A half day?"

She squirted soap into the water, the question apparently not needing a response.

"Okay, fine. At least take a quick walk with me before we start working." He grabbed her hand, but she held on to the sink with the other.

"I have to do these dishes."

"They'll be there later." He tugged again.

"I've never left them undone."

"Wait, what?" He studied her guilty face. "You mean, like, *ever*?"

She let go of his hand. "In the city, you learn not to leave dirty dishes out, all right?"

He blocked the image of roaches crawling all over her counters. "Good call. But we're not in Queens right now."

Grinning, she crossed her arms. "Not all of us are slobs, like you."

He feigned a look of offense. "Me?"

"Mm hmm. I've been in your Jeep, and I've walked by your room, Pigpen. Definite slob material."

He returned her grin. "What's the point of making your bed if you're gonna get right back in it that night?"

She rolled her eyes, and he grabbed her hand again. "C'mon. It's good to let your hair down sometimes."

Resigning this time, she followed.

They strolled side by side toward the softball field. Without her bandana on, her long curls flowed around her face and down her back. Free, no restraint. Exactly the way he wanted her to feel. She had every reason not to take people at their word. He only hoped showing her how much he cared would be enough to earn her trust. He had to try.

"So, what was that crazy accountant scheme you had going on earlier?"

The slightest hint of pink covered her freckles. "Sorry about making all that noise. I was going through the books, trying to get a feel for cash flow. There's this consistent monthly deposit I can't account for."

She let out a gruff exhale. "We're not talking chump change, either. From what I can tell, it's pretty much been floating the camp for the last twenty-plus years, right up until Grandpa died. But there are no records of who it's from." She threw her hands in the air. "It's so frustrating. Why would a donor want to stay anonymous for that long?"

"Who knows? Lots of people like to keep their finances private."

"Maybe. But the person obviously cares about the place. If they'd been willing to support the camp before, maybe they still will be. Lord knows we could use it." She broke off a twig from a tree lining the driveway and twisted it while they walked. "I put in a call to one of my business contacts to see if she can trace the deposits. Worth a try, right?"

"Absolutely."

She tossed the twig into the woods. "I mean, it might be a long shot, but . . ." Her feet slowed in front of the path. She darted a glance from the mended bridge back to him.

Smiling, he pointed ahead of them. "C'mon."

She stopped on the other side of the footbridge, wide-eyed. "Did you sleep at all last night?"

"A little." A small price to pay to show her she wasn't alone in this. He walked to the home plate he'd set up after mowing the field.

"I don't know what to say."

He rubbed his cheekbone as she sauntered over. "Most people say thank you when someone helps them out."

"I've never been very good at that."

He faked a look of shock. "You're kidding."

She shoved him.

Laughing, he stumbled backward into the rock wall. "It's okay to accept help from people, you know. Not everyone expects something in return."

She settled on the rocks and stared across the field. "Guess it's easier to expect the worst in people. You avoid disappointment that way."

"And friendship." He sat beside her.

She toed her sandals off and ran her feet through the grass. "Better than risking betrayal."

"Did someone leave you at the altar or something?" He hadn't meant it to come out like that. Or to come out at all. And the second her face flinched, he wanted to ball the words up and punch himself in the mouth with them.

"The altar? Ha. That'd be too respectable for Jesse. Try the bed of his pickup."

The rocks' ragged edges bore into Ethan's palms the tighter he clutched them.

"My fault, though. Before Dad left, he used to tell me never to mix personal with business. Turns out we both failed on that one."

"Wait. This dude worked at the flower shop?"

"Prize employee. Hustle the boss, and you get all the perks, including sharing your bed with a naive girlfriend." She plucked a dandelion from the ground and coiled the stem around her finger, looking almost nauseated. Was she worried what he thought?

"Cass, the guy's obviously a jerk. There's nothing to be ashamed of. We all make mistakes." Ethan's list probably outstretched hers tenfold.

She flicked the weed into the grass. "I wish that were true."

He set a hand on her arm. "Whatever it is, it's in the past."

"Doesn't mean it can't still haunt you." She pushed up from the rocks, strode a few paces ahead, and stopped with her hands through her hair. "I got pregnant. Found out on prom day, of all things. And to top it off, he stood me up that night for some chick he'd had on the side the whole time."

Fury heated Ethan's veins. Ti wasn't exaggerating about Cass having a reason to keep her guard up. After an experience like that, who could blame her for being scared to cross work boundaries again? Had she been worried he'd treat her like this Jesse creep had? He gripped the rocks harder, not trusting himself to move.

She turned, head lowered. "I rode the subway in my stupid prom dress all the way to the Bronx to tell him off." She rubbed her hand. "Hooked him in the cheek so hard, my knuckles were bruised for two weeks. But it was worth it."

Compassion tempered his strides toward her. At her side, he cupped her hand in his.

"They're not the kind of scars you can see." She withdrew and laced her arms across her stomach. "I miscarried a month later. And you know who went to the doctor's office with me? A cab driver. Waited the entire time. Running the meter, of course."

An ache like he'd never experienced clawed through him from the inside out.

Glassy eyes found his. "I didn't wake up one day, deciding I was on my own, Ethan. I always have been. But that day, I finally realized I had to start living like it."

Without hesitation, he closed her in his arms and rested his cheek over her head. "Not anymore."

―――――― ❧ ――――――

In the safety of Ethan's arms, hidden from everything else, Cass almost could've believed him.

The sun beat through her hair and warmed the back of her neck. She ran a finger under her eyes, pulled away, and escaped toward her sandals. "The day's going to get away from us if we don't get started."

With a tender expression, he nodded and followed beside her.

She twisted her shirt cuff, debating whether to say more. After pushing through endless hours to get work done, he'd proven himself faithful enough to trust, hadn't he?

Her body tensed at the thought. So had Jesse, at first. And look where her trust had led her last time.

Dew glistened across the pristinely manicured lawn. He had to have stayed up almost till morning to get this field ready. She drew a deep breath. Even if she didn't understand why, he was still here, and she couldn't deny needing the support. "I haven't told you and Ti yet, but an inspector's coming in a month."

His face scrunched into a guilty expression.

"What?"

He rubbed his neck. "Don't be mad, but I saw the notice. It fell out of your book the other night."

He was snooping? She suppressed her immediate reaction. Truth be told, she was relieved he knew. Now, maybe he'd understand why she had to stay so driven.

"Then, you know we don't have time to mess around." Her sideways glance caught a smile she was starting to love more than she should.

Across the bridge, he jutted his chin toward the canteen. "Two or three coats of lacquer, and I think it should be about finished."

"Great." She dragged her sandals through the gravel. "You know, I was thinking of asking Ti to paint a mural on the side facing the driveway, so it's what people see when they first pull in. Do you think that's a good idea?"

There was that grin again. "I think it's perfect."

Borrowing his confidence, she exhaled. Maybe this would all work out. Somehow.

He motioned to the boathouse on the backend of the property. "What's that building?"

She wriggled her keys out of her pocket, hardly containing a smile. "Wanna see?"

"After that expression, now I'm gonna have to."

Laughing, she led them across the lawn to the oversized shed-like building and unlocked the door. "I think this might've been my grandpa's favorite part of the camp."

A musty odor poured out from inside. Her face fell. She swatted cobwebs with both hands, struggling to untangle the strings and her thoughts.

Ethan moved her behind him and tore down the webs to clear a path.

She wandered over to a pile of mildew-covered life vests on the floor. "He never would've left it like this."

Ethan lifted a paddle from the ground and rubbed the caked-on dirt off. "The last group of campers probably didn't clean it out. Maybe he just didn't get to it before . . ."

"No, you don't understand. This building used to be like a sanctuary for him. A place to de-stress. He'd spend hours out here, cleaning the vests meticulously, building canoes."

"Building?" His gaze swept over the boats. "You're saying he actually carved these himself?"

She traced her fingers over the engravings in the one he'd made for her. *To C. M. from Grandpa McAdams.* "Some of them."

He looked over the canoes again, eyes beaming like they'd struck gold. "That's incredible. We gotta take these out."

The guy loved the outdoors, didn't he? Her stomach clenched at the thought. Jenni had a canoe on her SUV the other day. Was he thinking about memories with her?

Canoeing, bridge jumping, camping . . . She obviously loved mountain adventures as much as he did. Wasn't hard to see why he'd proposed to her. Or why he'd kept telling Cass to let her hair down. The contrast between her and Jenni was so palpable it hurt.

She batted away the sting and shook her head. "We have—"

"Work to do. I know." He hung the paddle on the wall. "Sometime, though. I'm pretty sure he made these canoes so you could have some fun. Just sayin'."

As if his dimples weren't disarming enough, those darn blue eyes could leave her in a puddle if she didn't look away.

She turned toward the moldy vest, smile falling. Too much was going on for her to be fretting over some imaginary love triangle. Especially after finding this building in shambles. She could buy the possibility that Grandpa might've gotten too weak at the end to maintain the grounds, but not the boathouse.

Ethan came up beside her and wiped pine needles off another vest before hanging it up. "It shouldn't take us long to clean this place up."

"It's not that." She walked outside, pushed her hair away from her forehead, and inhaled.

"What is it?" Ethan said from behind her.

"This." She flung her arms out to her sides. "This whole place. How rundown it's gotten so quickly. All these crazy things happening since I got here—that roach infestation, slashed mattresses, those stupid raccoons on the roof. Is it really some punk kids playing a joke?"

He rubbed his shoulder. "You think someone's sabotaging the place?"

"I'm starting to wonder." Would it be so far-fetched? He probably thought she was overreacting. Maybe she was. But even if upstate New York was safer than Queens, something didn't add up. And with so much stacked against her getting the property ready for sale in time already, she couldn't afford to add malicious intent to the list.

"Did you ever hear back from Deputy Harris about the cabins?"

She twisted her hair into a bun and tried not to scoff. "He said there wasn't enough conclusive evidence. Basically gave me a pat on the head like I was some paranoid city girl."

A tendon on Ethan's neck pulled taut. Raking a hand through his hair, he stared at the pine needles under his boots. "Cass, I don't know if my mom will see me, but I can try to talk to her if you want. See if she can put some pressure on Harris to take this seriously."

He'd be willing to talk to his mom for her? "I can't ask you to do that."

"You're not asking." The corner of his mouth sloped to the left. "It's okay to accept help, remember?"

He really loved pushing that pressure point. She blew out a breath and met his crippling blue eyes head-on. "Thank you."

"Now, that wasn't so hard, was it? A little more practice, and you'll be a pro."

She shouldered past him. "You're maddening. You know that?"

He laughed while swatting a mosquito away. "One of my superpowers."

Too bad one of hers wasn't resisting his charm. She locked the door and almost bumped into him as she turned.

"I still think we should take the canoes for a spin."

"And *I* still think we should get back to work." She side-stepped around him.

He hopped in front of her. "At least let me get them ready. The canteen's going to take a few coats of lacquer. I can air out the place and clean the vests in between rounds."

Twiddling the keys, she looked back at the building. The boathouse needed to be cleaned. And to be honest, the thought of how many spiders were crawling in there kind of freaked her out. But this project was more special than the others. Could she trust him with it?

She finagled a key off the ring and handed it to him but held on. "This is important."

"Understood." He tossed the key in his palm.

"Don't let it go to your head."

"Too late."

She pivoted away from his goofy grin and started up the hill before he got on a roll.

"Cass?" he called from behind her. "Since you won't let me take you out in the canoes, let me make you dinner tonight instead."

She turned.

"*After* a hard day's work," he added when she hesitated.

If he cooked dinner as well as he did breakfast, she'd be crazy to decline. Giving in, she nodded and spun around, but not before his dimples bookended a smile she'd have to spend the rest of the day trying to work out of her mind.

She hustled around the mess hall as if distancing herself from him would make a difference. Her cell rang right before she reached the deck. She shimmied it out of her pocket. Maybe it was Britt getting back to her about that mystery donor. One glance at the screen, and she sighed. "Hey, Ma."

"Cass." A shaky inhale turned into a cry.

"Ma? Are you all right?" Her stride slowed until she barely moved. "What's going on?"

"I don't know. A letter from the bank came in the mail yesterday. Something about a default. It's too much jargon. I can't make sense of it, but it's bad, isn't it? Are they trying to take my shop away?"

A notice of default? Cass patted around for the railing and any clue of what to say. Yeah, they were behind on payments, but they were trying. It wasn't supposed to get this far. "Did you deposit that last check I sent you?"

Her pause sank into the pit of Cass's stomach and weighed her whole body onto the nearest step. She'd seemed off the night before Cass left to come here, but she assumed it was from mixed emotions about being on her own for a while. "Ma?"

"Oh, baby, you know I wanted to. But things got so stressful with your leaving. I—"

"Don't say it." Cass refused to hear she'd started pills again. Not after how far she'd come with breaking the addiction. She promised she was clean.

Another ragged inhale shook through the line. "You don't know what it's like. Ever since you went off to college, this place has been falling apart. I can't do it on my own."

"On your own?" The phone trembled in her hand. Sunlight beat against her and doubled the heat fuming through her skin. Did she honestly think Cass hadn't spent most of her life helping her? That she wasn't here now, busting her butt for *her*?

"I'm sorry, Cass. We'll work this out together, right? . . . Baby?"

"I can't talk about this right now." Not if she wanted to avoid saying something she'd regret. She hung up and forced herself to focus.

A notice of default only gave her three months to come up with the money before the bank assumed possession of the shop. If she made the right connections, she might be able to sell the camp in that timeframe. But if the inspection shut her down before then, what would it matter?

Ethan trailed up the hill from around the building, carrying a can of lacquer in one hand and a paintbrush in the other. Faithfully hard at work.

She hugged her arms to her sides, wishing they were his instead. He'd held her with such affection earlier, warm eyes begging her to trust him. Her lashes creased together. How could she trust when no one kept their promises?

Ti's words rushed back over her. *"He might just be your saving grace for this place."* Maybe he was. But what happened if grace wasn't enough?

CHAPTER FIFTEEN

Awe

Ethan flipped on the oven light to check the lasagna for the twentieth time. He might as well have been standing in front of the canteen, watching the lacquer dry. Staring at it wasn't going to make the last five minutes on the timer tick any faster.

He ducked into the fridge and fished through the crisper for a cucumber. Maybe the cool air would knock a few degrees off his body temperature.

What was with his nerves? It wasn't like this was his first date. Or a date, period. He was just fixing her dinner. That didn't count as making a move, right?

Okay, maybe it did. He shut the fridge and dropped his forehead against the freezer door. Cass had opened up so much in the past two days. He couldn't risk her pulling away again. But holding back what he felt for her was about to kill him.

"Mmm. Something smells delish."

Flinching at Ti's voice, Ethan juggled the cucumber in both hands. Nice.

But instead of teasing him, she flitted over to the salad bowl and picked out a carrot. "I told Cass you were a keeper. Think you just sealed the deal."

If only it were that easy. Ethan peeled the cucumber. "It's just lasagna."

She snagged a bottle of red wine off the counter without bothering to tame a grin. "Sure it is." She strolled over to the table at the same time Cassidy breezed in from the hall.

A simple pair of jeans and a green shirt that looked softer than her curls shouldn't be that radiant. Effortless beauty. The girl had it in spades and didn't even know it.

Unable to take his eyes off her, he sliced somewhere in the general direction of the cutting board.

"Smells amazing in here." She drifted closer.

He slid the cucumber slices into the bowl and searched for his voice. "Family recipe."

She peeked in the oven. "Ahh. Your *other* superpower. Almost forgot about that one." She smiled, but her laugh didn't quite override the strain around her eyes.

Had something happened since he last saw her? With his back shielding Ti behind them, he mouthed, "Are you okay?"

Her gaze plummeted to the ground. "Yeah. It's nothing."

Her shoulders didn't tense like that over nothing. "You want to talk about it?"

"Not tonight." She looked up at him. "Can we forget everything else for a few hours?"

If she kept looking at him with that sense of helplessness, he'd do anything she asked. "You got it."

She ambled over to the table.

"You should rub a banana peel over those," Ti said.

He peered behind him. "Huh?"

"Mosquito bites. Rub the inside of a banana peel against them. It'll take the itching away."

He removed his hand from the bites on his arm he didn't notice he'd been scratching and glanced at Cass for some cue on how to respond.

Ti looked at them both. "What?"

Cass cracked up. "Ethan's not used to your homeopathic gibberish yet."

"Hey, just 'cause it's unconventional doesn't mean it won't work. And you, missy, should try a little red wine with dinner." She dipped the bottle at her. "It'll ease that tension right out of your muscles. I'm telling ya. You want to unwind? Here's the trick."

"If I could stomach it, I might." Cass picked Jax up from the floor, nestled her nose against his, and put him back down.

"You don't drink?" Ethan placed the salad on the table.

"Never acquired the taste."

He hooked a thumb toward the oven. "There's a little wine in the lasagna, but the alcohol cooks out and leaves a sweetness behind."

"I'm sure it's fine."

Ti set the bottle down. "What else did you put in that lasagna, Chef Ramsey? There's no meat, is there?"

Was she serious? He squeezed the base of his neck. "Uh . . ."

Ti scooted her chair away from the table, got up, and strode across the room.

"Where are you going?"

"To make restitution for you," she called over her shoulder.

Cassidy's gaze intersected with his. "Don't ask."

"Not sure I want to." He grabbed potholders from the drawer, pulled the apparently offensive main dish from the oven, and positioned it on the table beside a vase of wild daisies Cass must've picked to replace the flowers Nick had brought her.

She breathed in the aroma rising from the pan. "Don't worry. I'll eat her portion."

And he'd try to hold a halfway normal conversation while sitting opposite eyes greener than he'd ever seen them.

On the floor, Jax extended his hind leg, stretched his paw apart, and gnawed on his fur. Nothing like a little ambiance. At least Cass didn't seem to mind.

"You think the guys at the station are missing you?"

He dished out a piece of lasagna. "Shoot, as much as I watch their backs, they better be." He laughed, missing them, too.

"You really wanted to get out of Haven's Creek, didn't you?"

"Left the first chance I got." He cut into the pasta with his fork to release the steam.

"Any regrets?"

He shook his head.

She kept her eyes on a cucumber she swirled around her plate. "What if you had a reason to stay?"

Almost choking on a bite, he bumped his fork onto the floor and bent under the table for it. Regrets? Not as many as he'd have leaving now that he'd met her. He could hardly keep his cool sitting across the table from the girl.

If she meant stay for her—that she wanted him in her life—there was no way he'd make it through the rest of dinner without telling her how much he wanted that, too.

He banged his head on the way up. Way to pull off the Rico Suave smoothness tonight.

"You all right?"

Nowhere close. He grabbed his glass. "I'm just gonna . . . get some ice." *And maybe lock myself in the walk-in freezer for five minutes.* At the fridge, he considered dumping the entire ice tray over his head but dropped a few cubes in his cup instead.

"You could run this place, you know," she said between bites. "If you wanted."

He poured a bottle of water into his glass. "And manage together?"

"I'm selling, Ethan."

She's said it so softly, he whipped around to make sure he'd heard her right. Chin lowered, she rested her hands in her lap.

Selling? So, *that* was his reason to stay. Business. His chest caved. And here, he'd been ready to pour his heart out to her. He stared at the ceiling and shook his head. Mom told him he'd end up making a fool of himself by letting his heart lead like he did. She'd gotten one thing right, at least.

He turned toward the wall and flexed his palms on the counter. "Looks like I'm not the only one anxious to get out of here."

"It's not that. It's . . . complicated."

Always was. He never should've hoped that would change. He chugged his water, the rejection harder to get down.

Her fork clinked against her plate. "You'd be so much better at running the camp than I would."

And better off alone, apparently.

"You have my grandpa's same drive. That strength is one of the reasons he named the camp *Misneach*. He loved his Irish proverbs."

A light smile in her voice drew him around. "The man of courage has never lost," she said with what must've been her grandpa's Irish accent. She looked up at him, eyes full of courage of their own. "He could've named it after you."

Courageous? She had the wrong guy.

"Or you could go to Cornell," she said softly. "Have you thought any more about that?"

He returned to his seat. "Nothing to think about. Life moves on."

She set her fork down again. "Too bad it can't move backward."

Her words held enough ache to override his own. Especially now that he understood the extent hers reached. He was supposed to be helping her without expecting anything in return. Yet, that was exactly what he'd been doing. Expecting her to want more than a business relationship.

Was that what she'd been stressed about earlier? Worrying he thought this was a date? Or was it financial pressure? If she wanted to sell, she had a reason. It wasn't his place to pry. But if she needed a night free of tension, the least he could do was not add to it.

He buried his feelings and set a hand over hers. "Your grandpa's not the only one who's pushed through uncertainty. Whatever happens, I'm sure he's proud of you."

She batted away the beginning of tears and returned his smile. "I hope you're right."

He didn't get much right, but that he was sure of. If she needed a friend to lean on until she believed it herself, he'd spend all summer trying. Starting with tonight.

Easy conversation carried them through the rest of dinner until she finally stretched away from the table. "Pretty sure I'm not going to need to eat for the next month."

"I'm with ya." He winked. "Except for dessert, of course."

She stopped him halfway out of his chair. "Dishes first."

"You kidding me?"

"C'mon." She grabbed his hand and led him over to the three-sink setup. "It'll take five minutes." She turned on the hot water, swirled dish detergent into the first sink, and squirted some kind of cleaner into the third.

"Why do I get the feeling I'm about to be schooled?"

She edged closer. "Jack of All Trades isn't intimidated, is he?" She unbuttoned his cuffs and rolled up his sleeves, soft fingertips grazing his skin.

His pulse doubled. Intimidated? More like incapacitated.

"First step is washing." She pushed up her own sleeves and scrubbed their plates in the soapy water. "Then rinse," she said while swishing them in the next sink. "And sanitize." She dunked them in the third.

"Easy, right? Oh, and don't forget to air dry. *Never* use a towel. I don't know if the head cooks will be like they were back when I was a dishwasher, but trust me. You don't want to be on their bad side."

Standing there with soapsuds crawling up her forearms, she flashed a smile that made Ethan's skin flush without getting near the hot water.

"Maybe this isn't such a good idea."

"Aw, c'mon." She reached for his hands. "These calloused fingers can use some softening."

"What, you don't like a man with tough hands?"

"I like a man who's willing to make sacrifices." Her green eyes were two seconds away from consuming any shred of willpower he had left.

He backed away.

"What are you doing?"

"Making a sacrifice."

Hand on her hip, she cocked her head. "By not doing the dishes?"

"By not kissing you."

Her pink cheeks lured his focus to her lips even more.

Ti trekked in from outside.

He tipped his head back, relieved for the interruption. God really did have a sense of humor if he thought Ethan could handle not acting on his feelings.

Ti set her camera and a paper grocery bag onto the counter. "Two words. Chubby. Bunny."

"No, you didn't." Cassidy jogged over and peeked into the bag. "You did."

He looked between them. "Chubby what?"

They both laughed. "It's time we show DeLuca, here, how to be a camper. I'll officiate." Ti steered him to his seat, dumped a bagful of marshmallows into a giant bowl, and assumed a position at the front of the table like a referee.

Marshmallows weren't the dessert he'd planned, and definitely not the one he craved, but he'd take the distraction. "Okay, what are the rules?"

"You and Cass alternate adding a marshmallow to your mouth and saying Chubby Bunny." Ti stuck one into her mouth to illustrate. "Whoever can't fit any more in or can't say Chubby Bunny loses."

Cass scooted in her chair. "Maybe you should play instead of him. It'll be unfair otherwise."

"Don't worry. I'll go easy on you." He flexed his laced fingers.

She flaunted that sassy look again. "I meant it'll be unfair for you."

"You've got a bit of a competitive edge, don't you?"

"You're in for it now." Ti laughed. "By the way, when are you two getting married?" she said right before snapping a picture. "That one's definitely going in the scrapbook."

Shaking off any embarrassment, Cass snagged the first marshmallow, tucked it behind her cheek, and grinned. "Chubby Bunny," she said like a pro.

After three, she could've passed for a chipmunk who'd had her wisdom teeth pulled. Her carefree laughter sang over him. Regardless of how crazy he looked, too, he'd stuff five more in his mouth if it'd keep that sweet sound lingering.

Seeing her like this—full of joy, reliving her childhood—drove an unexplained sense of loss onto his shoulders for all the years they could've spent together if he'd kept coming to the camp as a kid.

Her cell buzzed from the corner of the table. "Hewwo." Her smile fell as she hustled to free her mouth. "Yeah, hey, Britt. Sorry. What'd you find?"

Her face paled whiter than the bowl of marshmallows. "What? Are . . . are you sure?" Her gaze ping ponged from Ethan to the table. "I understand. . . .Yeah, yeah, I'm fine. Thanks for checking on this for me. I appreciate it. . . . You, too. Bye." She hung up but didn't move.

He slipped a hand over hers. "What is it?"

Her lashes lifted slowly. "I know where the money's been coming from."

Ethan set the last dish in the drain rack and stared out the window. Cass hadn't moved from her spot on the hill for the last thirty minutes. "Should we check on her?" he asked as Ti walked by.

"You're the bold one."

Or the naive one. What could he say to comfort her after the bombshell she just received? Did she even want his comfort? Regardless, he couldn't leave her out there alone.

He dried his red hands, draped the towel over the sink's edge, and winked at Ti. "If I'm not back in an hour, send backup."

"Ten-four."

Outside, Sandy rose to his feet as Ethan approached. "You've got a good watchdog, there."

Cass rubbed Sandy's head. "A good friend, too."

Ethan sat on the other side of her. Humor had defused her before. But in the silence, something told him not this time. He gently pressed his arm against hers and motioned to the dark sky. "It's pretty amazing, isn't it?" He clasped his fingers behind his head and reclined onto the cool grass.

She followed and peered above them. "The stars always felt so close up here. Almost close enough to touch."

"But still out of reach."

"Exactly." She turned, eyes full of hurt and longing.

Releasing a breath, he forced his gaze from her toward the sky. "It's like this giant mystery. As a kid, I used to think if I stared at the stars long enough, I'd figure it out."

"Ever find any answers?"

"Not the ones I was expecting." He twirled blades of grass around his fingers. "But I guess I finally accepted I'm not supposed to have all the answers. Without mystery, there'd be no awe."

In the quiet, her soft inhale drew him near. He leaned on his elbow beside her, not wanting to push.

Her lashes squeezed shut. "How can it be my dad? All this time, he kept the camp running yet never once invested in me. Why?" She faced him. "I don't want awe, Ethan. I want answers."

And he wished more than anything he had them to give.

A tear coursed down her chin and mixed with the dew on the grass. "I just wanted him to love me."

Forgetting boundaries, he tugged her close. "Sometimes we express love the only way we know how."

More tears soaked into his shirt. "I wish I could believe that." She rolled back and brushed off her cheeks. "You know the last thing he ever gave me was a journal. I opened it every day the year he left us, but I never wrote in it. Not once. I kept thinking, if I could just figure out how to rewrite my story, it'd be good enough that he'd come back."

Ethan could've decked her dad for letting her think that. He met her eyes so she could see his sincerity. "You have one of the most moving stories I know. Full of bravery and sacrifice. That life's worth sharing, Cass." Even if it wasn't with him.

Rather than say anything, she rested her head on his chest and simply let herself be held.

Maybe it wasn't fair to judge her dad. He'd probably supported the camp all this time for her. Not that money made up for leaving, but who was Ethan to talk about letting people down?

He ran the backs of his fingers over her soft hair. "Have you thought about calling him? I'm sure he'd reinstate those deposits if you asked."

She shook her head against his shirt. "I can't. I promised myself I'd never ask him for money." A sad laugh followed her admission. "He doesn't even know I'm here."

Ethan lowered his lips to the top of her head before he could stop himself. "Then we'll figure it out together."

Her warmth blended into his as she clutched his shirt tighter. "Thank you," she whispered.

The trees stirred above them, minutes drifting. His embrace didn't offer answers. It couldn't restore what she'd lost. But if it brought her any comfort at all, he'd hold her all night.

She peeked up at him with a genuine smile returning to her eyes. "Can I show you something?"

Sandy hobbled to her side at the same time she pushed to her feet. "I'll be right back." She ruffled his ears. "Stay."

Sandy whimpered as she disappeared into the mess hall.

Ethan angled his head the same way Sandy always did to him. "Thought I was your favorite." Chuckling, he gave the dog's shaggy head a good rub. "I don't blame you, buddy. There's something about her."

He smiled at the strands of red hair left on his shirt, pressed his palms into the cool ground, and lifted his gaze toward heaven again. This was one time he wouldn't mind an answer. Or at least a little extra strength. 'Cause if she was selling and leaving, he had to get control of his feelings.

And fast.

CHAPTER SIXTEEN

Escape

Cassidy returned to the hill five minutes later, blinking a flashlight on and off. "Up for an adventure?"

Ethan stretched an arm in front of him to block the glare. "As long as you stop blinding me."

She turned off the light, but her impish expression continued to glow as she brandished a hammer.

What was she up to? "Should I be nervous?"

Tight-lipped, she shook her head and nodded toward the cabins hidden in the far corner of the property. Traces of the earlier moment still lingered around the corners of her eyes, but it was clear she'd tucked it all away. At least, for now.

Twigs and pine needles crunched along the path. Slightly ahead of them, Sandy dragged his nose on the trail until something scurried in the bordering woods. His head shot up, ears at attention, but Cassidy didn't flinch. She was becoming more at home here than she probably realized.

Her face beamed with something palpable when they reached the steps to the second cabin. Not mischief. Something deeper.

"Maybe it sounds corny, but this camp was sort of a safe haven for me growing up. This cabin, especially. Dreams were never out of reach here." The leaves rustled again. She laughed. "Bats either."

"Bats?"

Sandy followed her up the stairs. "I don't mind them outside. But when they get caught in the rafters . . . Ever hear thirty girls scream at once? Brings a whole new meaning to acoustics." She handed him the flashlight and unlocked the door. "But that's how I figured it out."

"Figured what out?" Behind her, Ethan rubbed Sandy's head.

She raised a brow and grinned—this time, definitely full of mischief. "The secret."

He crossed his arms. "Let me guess. Vampires live in the cabins."

Without denying it, she grabbed the bottom of his shirt and tugged him inside. A dim overhead light barely added to the glow coming through the windows.

Sandy only made it a few steps inside before backing out to the porch. Ethan didn't blame him. As the floorboards creaked under their feet, he couldn't help glancing up at the rafters. Just in case.

In the back left corner, Cass scooted one of the bunk beds to the side and knelt to the floor. She pulled the hammer free from her belt loop, jimmied the claw in between the boards, and pried one up.

"Okay, now you're sorta freaking me out." He peeked into the darkness below. "You're not seriously gonna stick your hand down there, are you?"

"Are you volunteering?"

"And give up my flashlight duties? Not a chance."

"Mm hmm. Then shine that light over here, will ya?" She tugged on his pant leg until he knelt beside her. Her whole arm disappeared into the hole. She really *was* tougher than he thought. "Got it."

The light reflected off the non-rusted portions of a tin container the size of a shoebox. He scratched his head. "Time capsule?"

"More like buried dreams." She sat back and set the dusty box on her lap.

The slight quiver in her hands sent nerves fluttering all the way across Ethan's chest. He backed up to the bed behind them, wanting to give her some space.

The container's hinges squeaked open. She laid the box aside, carefully unrolled something wrapped in plastic, and smoothed out a stack of papers. Whatever it was had to be special.

He gripped the bedpost to keep from moving toward her. He had no right to know her dreams, no right to ask.

She met his gaze and handed them over freely. "Please," she said as if reading his mind.

Torn between reluctance and curiosity, he scanned the pages. "Songs?"

"Handwritten originals. Every one." She rose to her feet and brushed dirt off her thighs. "I used to come here to play the guitar because of the acoustics."

"You're a songwriter?"

"Was." She crossed the cabin to a window by the door and leaned on the sill. "I knew once I outgrew coming here, it was time to let go of childhood dreams. Face the real world. But I couldn't get rid of them." She turned as he reached her side. "It probably sounds silly. But I guess I thought if I buried them, I wasn't fully letting go."

It took herculean strength not to pull her into his arms when she stood before him with such vulnerability.

"Why didn't you pursue it?"

"And add to New York's fine collection of starving artists?" She rested one arm on the sill. "I've seen it, Ethan. Too many kids, wasting their lives chasing stars. Some dreams are meant to stay buried. At least here, they're safe."

He inched toward her. "From what?"

"From everything."

Did she honestly believe that? "Without risk, there'd be no art."

She brushed off his comment. "You sound like Ti."

"She's brighter than she lets on."

"You noticed that, huh?" She laughed softly. "Music was always an anchor for us growing up. Like a safety zone in the midst of chaos." She lowered her head. "I honestly never wanted to pursue it as a career. I was just afraid of losing it altogether." Moonlight draped across a pensive expression and filled her pause.

Of all the things he wanted to say, nothing came out.

She looked up and studied him, eyes soft and genuine. "How do you do it?"

"Do what?"

"Live without fear."

Was she joking? He rubbed a knuckle over his cheek. "I think you've got the wrong guy."

"No, I'm serious. You meet life head-on, always finding the best in things. You see people's potential, even when they can't." She pushed off the sill. "How are you able to do that?"

The wooden floorboards held his gaze as Izzy's face flooded his mind. Her unshakable smile. Her optimistic spirit. Her unassuming compassion.

A long inhale raised his head. "Because someone once did the same for me."

Cass's lips parted slowly, but she didn't speak. Her chest rose and fell with a breath he could almost feel. Without saying a word, she led him to a bunk bed in the middle of the room and gestured for him to sit.

His already-sprinting heart took off in double time when she lingered in front of him.

"Wait here."

As if he could move even if he wanted to.

This wasn't good. Being in a place that was so intimate and personal to her. The way she was opening up to him. After just finding out about her dad, on top of the stress of getting this place ready to sell, she obviously needed a friend. Someone she could feel safe with. And God knew he wanted to be that person, but he only had so much strength.

She disappeared into the shadows and came back with a guitar in hand. Seated on the bed opposite him, she spread the sheet music on the mattress and strummed a few chords.

The longer she played, the deeper she seemed to connect with the music, as if the sound transported her back to the moment she wrote it.

"Home, so far, don't leave me now. Pain, so near, I don't know how. To find where time stops and I begin. So, pause the sun, breathe deep and long. Hold on before the moment's gone."

She wasn't exaggerating about the acoustics in here. But the sound wasn't what mesmerized him. Or even a young girl's honest lyrics. It was the woman before him. The woman, igniting something inside him he didn't fully understand.

All he knew was if he stayed any longer, his heart would win the battle over resolve, no matter the casualties.

"I'm tired of this sting, tired of being alone. So, take this blank page and write me, write me home." She ended the song but kept the guitar close a little longer.

Her fingers drifted down the face of the wood to her lap, her gaze following. "There's some stuff going on with my mom. And then finding out about my dad's payments. I don't know. I just wanted to get away from it all for a few minutes. Music used to help me do that. Like a home I could always run to from a world of instability."

"I can see why. That song was amazing." And so was she.

She rested the guitar against the bed, curved a strand of hair around her ear, and slowly found his eyes. "I've never played those songs for anyone."

"Why me?" The words hardly came out.

She didn't lower her gaze. "Because you make it safe to feel again."

His heartbeat thudded against his ribcage with longing. It was more than attraction. But the burning desire to sweep her onto this mattress was part of the same love keeping him from moving. He couldn't do anything to risk losing the safety she felt with him.

She lifted off the bed and wandered toward the window again.

He craned his head back, blew out a hard breath, and counted to ten before joining her. Just because he was losing his heart, didn't mean he could ask for hers.

She stashed her hands in her back pockets and bit her bottom lip. "You work so hard, Ethan. I want to make sure you know how much I appreciate you." She pulled some papers from her pocket and handed them to him.

He unfolded two printed-off tickets to a Broadway show. In the city.

"It's on a weeknight." She nudged him in the shoulder and laughed. "Aren't you proud? I'm learning to let my hair down. Be spontaneous."

Memories of the night Izzy died throbbed behind his eyes, pulse pounding in his ears.

Smile lost, she took the tickets right back. "I'm sorry. I shouldn't have thought . . ."

That he was falling in love with her? That he wanted to be anywhere with her? 'Cause he did. Anywhere but the city. Anywhere but the past that haunted him.

He couldn't meet her eyes. "I'm sorry, Cass."

"Don't be." She returned them to her pocket. "I'll give them to Ti. Lord knows she's been dying for a dance with city life again."

The forced lightness in her tone didn't hide the hurt beneath it. She couldn't possibly understand his reaction, and he didn't want her to. He wanted to hide that part of his life and shield her from his failures.

She fidgeted in front of him. The outside light flickered over the disappointment and confusion in her eyes until he couldn't stand it.

Heart taking over, he pulled her into his arms. Everything inside him melded into a kiss less cautious than their first. Against her softness, desire escalated. He forced his lips to slow and linger against hers. But he wasn't ready to let go, wasn't sure he had the strength to. "Cass . . ."

A gentle touch to his face brought her closer instead of away. At her response, an ache seized him. He couldn't hold her tight enough. His lips skimmed her cheek to the skin below her ear.

Her heart raced against his chest, each beat echoing the words she'd shared about her past hurts. He couldn't add to them. Not when she finally trusted him.

Finding strength outside himself, he rested his forehead to hers, breath raspy. "I'm sorry."

She pushed back slightly and studied him, like she was trying to piece together a puzzle.

Would she understand? "I should go." Still cupping the base of her neck, he kissed her cheek. "Self-control isn't one of my superpowers." He looked away, too afraid her green eyes would make him stay.

Outside, the cool air slammed into his overheated body, but it wasn't enough. He needed wind, speed. He jogged to his bike, hit the pavement, and prayed the open road would let him escape himself. One more time.

CHAPTER SEVENTEEN

Release

Cass scrubbed around the base of the shower stall in the bathhouse, hands and knees pressed against the cold tiles. Disinfectant fumes had plagued her all morning, but not as much as confusion about Ethan had.

Maybe she'd been misreading him. Sometimes, she would've sworn they'd been best friends for as long as she and Ti had. The effortless camaraderie, the playful banter, the honest conversations—all of it.

Then there were times like last night. The way he'd held her, kissed her. He couldn't fake that, could he? But why'd he back off?

She chucked the scrub brush into the bucket, pushed it away, and stared at her raw fingernails. What was she doing, slaving in here at the crack of dawn? Cleaning might change her surroundings, but the stains inside her never left. She should know that by now.

She pulled herself up as always, adjusted her bandana with her wrist, and looked the place over. It was as good as it was going to get.

Outside, the misty morning kept the quiet property covered in shadows. This early, Sandy was likely still asleep by the canteen. No way Ti was up yet, and who knew where Ethan was. Had he even come home last night? Or was he still out somewhere, trying to figure out how to redraw the lines she'd blurred between them?

All the questions swirled around her stomach with an answer she should've realized sooner. After everything she'd told him, he was probably confusing sympathy for affection.

Of course he ran away. He might've been attracted to her physically, but he was too nice of a guy to take advantage of her. And she never should've put him in a position to make that call to begin with.

Her chest caved at the thought. He'd been a good friend to her. The least she could do was let him off the hook for more.

Ahead, the door to the boatshed rocked open in the wind. A breeze rushed over her but might as well have cemented her feet to the ground. Spouting off the conversation in her head was one thing. Actually having it with Ethan was another.

She pulled off her bandana, shook out her hair, and picked at the knot as she walked. No point in trying to subdue the frizzed-poodle-look in this weather. At least it might give them something to laugh about. Maybe they could forget last night happened and go back to being friends.

Shoving down her nerves, she approached the doorway. "Ethan, I . . ."

The bandana fell to the ground, her heart right after it. Splintered pieces of smashed canoes covered the floor, other canoes and gear missing. The musty scent closed in on her. She gripped the trim. *Not the boathouse.*

"Cass?" Ethan called from up the hill. "I know you need your space, but can we talk about last night? I don't want you to think—" Right behind her, he almost dropped the can of lacquer in his hand. "What happened?"

Heart pounding, she turned. "You tell me."

Confusion raked down his face. "I locked up last night. I swear." He set the can on the ground and examined the lock. "I double-checked everything."

"There's no forced entry. Did you leave the key out somewhere?"

"Of course not." He wrangled his keys from his pocket. "They've never left my side."

She coiled the bandana around her fingers, thoughts circling. It didn't make sense, unless someone got close enough to him without his noticing. The possibility wrung around her as tightly as the fabric cutting off her circulation.

"Did you go to Jenni's last night?"

"What?"

Steeling herself, she looked up. "Jenni showed up with a canoe the other day, so she'd obviously have an interest in all this gear. Not to mention motive, if she's not over you."

She dropped her gaze, not wanting to see if the feeling was mutual. "And if her dad owns a pest control business, would it be a stretch to think she came up with the idea to dump those roaches in the shower hall?"

"Uh, yeah, actually. A huge stretch. You can't honestly think she's involved." He arched an unconvinced brow. "She may resort to a lot of things, but vandalism isn't one of them."

"Just because we want to believe things about someone doesn't mean they're true." Head down, she hurried through the door. Away from what she wanted to believe herself.

"Cass, wait. Can we please talk about all this?" He reached her side. "I didn't go to Jenni's last night. And I never let the keys out of my sight. I promise." He lifted her chin until she had no choice but to face the disappointment coloring his eyes. "I'd never hurt you like that."

His heart-wrenching honesty piled onto her regret for thinking he would. She released a long breath. "I'm sorry. You're right. We're both stressed, trying to make things happen that obviously aren't."

She treaded up the hill. Maybe with some distance, she could get a handle on her emotions.

"Trying to make things happen?" He followed. "What are you talking about?"

Already ahead of him, she turned, business mode back in place. Like it always should've been. "Please take pictures and send them to Deputy Harris. I'll call the insurance agent."

"Wait. Cass, don't shut me out."

What else could she do? It'd be easier for them both.

Her cell rang from her pocket. She glanced from the screen to Ethan. "I'm sorry." She turned, pushed up the slope, and answered. "Cassidy McAdams."

"Wow, that bad, huh?" Nick asked.

She stuffed the bandana in her pocket. "What is?"

"You've got enough stress in your voice to give yourself a migraine."

Was she that readable? "It's nothing. Just business stuff."

"Well, whatever it is, it sounds like a good reason for a night out. I'm leaving Manhattan now. Just crossed the George Washington. I should be back in plenty of time for dinner. What do you say?"

She stopped beside the mess hall. "I need to work."

"A drink, then?"

She looked at Ethan, taking pictures of the damage she still didn't know who'd caused. "I really shouldn't."

"Because of DeLuca?"

"Excuse me?"

A horn honked in the background. "Please don't take this the wrong way, but you're not his type. I mean that as a compliment. You're intelligent, conscientious—"

"Boring?"

He laughed. "I was going to say responsible."

Even worse. Was that all she was? The truth of it sent one realization chasing another. Nick had better add naive to that list. She'd opened up to Ethan these past few days, shown him more of herself than she did to anyone.

And he pulled away.

As much as he was drawn to a lost cause, he probably took one look at the real her and realized gluing her broken pieces back together wasn't worth the effort. She never should have expected him to want to get involved with someone this damaged.

And if that weren't bad enough, then she pulled the jealous girlfriend card, accusing Jenni of trashing the place. She dropped her forehead to her hand. The whole situation couldn't get any more humiliating. "Thanks for the compliment."

"Aw, don't be upset. All I'm trying to say is he's not worth it."

The knot in her neck tensed. "Not worth what?"

"Whatever he has you worked up about."

"I'm not worked up." If her voice stopped shaking, it might've been believable. "And I don't mean to be rude, but this is really none of your business." Okay, maybe that *was* rude.

His pause stretched. "You're right. I just don't want to see you get your heart broken. That's all."

Ethan's glance swept toward her from down the hill. She averted her gaze and scuffed her shoe against the rock propping open the mess hall's side door. "In order to break my heart, he'd have to have it first."

"He doesn't?"

Why had she said anything? She couldn't answer him. Not truthfully.

He breathed into the phone. "At least be on your guard. The guy couldn't get out of Haven's Creek fast enough when he left. Don't you think it's weird he's back, working at that camp for free? If he's got some kind of ulterior motive, I don't want to see you get hurt in the process."

Her insides flinched. She released her balled-up fingers and the thought. No, Ethan wasn't Jesse. He might not want to be with her, but he wouldn't try to con her. "I know you two have history, but he's a good guy, Nick." Better than she deserved.

An exhale seeped through his end of the line. "For your sake, I really hope you're right. If not, I'll be here when you need me." He hung up, but Cassidy didn't move.

Ethan plodded around the opposite side of the main building. Away from her.

Jumbled emotions from this week latched on to ones from her past until it was hard to breathe. Memories pressed in and launched her forward.

She ran. Down the hill, past the shower hall, through the pain. Once her sneakers hit the pavement, she pushed even harder but couldn't block out the voices pounding her thoughts, one after the other.

"*You're not his type.*" Nick's words bled into Jesse's. "*If you knew how to have fun, I wouldn't have to go searching for it with someone else.*"

Images of Mom's comatose stare shadowed her voice. "*If we were good enough, Dad wouldn't have left. Don't ever give a man a reason to leave. You hear me?*"

"*Always the responsible one.*" Ti's singsong tone rang against the wind.

Memories kept blaring until a car horn overpowered them. An SUV came into focus directly ahead. Jarred back to the present, she skirted along the mountainside as the vehicle swerved past her. A ring of sweat soaked into the top of her shirt, frustration seeping through her pores.

She slapped her palms on the rocks, hating that they were right. All of them. She'd kept herself too guarded to be spontaneous, too afraid to risk letting anyone in. She'd pretended to be strong all her life. Hid behind responsibility, worked to prove her worth. But all she'd ever been was scared.

Fingers tight, she shut out every other noise, wanting to escape it all, but Ethan's voice wouldn't let her. Even in a whisper, it held her against the mountainside. "*Who are you trying to be?*"

Tears coated her cheeks with the answer she hadn't stopped chasing since Dad left. Someone worth loving. That was all she'd ever wanted to be.

The weight of missing the mark slumped her shoulders down the face of the rocks. If she were as confident and carefree as Ethan and Ti, would that change?

Another car passed by and stirred up a gust of wind and even more thoughts. The vehicle drifted out of view, leaving a hushed stillness over the street.

From the opposite edge of the road, the creek's steady current echoed up the cliff and rippled over her with reminders of how often she'd stayed behind while other campers had fun.

Not anymore. If she wanted to start living without fear and restraint, now was the time. She pushed off the wall and didn't slow until she reached the camp.

Ethan caught her glance from the top of the driveway by the canteen. He set a can beside Sandy and jogged down the hill. Face strained with worry, he stopped in front or her. "I know you're upset with me, and you have every right to be.

Someone broke into the boatshed on my watch. I take full responsibility for that. If you want me to leave, I understand."

She lifted her head, far past ready for things to change. "I don't want you to leave, Ethan. I want you to take me out."

Working the rest of the day hadn't gotten rid of the unease chafing against Ethan's insides. He tossed a towel into his Jeep's back seat. "This is a bad idea."

"Bridge jumping?" Ti swung her camera over the side and leaped into the back. Cans rattled in the floorboard. "It's an awesome idea."

"Yeah, if we were teenagers, maybe." He closed his door but couldn't shake the look on Cass's face when she'd asked him to take her. Something wasn't right. He'd thought for sure after talking her into putting it off most of the day, she'd have changed her mind by now.

"Oh, lighten up. She was always too chicken to do it when we were campers. Let her be fearless for once. You're the one urging her to let her hair down, right?"

Ti's comment caught him dead in the gut. Was that what this was about?

His cell buzzed in the cup holder. After waiting for Mom's call all day, he scrambled to grab it. His shoulders sank at the sight of Jenni's number instead. What made him think his mother would actually get back to him?

He ignored the call as Cass jogged over in a pair of board shorts and a T-shirt over a bathing suit.

Ti whistled. "Ready for some fun, girlfriend?"

"You have no idea." Cass jumped in and pulled her sunglasses off her head.

Ti drummed her hands on the top of Ethan's seat. "Let's rock and roll."

Muscles taut, he let off the clutch. This morning's confrontation at the boatshed added to the tension left over from yesterday. Now this. Why wouldn't the girl just talk to him?

Not that he had room to say anything. Explaining his reaction to those tickets meant opening the part of his past he wasn't ready to share yet. But surely, she knew his leaving last night had nothing to do with a lack of attraction. Didn't she?

Once on the road, Cass stood up and flung her arms in the air, fiery hair blowing behind her. Ti's laugh followed several camera flashes and blended into Cass's squeals.

He snagged the bottom of her shirt. "What are you doing?"

"Letting loose." She gripped the top of the Jeep with one hand but didn't take her eyes off the sunset on the skyline. "Freedom, space—just you and the wind, remember?"

He never expected to eat those words. Now, he wanted to throw them up.

She sat and slid her glasses along her nose to meet his eyes. "A little adventure's good for you." She had his voice down perfectly.

Was she gonna dish out any other reminders of all the stupid things he'd said to her this week? Sure, he wanted her to enjoy herself. Wanted her to laugh, experience life outside of work. But not like this. Not if she was doing it because she thought he wanted her to.

He parked in the turnoff twenty feet away from the rusty steel bridge. Ti slipped out the back and shot a few pictures. Stomach still churning, he grabbed Cass's hand before she opened the door. "Can we talk first?"

"I'm tired of talking, Ethan." She clambered out. "I'm ready to live."

Ti tossed an arm around her and snapped a picture of the two of them together before running to the bridge.

Ethan jogged after them, not ready to give up.

They ducked under the first railing. Ti shot another picture and lowered the camera. "It'd be perfect if Mr. Pouty Face behind you weren't ruining it. Relax, Ethan. It's not that far of a drop."

The drop wasn't the problem. "I'm sorry. I just don't think this is a good idea."

Head to the side, Cass glowered at him. "You're telling me you've never made this jump before?"

His jaw flexed, and she flashed a that's-what-I-thought smirk.

"Yeah, in August, after the water's had a chance to warm up. At least go down and feel it first." If the wind hitting them in the face right now didn't change her mind, dipping her toes in that frigid water would.

"I'm a big girl, Ethan." She finagled her T-shirt over her head and handed it to him, followed by her shorts. "If you guys can do it, I can do it."

He darted his gaze to the arch above them. This wasn't the time to react to his attraction. A long exhale lowered his eyes no farther than hers. "It's not a competition."

A pained smile looked back at him. "Wrong. It's always a competition." She climbed under the outer rail and held on to the bar behind her.

"Cass, please." Gripping the cool steel, he set his free hand on her arm. "You don't have anything to prove."

Her hazel eyes carried waves of sadness. "Wrong again." She faced the wide creek carved through the mountains. Wind rushed through her hair. And with a deep inhale, she let go.

The thrill of release tingled through her. For the first time, nothing held her back. Nothing grounded her. No restraint, no responsibility. Just air. Freedom.

Until she hit the water.

Knives. Thousands of ice-cold knives stabbed her body from every direction, stealing her breath, her movement. She gasped for air.

"Cassidy!" A garbled voice rang from somewhere above her.

She strained to push the weights surrounding her. Limbs numb, she couldn't swim against the current. Couldn't call for help.

Shivers racked her lungs. So. Cold. She closed her eyes. Time slowed as panic gradually surrendered to the drowsiness taking control of her pulse.

Downstream, a blurry silhouette crested the bank. Ethan. What little fight she had left in her thrust her arms out, but the pull of the water tunneled her backward over a cluster of shallow rapids. Adrenaline recharged her muscles and shot her up from the surface for air.

"Eth—" Her back smacked into a bolder behind her. With the wind knocked out of her, darkness compressed until everything went black.

Something firm pressed into her chest. Once, twice. A burning sensation trekked up her throat. She turned and coughed. Water spilled over her cheek as Ethan blinked into focus.

Soaking wet, his whole body nearly crumbled above her with an exhale of relief. He drew her into the crook of his arm, heart racing. Instead of saying all the things he had every right to, he wrenched off his wet shirt, wrapped a towel around her, and kept her close.

He brought her numb fingers to his mouth and blew warm breath over them, but she couldn't stop her teeth from chattering. "I . . . c-can't even . . . h-have f-fun . . . when I t-try."

He smiled against her hair. "Maybe you shouldn't try to cram it all into one day."

It hurt to laugh. Almost as much as it hurt to admit what a stupid idea this was. Had she really thought he'd see her differently after this? That she'd see herself differently?

"Cass!" Ti flew down the bank. "I'm so sorry. I shouldn't have—"

"I s-seem to r-remember . . . jumping . . . on . . . m-my own."

Ethan took Ti's towel, layered it on top of the other, and scooped Cass up from the ground.

In the Jeep, he angled all vents toward her and blasted the heat. Yet as soothing as it felt, the warmth didn't touch the comfort that being carried in his arms had given her.

The main building fluttered into view, the ride home a blur.

He jogged around the front bumper to her side, like he was getting ready to carry her to her room.

"I can walk, Ethan. I'm fine, really." Aside from being mortified, anyway. She planted her feet on the ground and steadied a hand against the Jeep's door panel. "Nothing a hot shower can't cure."

His gaze flitted to Ti, and she was glued to her hip before Cass could argue.

Once inside, Ti started the shower and set her robe out. Cass peeled the wet bathing suit off her skin. Rash marks ran down her arms and legs where the moss-covered rocks had scraped against her. They'd sting in the shower, but it'd be worth it to feel her toes again.

As soon as Ti closed the bedroom door, Cass shut herself in the steam-filled bathroom. Hot water jetted onto her back, unlocking her muscles one at a time.

If she stayed in here long enough, maybe it'd wash away all traces of what had just happened. Better yet, traces of the entire week. All she'd done was make one blunder after another. She didn't even want to imagine what Ethan must think of her now.

Twenty minutes in the shower hadn't erased the effects of the day, but there was always the chance her bed would work its magic. She pulled on her bathrobe, flopped onto the mattress, and covered her face with a pillow.

A scream jolted Cass straight up in bed and sent her gaze shooting across the dark room toward her clock. Midnight. That cold water must've taken more out of her than she'd thought.

She slid her legs off the side of the bed and waited to regain her equilibrium. Sandy's bark joined some other commotion outside. What in the world?

She tightened the belt on her robe and hurried down the hall. "Ti? What's going on?"

A draft blew in from the wide-open front door. Adrenaline took over exhaustion and propelled her outside. "Ti?"

Barely halfway across the deck, she buckled at the knees. Massive flames roared from the canteen. Ti held Sandy on the edge of the driveway while Ethan combated the fire with a hose. Waves of heat and smoke barreled over her, but all she could do was stare.

No. This isn't happening. Breath came hard and sharp, launching her down the stairs.

"Cass, don't." Ti rose but couldn't grab her. "Ethan!"

He dropped the hose and caught Cass around the waist.

"Let me go. We have to stop it."

His hold tightened. "The truck's on its way. There's nothing we can do."

"No." She wrestled to break free, thrashing and shrieking.

The roof collapsed. A gust of heat and debris flooded toward them. Ethan turned her in his arms and cradled her head to his chest. Too weak to fight him, she held on.

Sirens struck the air while red lights led a fire truck up the driveway. Ethan called Ti over. "Get her inside. Stay with her." He rested a hand on her arm. "Please."

Ti shouldered most of Cass's weight while guiding her up the deck. In the bedroom, Ti curled beside her on the mattress. "It's gonna be okay."

Would it?

"I should be out there."

"Shh." Ti held her tight until the fight drained from her.

The blare from the sirens stopped, but the turmoil outside kept pulsing. The truck's lights flashed against the shadows in the room. Clutching her pillow, Cass squeezed her eyes shut.

Ti rubbed her arm and sang the way they did as kids when they wanted to pretend nothing bad could reach them. "When the lights turn dark and the shadows deep, close your eyes and drift to sleep. To the place of dreams that sweep us away, together we run. Best friends, always."

Cass clasped Ti's hand, grateful not to be alone. Fears coiled around questions of who was behind this and what lengths they'd go. Would she and Ti be in danger next? Ethan's protection could only stretch so far, and she had no one else to turn to for help.

Their childhood song replayed in her mind. As scared as she was, she couldn't run away from this. Her only choice was to fight.

CHAPTER EIGHTEEN

Smolder

Brisk air poured down the mountainside and amplified the dull chill seeping through the grass into Cass's knees. In front of the canteen, she sat back and faced the wind head-on. It couldn't sting any worse than the ache that'd kept her awake all night. After shivering out here in her pajamas before the sunrise, her body was already numb, anyway.

She lowered the sledgehammer she'd dragged up from the garage and covered her face with her shirt to block out the charred stench scraping down her nostrils.

Who'd be so cruel to set the canteen on fire? Hadn't vandalizing the boatshed been enough? And what did they want her to do? Leave? She was trying. But she couldn't sell a destroyed property.

Surrounded by loss, she rummaged through the soot-covered debris and clutched a piece of blackened plywood. The wood bore into her palms, thoughts of Grandpa cutting deeper. Guilt compounded the anger surging through her. After all he'd sown into the camp, she couldn't stand by and watch it fall apart. She had to restore it. No matter what it took.

The door on the deck opened. In flannel pajama pants and a dark T-shirt, Ethan stumbled toward the stairs while rubbing his eyes. "Cass? It's six o'clock."

"Go back to bed." With shaky arms, she swung the hammer into what remained of the canteen's burnt structure. She didn't have the emotional energy to argue with him right now.

He jogged across the gravel on bare feet and caught her arm. "Cass, stop."

"I can't." There was no time. Whoever'd done this wasn't going to shut her down. For Grandpa and Mom, she had to pass that inspection.

Ethan pried the hammer from her hands. His warm arms closed around her, and she almost broke right there. "You're freezing. How long have you been out here?"

Not long enough. She had to keep working.

He rubbed her cold arms. "Please come inside. I know you're upset, but you need to rest. I promise we'll work this out . . ."

Headlights came up the driveway and cut him off. Jenni parked her SUV beside the grass and rounded the bumper. A confused gaze flitted between them and the wreckage as she slipped on her jacket.

Ethan tightened his hold around Cass's back. "What are you doing here?"

Jenni zipped her jacket up to her chin and buried her hands in the pockets. "You said to meet you here."

"What are you talking about?"

"Your text last night." She pulled out her phone and scrolled through her messages. "You said it's done and to meet you here at six."

Cass's body stiffened. She looked up at Ethan, stomach twisting. It's done. He was a part of this? He and Jenni, both?

Wide-eyed, he met her gaze, shook his head. "Cass . . ."

She pushed away. "Don't."

She turned and folded in half. The memory of her phone call with Nick echoed off the pile of rubble. *"Don't you think it's weird he's back, working at that camp for free? If he's got some kind of ulterior motive, I don't want to see you get hurt in the process."*

Ulterior motive. Waves of nausea seized her. This wasn't happening. Not again. Not with Ethan.

Each attack played back in her mind. He was always there, ready to rescue her, earning her trust. And she'd fallen for it, same as she had with Jesse.

She caved to her knees and hugged her arms to her sides. Scenes from this week clashed with scenes from her past until she felt as helpless as that broken teenager in her prom dress, huddled in the back corner of the subway.

Jenni's SUV trailed down the driveway. Ethan must've told her to leave, but Cass couldn't hear anything except the throb of questions she didn't want to answer. How could she be this gullible? She'd opened up to him, talked herself out of doubting his motives.

His hand smoothed over her back. "Cass, please . . ."

She flinched away from his touch, hating how much she wanted to draw from the strength and safety of his arms. Hating how, even now, she wanted him to hold her and tell her she was wrong.

Past the point of restraining her tears, she rose and faced him. "Why, Ethan?"

The look of betrayal on her face almost crippled Ethan on the spot. She couldn't honestly think he was involved in any of this. Especially a fire.

She had no idea how hard it'd been for him to see those flames that close to her last night. To see her now with arms covered in scrapes and ash, breaths strained against the smolder.

Flashes of Izzy's lifeless body struck him like physical blows. Chest tight, he strained to box out the memories and focus on Cass instead.

Dark circles underlined her bloodshot eyes. She was past fatigued, on the verge of collapsing. She wouldn't be saying any of this if she'd gotten enough sleep to think straight.

He reached for her. "Look at me. I didn't text Jenni. Someone must've gotten my phone."

"Like someone got your keys to the boathouse?" Tears streamed.

Every inch of him ached to hold her and make it all right. He pulled her close.

"Stop. Just stop." She shoved him back. "The con's over, Ethan. Just tell me why you did it. What are you and Jenni getting out of this?"

The jab stung, but seeing her pull away hurt worse. "How can you ask me that?"

"You showed up on my property, ready to save me at every turn." The delirious look in her eyes backed him away. "The roaches, the mattresses, the raccoons. You were the only one with access to the boatshed. Now this?" She jerked her head toward the canteen. "You knew the fresh lacquer would go up in flames."

He stopped her by the wrists. "Jeez, Cass, are you even listening to yourself right now?"

"Was this your plan to get me to fall for you? 'Cause it worked, Ethan. Is that what you want to hear? It worked."

A flicker of relief shot through him at hearing she had feelings for him, too. Until every past hurt and betrayal tore down her face with such transparent pain, it nearly speared him in two.

He would never add to her heartache. "I don't know what's going on here, but I swear you can trust me." He lifted a hand to her hair, scared to let go.

She closed her eyes at his touch and hung her head so long he almost drew her to him, no matter what fight she might've put up.

Tears clung to her lashes when she finally faced him. "You don't know how much I want to believe that. Please just go." She walked away, and all he could do was let her.

After that incriminating text, he couldn't fault her for second-guessing him. He'd give her time and space if she needed it, but he wouldn't stop fighting for her. Not if she was still in danger.

His legs carried him up to his room, confusion and anger mounting with each step. Jenni had looked as shocked as they were when she saw the wreckage from the fire. She didn't have it in her to risk harming anyone. But who'd try to set him up? And why involve her? He changed, grabbed the keys to his bike, and jetted right back outside.

Instead of cooling him down, the open highway fed his indignation. Someone had to get to the bottom of these attacks. Last night crossed a line. Any of them could've been inside the canteen. What was next? The main building? He wouldn't let another fire steal someone he loved.

He revved the throttle as his tires hugged the curve. Mom might be too busy to take his calls, but she couldn't avoid him in person.

Thirty minutes of riding unlocked his muscles. But the second he pulled his bike up to the pillars in front of the city clerk's office, irritation claimed every tendon again.

He left his helmet on the bike's handle, whisked the glass door open, and headed straight for Mom's wing.

Her longtime assistant glanced up from her computer as he approached the desk. "Mr. DeLuca." She sat higher in her chair and fiddled with items on her desk. "What a nice surprise."

"I need to see her, Mary."

With a trained smile fastened on her face, she raised her glasses from her blouse and pulled the keyboard forward. "Let me take a look at her schedule."

He stretched a hand over the desk. "Now." He kept his voice even, but she couldn't have missed his resolve.

"Forgive me, Mary. My son seems to be short on manners today," Mom said from behind him.

Outside the doorway to a conference room, a handful of employees in suits almost as starched as hers flanked either side of her. No one moved.

The air conditioning clicked on and dragged the weighted silence from the ceiling to the floor. Each of her sidekicks scattered to other rooms in response to the slightest flick of her chin.

She strode into her executive office without stopping to greet him. Ethan unclenched his jaw but equaled her confident strides.

Beside a filing cabinet in the corner of the window-lit room, she opened a drawer and withdrew a folder. "What can I do for you, Ethan?"

Her sleek, tightly wound bun held more give than her voice. Was he just another business client to her?

"Do you really have to ask? You already know about the fire."

She didn't release her gaze from the papers in her hand. "Fire?"

Her nonchalant tone jacked up his blood pressure. He gripped the chair in front of him. "Cut the crap, Mom. Nothing happens in this city without you knowing about it."

A glare sharper than the prize letter opener on her desk sliced into him. "My, my. Aren't we full of compliments today?" Her practiced smile quirked. "And what would you like me to do about it?"

He dug his fingers into the chair. "Anything." Couldn't she see that was why he was here? "I don't know, Mom. Call Harris. Get him out of his desk chair for a change. Do something."

She swept her focus back to the folder. "I don't control the sheriff's department."

He scoffed. "Except when it pleases you."

"That's enough." She snapped the folder shut, banged it on top of the drawer, and stalked across the floor in her heels. "You stay off in your fire station, hiding from responsibilities." Her gaze drifted to a strand of Cass's hair on his shirt. "Or prancing around with God-knows-who." She stopped less than a foot in front of him. "And you think you know what it takes to run this city?"

He looked away from her cutting blue eyes, sneered, and returned her glare. "No. But I know what it cost you."

Her rigid composure gave way to a flash of something he couldn't read. She thwarted his eye contact and adjusted her suit jacket.

His shoulders sank. Why did it have to be like this?

Swallowing his pride, he stepped forward and softened his voice. "I didn't come here to fight. I came because we have nowhere else to go. The girls at that camp are in danger, Mom. Don't brush this off." He set a hand on her arm. "Please."

Despite everything else between them, she had to see it was the right thing to do.

A single pause shouldn't cause his stomach to tighten this much.

Etched stoicism crept down her face as she shifted her gaze toward him. "Policies are in place for a reason," she said mechanically. "If there's a disturbance, file a report with Harris. I have every confidence he'll address it with the urgency it requires. Mary can provide—"

"Stop." He let go of her arm but not her eyes. "Don't patronize me with regulations and protocol. I'm not a constituent. I'm your son, for God's sake. Does that mean anything?" Twenty-eight years old, and he stood in the middle of that office with every vulnerability of his eight-year-old heart laid before them.

The slightest flutter touched her lashes, but she clung to her unyielding stance. "I'm sorry."

Not as sorry as he was. Fury reheated his body in two point five seconds. He hustled through the doorway without looking back.

Mary rose from her chair as he turned, but he kept trucking to the exit before he took his anger out on anything but the pavement.

He lugged his helmet on and peeled out of the parking lot. The miles passing under his tires couldn't draw him far enough away. He never should've hoped Mom might've changed. That *he* might've changed. Izzy'd taught him to believe nothing was past mending. Maybe it was better she wasn't here to see him let her down. Again.

Hours of open road and wind siphoned out his adrenaline and left the ache underneath more exposed than ever. Not knowing where else to go, he idled in Nonna's driveway.

Was Cass ready to talk to him yet? Would she ever be? Even if she came around and believed he wasn't involved, how could he expect her to feel safe with him again when he kept failing to protect her?

Drained, he didn't move until his cell rang. He shucked off his helmet and answered, but Nonna didn't give him a chance to say hello.

"You gonna sit in my driveway all day, or are you coming inside?"

He glanced at the house. "Sorry, I'm not very good company right now."

"Then what are you doing here?"

Sliding the helmet onto the handlebar, he shook his head. "I don't know."

"Well, I do. You're hiding."

Not Nonna, too. The last thing he needed was another lecture. "Now's really not the best time—"

"Now's all you've got. Or are you waiting for a heart attack to remind you of that?"

She had to throw that in there, didn't she? Knowing her, she was probably standing at the window, waving her hand around at him with that feisty Italian flair of hers.

He lifted his boot to the footrest and let out a breath. "Thanks, but I'd rather rewind time instead. Do things differently."

He might not've been able to stop whoever'd been wrecking the camp, but at least he could've kept his feelings for Cass in check. Been the friend she needed instead of complicating things and hurting them both.

"Nonsense. Everything you've done is exactly why that girl's in love with you."

The hurt on Cass's face earlier ripped into him all over again. "Love can't survive without trust, Nonna."

"So, be trustworthy, then."

His foot slipped onto the gravel. "You don't think I'm trying?"

"I think there's a girl over there, needing you to do more than try."

"What am I supposed to do?" He wiped off the dew already collecting over the gas tank. Even if he could reason with Cass now, the damage was done. "I can't make her trust me."

"No, but you can show her a love worth trusting in."

Ti's words crashed right into Nonna's. *She has a reason. But that doesn't mean you can't prove her wrong.*

Jesse and her dad had both abused Cass's trust and ruined her faith in commitments. If he walked away without fighting for her, he'd only prove her right.

"Go on, now. That eyesore of a motorcycle is scaring the deer away."

Smiling, he leveled his feet on either side of the bike and gazed toward the house. "Thanks, Nonna. Love you."

Her shadow swayed with the curtains beside the door. "You, too."

Grateful for a love worth emulating, he pulled on his helmet and hoped he still had the chance to try.

Cass opened her bedroom door and shielded her eyes from the hallway's light. She'd meant to take an afternoon catnap, not sleep like a zombie for six hours.

In a pair of boxers, a long-sleeved T-shirt, and fuzzy socks, she shuffled toward the dark kitchen. The overhead light buzzed on and added to the crunching noise coming from Jax's food dish.

She massaged her forehead. What were the chances the last day and a half had been a dream? The quiet kitchen stared back at her with the answer.

No savory Italian roasted coffee aroma. No contagious sound of Ethan's laughter. Nothing but sterile shelves as empty as she felt. The memory of this morning ricocheted off them and punched a hole through her chest.

She pinched the bridge of her nose and tried to shut out the wounded look in Ethan's eyes when she'd accused him. She should've let him explain, should've—

Her cell rang from the counter where she'd left it before her nap. Pulse picking up, she fumbled the phone upright to see if it was him. Nick. Her thumb rested above the answer button but swept over to ignore instead. She wasn't up for talking.

The phone message icon at the top of the screen caught her eye. How many calls had she missed while sleeping? She leaned a hip against the counter and called her voicemail.

"Cass, it's Mom. I'm sorry about the check. Don't give up on me, baby. I just . . ." She sighed. "Please call me."

Cass hurried to the next message before the tremble in Mom's voice got to her.

"Miss McAdams, this is Joshua Wallis from the claims department at The Hardford, returning your recent call about damaged property. I've scheduled an insurer to come out 9:30

a.m. on Tuesday. Please don't dispose of anything until he's inspected each item. If you have any questions or need to reschedule, feel free to give me a call."

After the canteen catastrophe, she'd almost forgotten she'd called about the canoes. What would they think once she filed a claim for the fire, too? Probably that she was a hustler, trying to scam money out of them. Couldn't be any worse than what she'd accused Ethan of.

She planted her forehead against the fridge. He'd stood by her at every turn, helping her laugh and feel safe. It couldn't have all been a ruse. It didn't fit.

A dull pain pulsed from the crown of her head all the way down to the base of her neck. She opened the fridge in search of anything to deaden the ache. The bottle of wine from the other night practically glowed in the light.

Worth a shot.

Skipping a glass, she carried the bottle into the mess hall toward the loveseat at the opposite end. Her socks kept the cold from the cement floor off her feet about as well as her boxers kept the draft off her legs. She started a small fire in the fireplace and curled up on the couch.

From behind her, Jax leaped to the chair arm and climbed onto her lap.

"Right on time, buddy." She grabbed the bottle from the floor while he groomed himself. His warmth drove her deeper into the cushions. Between his steady purr and the wine, she might've relaxed if her mind weren't stuck in overdrive.

The longer she sat there, the worse she felt about how she'd treated Ethan. Despite logic pointing to him, the truth was, her heart wanted to believe him. *Needed* to believe him. Now, she might've lost the chance to find out if it would matter.

Time ran down with the fire. In the stillness, a chill trickled over her arms. She slid Jax onto the couch, stumbled off the cushion, and leaned a palm against the stones above the fireplace until the blood stopped rushing to her head.

Jesse wasn't joking when he'd called her a lightweight. If a little wine set her off balance, no telling what hard liquor would've done. Good thing she usually stayed away from both.

Cold air breezed in from behind her. She turned, and Ethan stopped inside the doorway, hesitating. The same worry in his eyes from the morning poured from them now and kept all the things she wanted to say lodged in her throat.

Head lowered, he strode over and added another two logs to the burned-down fire. His arms and back flexed as he moved, muscles taut under his pullover. The same muscles that'd provided her strength and protection again and again.

All the times he'd held her—they had to have been genuine. *Please.* Her heart rate picked up, fear raging against hope.

He straightened in front of her but didn't lift his head. "Cass, I know how things look, and I can't explain how someone got my keys or my phone, but I promise I'm not a part of any of it."

Meeting her gaze, he started to reach for her but stopped and breathed in. "Everything I've ever said or done with you has been real. I swear."

Studying his face, she traced her fingers over his stubble to the hairs on the back of his neck. The honesty in his eyes gripped her. Unanswered questions could wait. She had to know for sure how he felt. Would he push her away? Was it too late?

His breath quivered against her lips. She hovered until his hand found the small of her back. Sighing, she pressed in. Soft and tender, his touch matched hers. And everything inside her—the questions, the fears, the yearnings—crashed together until she lost herself in the feelings he stirred.

No matter what happened in the past or what happened next, this was where she belonged. With him.

He lifted back slightly, the vein on his neck pulsing in a disjointed rhythm. "I'm not as strong as you think I am."

"What if I don't want you to be?"

His eyes searched hers. "Then we're both in trouble."

Maybe that was what she wanted. To give him all of herself without questioning his motives or fearing the consequences. Without trying to stay in control or pretending to be someone she wasn't. Just him and her. Nothing else.

She moved his palm from her cheek to her lips and breathed in the cherry wood fragrance mixed with the scent of his skin. This was home. In his touch, his smell. She wanted every part of him as much as she wanted to give him the same.

The warm cobblestone wall pressed into her back. Bracing one hand against the rocks, he pulled her into him until her body molded to his.

She'd never experienced an all-consuming longing to be with someone like this. To block out every thought and just *be*. Wasn't that what he wanted, too? Her hands trailed down his stomach and lifted the bottom of his shirt.

He pushed it back down. "Cass, no."

The fire crackled, along with the very thing she'd fought so hard to keep from ever feeling again.

Rejection.

She let go of his shirt and cradled her arms to her chest. "You don't want . . ."

Eyes closed, he dragged both hands down the face of the wall and backed up. "I want what's best for you."

What did that mean? She faced the ceiling, feeling so small and foolish standing there with every vulnerability and desire accentuated in the glow of the fire. With her whole heart, outstretched before him. And unwanted.

Had she been wrong again?

Tears burned in her throat. Unable to stifle them, she fled to the door.

"Please don't . . ."

The door swung behind her, trapping his words on the other side. The cold air outside doused her skin but didn't come close to putting out the fire still churning inside her.

A *thud* shuddered from inside, followed by the door squeaking open. "What do you want from me, Cassidy?"

She kept her back toward him. "Nothing."

"Really? 'Cause that didn't seem like nothing a minute ago." He let out a hard breath. "I'm trying to protect you."

She turned. "From what?"

"From what? From that." He pointed at his Jeep. "Is that what you want? You want me to sweep you into the back of my Jeep right now like Jesse did."

That was a low blow, but she could mask the impact better than he could. She'd had practice all her life. "I wanted you to be different." Cut 'em at the base. That was what Mom had taught her.

The dig struck his eyes. He shook his head, backed up, and strode toward his Jeep.

Hand on the handle, he stood without facing her. "You can't have it both ways, Cass. Either I'm the jerk trying to play you, or I'm the man trying to show you what it means to love someone." His chin drooped to his chest as he opened the door.

Words wouldn't come out. The engine's roar stood in for her response. She hugged her arms to her stomach but couldn't stop trembling.

Taillights bled down the driveway, her heart dragging behind them. She'd crumble as soon as he was gone but not while he still had a view of the debris left behind.

The Jeep skidded to a stop halfway to the curve. He left his door open and jogged back to her.

She begged her body to stand tall as he approached, but the moment he pulled her into his arms, she came undone. She clutched his shoulders, overwhelmed by a love strong enough to let her fall apart in an embrace that made her whole again.

CHAPTER NINETEEN

Chances

Morning sunbeams filtered through the blinds and warmed Cass's face. One yawn stretched into another until her bedroom slowly came into focus.

Her gaze drifted down to Ethan's arm wrapped around her side. Every inch of her froze as memories pieced last night back together. The replay squeezed across her chest. Tipsy, fragile, and vulnerable. She'd given him a wide-open shot at taking advantage of her.

She shut her eyes at the humiliating image. More like she'd given him every reason to run away as far as he could from an emotional train wreck. But instead of doing either, he'd stayed and held her until she'd fallen asleep. How could he still be here?

She gingerly rolled over to face him. Beneath his pullover, his chest rose and fell in an unconscious rhythm, muscles relaxed. The strain of yesterday no longer lined his forehead. Yet even this peaceful, every feature still emanated strength. The kind that was tempered with a level of gentleness she'd never experienced from a man.

At the end of the bed, Jax flexed his front paws over Ethan's calves. *Oh no.* She swept a glance back at Ethan's face to check for any signs of an allergic reaction.

Poor guy. He must've taken a Benadryl sometime last night. Not that he would've needed something to help him sleep. He was probably as exhausted as she was.

They'd faced so much together in such a short time. Things that would've driven others apart. But he never left, not even when she pushed him away. He gave of himself without expecting anything in return.

She ran a hand over his scruffy cheek. No one had ever taught her how to love.

Until now.

She lifted the covers, slid a pillow in her place, and eased off the mattress. The cool floorboard pressed into the bottom of her feet and sent a shiver up her legs.

She tugged her shirtsleeves down and curled her fingers around the cuffs as she studied him. He'd slept above the covers, still in his clothes from yesterday.

Jax stretched his back and burrowed tighter against the crook of Ethan's legs. She held in a laugh while snapping a picture with her cell. At least maybe they'd kept each other warm all night. She snagged a throw blanket from the chair in the corner and draped it over him.

Running her hand down his hair as gently as she could, she pressed her lips to his forehead and breathed in the scent of the man who'd protected her heart over and over again. Would he give her the chance to return the same kind of love?

She slowed beside the bathroom door to study him one more time before heading toward the shower and the hope of starting over.

Steam fanned through the bathroom door twenty minutes later. While rubbing her hair with a towel, she stopped short at the sight of the empty room.

If it weren't for Ethan's lingering scent, no one would have known he'd been there. He, of all people, had even made the bed. She laughed as she traded her robe for a pair of jeans and a knit sweater.

The glorious aroma of Italian roasted coffee lured her down the hall to the kitchen. Ti peeked over her shoulder while opening a cabinet. "Morning, Sleeping Beauty."

"Remind me never to guzzle over half a bottle of wine all at once." Cass shuffled straight for the coffeemaker. "Where's Ethan?"

Ti tilted her head. "Oh, you mean the-love-of-your-life-turned-psycho-conspirator?"

She cringed. "He told you?"

"I heard." Ti filled her mug to the brim. "Along with all of Haven's Creek."

The scene Cass had made yesterday morning colored over the one from last night. She hunched against the fridge and dropped her head to her hands. "What's wrong with me?"

"You sure you want me to answer that?"

Cass swatted her arm. But the truth was, they both could've filled in the blank with a list a mile long. She craned her neck toward the ceiling.

"You need me to sing?"

Cracking a grin, Cass shook her head. "Not sure it'll help this time."

"Psh, girl, singing always helps." Ti backed beside her and leaned into her shoulder. "You guys love each other. It's gonna work out."

Just like Ti to oversimplify things. Cass stared at the tiles. "I'm scared."

"I know." Ti rested her head on Cass's shoulder. "It's okay to be scared. Just don't hang on to the past so much that you let counterfeit versions of love keep you from experiencing the real thing."

Words of wisdom from Trina Russo. She smiled at the reminder of Ethan's comment from that day in the cabin. "*She's brighter than she lets on.*" Funny how easy that truth was to believe for someone else instead of for yourself.

She rested her cheek against Ti's hair. "Thanks."

"I gotta have *some* purpose in being here." Chuckling, she handed Cass a cup of coffee and prodded her toward the door. "Now, go tell the man how you feel already."

Cass laced her fingers around the warm mug and ambled onto the deck. Steam rose from a coffee cup on one of the chair's arms. He must be coming right back. His sketchbook caught her eye. That reminded her.

She scurried inside to Grandpa's office and pulled up her email. The notification she'd been waiting for had finally come in. She couldn't open it fast enough.

Her stomach did somersaults as she read over the recommendation. She printed off the pages, tucked them in a folder, and hustled outside while trying not to spill her coffee.

Ethan looked up from the Adirondack chair with a soft gaze that might as well have been a kiss. The somersaults intensified, turning her mouth dry.

He set the sketchpad aside and rose. "I was gonna make breakfast, but I wasn't sure what you were up for?"

Breakfast? After all they'd just gone through, he was worried about what to make her for breakfast.

She curved her bottom lip under her teeth and raised her shoulders. "Got any humble pie recipes in your repertoire?"

He rubbed his stubbly cheek. "Pretty sure I've eaten that one enough times to know the recipe by heart."

Not as much as she had. There couldn't be a recipe large enough for the pie she needed right now.

She set her mug on the chair arm and looked at him with every ounce of honesty she could offer. "I'm sorry, Ethan. For so much, I don't know where to start. I never should've doubted you."

"With the lineup you gave yesterday, I don't blame you." He laughed softly. "I almost started to doubt myself." His fingers found hers, face sobering. "I don't know who's sabotaging this place, Cass. And maybe we're on our own in finding out, but I'm not gonna leave until we do."

Protecting the camp should've been her top concern, but the fear of not selling it didn't scare her anymore. Through everything, Ethan had taught her what it meant to be brave.

Still holding the folder, she crossed her arms over her sides and walked toward the front of the deck. Ethan followed and settled beside her against the rail.

She took in the massive tree line and the realization of how much had changed since she'd arrived. "When I first came, it was out of respect for my grandpa mixed with a sense of obligation. It almost became a challenge, another notch on my belt to prove my worth."

Despite the damage from the fire, the quiet field still held a misty tranquility. She folded her arms beside the planter and breathed it in. "But then I remembered how much of a home the camp's been for me. I keep thinking of all the ways it's shaped my life. How can I risk not offering those same experiences to other kids?"

The smell of smoldering ash clung to the air and drew her focus toward the heap of burnt wood. "I don't know. Maybe I'm crazy for thinking about staying. I mean, obviously someone doesn't want me here. And I still have no idea if we can pass inspection, but I'm tired of being afraid."

She pushed up from the railing. "I don't know what or who I'm fighting against, but I've finally realized what's worth fighting *for*. Even if I fail."

Beside her, blue eyes held on to every word.

Her cheeks warmed. "What?" Was she rambling?

"Nothing." His dimples said otherwise. He faced the field and exhaled. "I was just thinking I'm not sure I want to leave, either."

"Are you kidding? After how long you've been trying to get away from this town?"

His gaze drifted back to her, deep and earnest. "Maybe I was just waiting for a reason to stay."

Would he stay if she asked him? Her pulse drummed, her lips barely holding back the words. He'd cared for her so self-lessly. It was time she did the same for him. As much as she wanted to be with him, she wanted his happiness more. "You deserve to live your dreams, Ethan."

"I think I already am." He moved in, and she almost dropped the folder.

She clasped it and forced her eyes to pull away from his before she caved. "You have another place to be."

He looked from her to the folder she extended to him and took it slowly. "What's this?"

"New beginnings." The very thing he'd shown her how to believe in.

His focus trailed down the first page and returned to her. "An application to Cornell?" He shut the folder. "This is sweet, but they're not going to accept me."

"Actually, they pretty much already have. The application is just a formality."

His face went blank. "What? How?"

"You'd be surprised what a glowing recommendation can do."

"Recommendation? From who?"

She opened the folder and slid the last page over the first. "A well-known, highly respected New York architect, who happens to be an alumnus."

He scoured the page and froze. "Your dad's Connall McAdams?" The pieces visibly fused together. He turned, forked his fingers through his hair, and shook his head. "I'm such an idiot. I can't believe I didn't realize . . ."

His arms slid to his sides. Back straight, he whisked around again. "Wait a sec. You contacted your dad for me?"

She shrugged. "It was important."

He lowered his chin and closed his eyes. "I don't know what to say."

"People usually say thank you when someone helps them out."

He laughed. "How did I know you were gonna make me eat those words one day?"

She sauntered to him, unable to shake her smile. She picked strands of Jax's and her hair off his shirt. "I might not be able to make a mean lasagna, but I have a few recipes of my own."

He flaunted a sideways grin. "You should have your own theme song." He swept her curls off her shoulder, slid his fingers behind her ear, and pressed in until her breath hitched at his touch. Slow and tender, his kiss said everything he didn't have to.

She'd never felt more safe and cherished. Never knew she could feel this way. In his arms, she returned his affection and breathed in the truth she was no longer afraid to embrace. "I love you, Ethan."

Regardless of where life led either of them, that assurance would always anchor her.

He rested his chin over her head and held her so long the air felt ten times cooler when he let go. He grabbed her hand. "C'mon. We're gonna be late."

Late? "For what?"

"Our date in the city."

CHAPTER TWENTY

Undone

S teamy, tantalizing aromas rose from the two plates the waitress set in front of them.

When Cass had first led him to this sketchy, hole-in-the-wall Colombian restaurant in the middle of Queens, Ethan thought for sure she was playing him. The cramped inside didn't do much to counter the drug cartel image it had going on, either, but the fragrance . . . Wow.

Cass stopped the young woman before she turned. "Can you bring some habanero sauce, please?"

Ethan grabbed his knife, but the rotisserie chicken fell apart at the slightest touch of his fork.

Cass pulled the utensils from his hand. "Use your fingers. Trust me."

Happy to oblige, he smeared a piece of chicken in the beans. She caught his hand before it reached his mouth. "Wait, you're missing the best part." She sprinkled a shredded green herb over his food. "Your taste buds are about to be in heaven. Cilantro makes the world go 'round."

Her almost-intoxicated expression made it hard to doubt her. And after the first bite, he understood why. Now he was the one fluttering his lashes.

She doused her plate in a green sauce the waitress had brought by and held the bottle out. "Want some?"

He read over the ingredients. "I put fires out for a living. Why would I purposely set one in my mouth?"

"Wuss." She slid a bite off her fork and faced the ceiling as if she just entered another stratosphere. "I can't believe I let you talk me into coming, but I gotta admit. I'm sort of glad." She took another bite and waved a hand over the dish. "'Cause this, right here—totally worth it."

Who knew food was the way to her heart?

"I still feel bad about leaving Ti at home, though." She smashed a slice of avocado into a tortilla with her fork. "What if something happens while we're gone?"

He licked the juice running down his thumb. "Sanders is a sharp guy. He'll look after things."

"Thanks for asking him to spend the day there, by the way. Ti hates to be alone." She wiped her nose with a napkin while sweat beaded over her forehead.

He laughed. "How can that be enjoyable?"

"It's not something wimps would understand." Grinning, she ran the napkin up her temple.

"Wow."

"*Mi* Cassidy." A short, round woman approached the table and intercepted her laughter. "*¡Qué bueno verte! Hace mucho que no te vemos por aquí. Te extrañamos.*"

Cass rose to kiss her cheek. "I've missed you, too, Mrs. Moreño."

The grandmotherly woman squeezed her hands, about to say something else, but a crash from the kitchen drew her around. "Aye," she said with hands in the air.

Cass returned to eating, smiling to herself until she looked up from her plate. "What?"

"You speak Spanish?"

"Hey, when you grow up in the city, you—"

"Learn how to speak Spanish." *Of course you did.* He added more cilantro to his rice. "Is there anything you don't learn on the streets?"

A sad gaze wandered out the window toward the run-down neighborhood. "Hope."

And yet she'd still managed to find enough to share with him. He couldn't imagine coming back here with anyone else.

After they finished their meal, she rose from her seat. "Ready?"

To spend the rest of the evening with her? Absolutely. To face whatever the night might stir up? Nowhere close. Seeing the Broadway show earlier hadn't been as bad as he'd expected. But now that night was falling, memories from the last time he was in city started creeping in.

Outside on the dark street, she looped her arm through his. "Mmm. Smell that?"

"Exhaust?"

She laughed. "Better than skunk."

"I think we have to call it even on that one."

She leaned into him. "Deal."

Deep voices sailed around the corner right before two oversized Hispanic guys did. Ethan instinctively tightened his hold around Cass and backed up.

The guys exchanged a glance and headed straight for him, their forward strides equaling each of Ethan's backward ones. The guy wearing a black ball cap smacked his friend in the chest while their digs in Spanish rebounded off each other.

Cass moved out from Ethan's hold and perched her hands on her hips. "Stop messin' with him before he decks you."

Eyeing Ethan's bicep, they both sneered like she'd just made the joke of the year. "You kiddin' me, Cassidy?"

Ethan released his tight muscles and his nerves. "You know these guys?" Why did he all of a sudden feel emasculated?

"Who, these two thugs?" She tugged on the one's hat and gave the other a shove.

"Ooh." The first one straightened his cap. "As cold as ever."

The taller one swept her in the air. "But still just as hot." He set her back to her feet. "Jesse wasn't happy when you bounced again. He know you're back?"

"I'm not back." Her face twitched, but she kept her shoulders level and her voice even. "Either of you seen my mom lately?"

"Naw. Her shop's been closed all week."

Her brows rumpled together. What was she not saying?

"Do me a favor and keep an eye out for her, 'kay?"

"You got it." The dude apparently had no problem letting his eyes roam wherever he wanted.

Ethan dug his fingers into his palms to keep from saying anything.

"Sorry, guys, but we gotta roll." She slipped her soft hand into Ethan's stiff one and ushered him forward, probably sensing his protectiveness more than he wanted her to. "Stay out of trouble," she called behind them.

Around the corner, she pressed her shoulder into his. "You have no reason to be jealous."

"Who said I'm jealous?"

She didn't miss a beat. "Your fingers."

Cracking a laugh, he relaxed his tense hands. "Old habits die hard."

"Tell me about it."

After a minute of walking in silence, he slid her a sideways glance. "Thought Jesse was an ex from high school."

"He is." She let go of his hand and looked from one side of the narrow street to the other. "But this is Queens. It's kind of hard to get away from people when your life's confined to a four-block radius."

He stopped. "You're saying he's been in the picture this whole time?"

"Other than when I was at NYU? Yeah, he's been around." A long exhale steered her focus to the asphalt. "Look, my mom lives here. I can't stay away just 'cause my ex-boyfriend runs these streets. The guy's a loser. He's never gonna leave."

His jaw ticked. "Does he bother you?"

She pulled her shirt cuffs under her fingers, still dodging his eye contact.

"Cass?"

"I can handle it." She strode forward again.

"That's not what I asked."

She turned and shuffled backward. "He's delusional, okay? Acts like he owns this neighborhood. Including me." She stopped and waited for Ethan to catch up to her. "We have our share of arguments, but it's usually when he's wasted. He sleeps it off and doesn't bother me again for weeks." She shrugged. "It's the way it is."

Ethan wrestled to strip his voice of the anger mounting toward this guy. "That doesn't make it all right."

"Yeah, well, the past doesn't really play fair."

"Doesn't let you outrun it, either," he mumbled under his breath.

That cold reality seized him the second they turned onto a block that looked just like the one he'd lost Izzy on. The nightmare he couldn't forget flooded in without warning, as if he was reliving it all over again.

The subway rumbling from one end, voices at the other. The couple fighting, the old man. Wind pummeled him with memory after memory. Izzy's motionless body on the ground. The sirens, the smoke, the thrust of the guy's shoulder who'd run into him.

He backed against the brick wall, chest tightening. He thought he was ready to face this.

Cass slid in front of him. "Are you okay?"

Though looking right at her, he only saw that night. "She died here."

"What?"

"My sister. She died on a street just like this." He looked away. "In a fire." The one he'd never been able to put out. He fought to blink away the images burned into his mind.

Cass moved her hand from over her mouth to his chest. "Ethan, I'm so sorry. I didn't know. I wouldn't have asked . . ."

He wanted to come. After she'd been willing to contact her dad for him, and the way she'd been so brave to want to fight for the camp, he couldn't keep hiding behind fear. But it was easier to believe he could be brave at home. Here, the darkness clawed into him with the truth.

He lowered her wrist and pushed off the wall. With his back facing her, he squeezed his neck. "You were right. About me always playing the hero. I spent so long filling in for my parents and trying to protect Isabella that I never stopped." He scoffed at the irony.

She cupped his shoulder from behind, but he couldn't bring himself to face her. "I couldn't save her, Cass."

"You were there?" Sympathy coated her voice. "What happened?"

Flashes of memories struck unrelentingly. "She was trapped in our car. There was gas all over the engine. It was windy. I don't know what sparked the fire. The investigation never gave us answers, but it doesn't matter. She died because of me." The pain in his confession streaked down his cheeks.

He shouldn't have left her in that car. One minute. If he could go back in time and change that one minute and take her with him to the gas station instead, she'd still be here.

"I've dedicated ten years to rescuing others, but it's never her. It's never enough." Regret collided with loss and broke his shoulders.

Cass turned him toward her, cheeks coated in tears of her own. Without any words, she held him with arms that absorbed the aches he'd kept buried for so long. Wave after wave, they poured out until he had nothing left to give.

Minutes lapsed. Noises clamored from all directions. But while standing in the middle of that dark alleyway, a whisper rose up inside him and overpowered every other voice roaring through his mind. *"You don't have to rescue her. I already did."* The words tore into the grip that'd been strangling him for ten years.

He looked toward heaven, cords around his heart unwinding. Izzy was safe, loved. Despite his failures, grace had been enough. Even now. Even for him.

Cass lifted back to search his face. Hazel eyes, full of compassion and assurance, steadied him. She was a part of that same grace. There were still so many things he didn't understand, but that much he was sure of.

He kissed her with salty lips and rested his forehead to hers. "I'm sorry for always trying to fix everything."

She grinned. "You'd make a lousy handyman if you didn't."

Laughing, he wrapped his arms around her and kissed the top of her head. "Thank you," he whispered over her hair.

He loosened his hold and tugged on his ear. Having a complete breakdown in the middle of the street wasn't exactly what he'd envisioned on the way down here.

She set her chin on his chest, looked up, and smiled. "Ready?"

He ran his hand down her hair and nodded. He might not ever be able to explain how much her being here with him right now meant. But if she still wanted to be with him after seeing him at his weakest, he'd never stop trying to show her.

She kept her shoulder tucked under his and steered them down the road toward an awning with *Freida's Flowers* on it.

Aside from someone clanking a lid onto a metal garbage can in the far corner, the block was empty. A few porch lights cast a dim glow over graffiti covering the brick walls on either side of them. He peeked through the iron window guards into a dark room of flowers. This was where she grew up?

Cass knelt to unlock an aluminum rolling gate. She heaved it up, pushed her key in the deadbolt, and paused.

"What's wrong?"

Without turning, she hung her head. "I just found out my mom's using again. I have no idea what we'll find in here, and I'm at a loss on what to say if she's home."

He steadied her hand with his and helped her turn the key. "You don't have to do it alone."

Exhaling, she gave him an affirming nod and opened the door.

A fragrant burst of warm air rolled out from the quaint shop. He eased the door shut behind them to keep from making too much noise. Something about the place evoked a sense of reverence. Maybe it was the way Cass's face came to life while taking in all the flowers. This was a part of her, even if it was a difficult part.

A noise stirred behind a back door. Shadows streamed in from under it. Ethan darted a glance toward Cass, but she moved toward the door without any hint of hesitation. He searched the room for something to use as a weapon. Bravery was one thing. Recklessness was another. "Cass, wait."

She whisked the door open.

A frazzled woman holding a lamp in the air about clobbered her. Sighing, she lowered her arm. "Cass, baby, you almost gave me a heart attack."

It had to be her mom. Loose curls framed an aged face with hair that looked like it might've been the same vibrant red as her daughter's at one point.

"Thieves don't usually have a key to the joints they rob, Ma." Cass pried her mom's fingers from the lamp and set it on the floor.

He could've been reliving the first day he'd met Cass, when she'd raised a lamp at him, thinking he was an intruder. He fixed his attention on a nearby plant to keep from laughing.

"Well, I don't know how you got in here. I just heard some rustling." Her mom snapped on the overhead light. "What are you doing here this late?"

"Sorry. It was sort of last minute." Cass circled around a counter and shuffled through some papers.

"Always business. You can at least introduce me to your friend, Cassidy." Her gaze trickled over him like a strobe light.

A hard exhale came from the counter. "Ma, Ethan DeLuca. Ethan, my mom, Freida McAdams."

"Pleasure."

He shook her hand. "Likewise."

Cass leafed through paper after paper. "How do you find anything around here?"

"It's organized chaos, baby." She moved beside her and patted the pages into a pile.

Side by side, there was no mistaking the resemblance. The same hazel eyes and all. Except her mom's were missing Cass's spark of life that had captured him from the beginning.

The crinkled skin around her mom's eyes and mouth bore the marks of age. But after all Cass'd told him, he wouldn't be surprised if life had left deeper marks of its own.

"It's late, Cassidy. Can we forget paperwork for now? Come upstairs and have some coffee."

Coffee. She'd just spoken the magic word. Ethan waited for Cass's response.

Her face fell instead of lighting up, but she recovered in a heartbeat. "Why don't you make some and bring it down?"

"Have it your way." Her mom rounded the doorway. "Sugar and cream for you, hon?"

Ethan nodded. "However you make it."

After a quick nod, she scurried up the stairs.

Cass smirked through a look of fatigue. "You might be sorry you said that."

"That bad, huh?"

"Don't say I didn't warn you."

He moseyed over and kneaded her shoulders from behind.

Moaning, she let her head hang as he worked out the knots. "Thanks. I needed that."

"You wanna talk about it?"

She leaned her elbows on the counter and released a long breath. "The economy's gotten so bad, people don't buy from specialty shops like this anymore. They buy bulk or from street vendors selling roses for a buck. I hoped if we gave it time things would turn around, but the bank's about to foreclose on the property. My mom lives in the apartment upstairs. If she loses the shop, she'll lose her home, her livelihood."

She dropped her arms to the ledge, pushed off it, and strolled toward the displays. "I thought if I could sell the camp, I'd have enough to pay off her mortgage so she wouldn't have to worry about it anymore."

The fragments came together and almost butted him straight in the head. The weight she'd been carrying, the stress of getting the camp up to code, the pressure to hurry. Why hadn't he seen it before now? And why didn't she just tell him? He could've been more supportive. Could've worked harder, done things differently.

Defensiveness stormed the heels of regret. Wait. How could her mom let her bear the weight of that kind of responsibility? Did she have any clue what Cass had gone through on her behalf?

Cass traced her fingers under a plant's petals. "But now, I honestly don't know what to do. I don't know how to help her anymore. Or if I even can."

As hard as it was not to hold her in his arms until the turmoil faded from her voice, it wasn't his place to fix it. He'd finally learned that. Behind her, he kissed the top of her shoulder. "Maybe you were never meant to be her rescuer."

She turned and found his eyes, and he prayed they held the assurance of everything he couldn't find the words to say.

"I hope decaf is okay." Her mom came through the door, holding a paper under her chin, and slid a tray of coffee mugs onto the counter. "Here." She handed the page to Cass. "I assume this is why you came. To take care of this."

She flaunted a proud smile at Ethan like she was brandishing an honor roll student bumper sticker. "My girl's a whiz with this business stuff. Always bails me out. Right, baby?"

Cass clenched the page, head down. "No." The whisper held such emotion, Ethan had to grip the display case beside him to keep from reacting.

Genuine confusion drifted down her mom's wrinkled face. "What do you mean, no?"

Cass's lashes lifted. "I mean, we can't keep doing this. I can't fix everything for you. You have to decide if you want to keep the shop."

"You don't think I want my shop?" Hurt touched her mom's eyes, but Cass didn't back down.

"You're sure not acting like it."

She clanked her mug on the counter. "What do you want me to do, Cassidy? You're not here. You don't know what it's like."

"Yes. I do." Hands balled up, she approached her mom. "You don't think I know the pain of having Dad leave us? That I wasn't here, listening to you sob in your room every night?" She snatched a handful of papers off the counter. "That I didn't stay in the shop past midnight every day, crunching numbers to make ends meet? I was here, Ma. I've *always* been here." Her arm drooped to her side, the fight dissolving from her voice.

"And now you want me to lose everything?"

Frustration crinkled Cass's forehead. "No. I want you to take a stand and finally see all you have that's worth fighting for." Her face softened as she let go of the papers and reached for her hands. "I want you to hold your head high and believe you can do this."

A glassy sheen covered her mom's eyes. "I can't do it on my own."

She cupped her shoulders. "Yes, you can."

The strain between them collapsed into a hug Ethan knew they needed to share alone.

He slipped outside. The street remained quiet, unaware of the reconciliation taking place on the other side of the door.

With his foot propped behind him, he leaned against the bricks and faced the sky. Despite the light pollution hiding the stars, they were still there. Always would be. If tonight hadn't taught him that, nothing would.

The door crept open minutes later. Cass strolled out with fresh tearstains lining her cheeks. The porch light caught her vulnerable smile, and Ethan caved.

Enough with resisting pulling her close. He rested his chin over her head as she curled her arms around his back.

Had they really only known each other a little over a week? He'd be telling any of his friends they were crazy if they thought they could fall in love that quickly. But math and logic didn't matter when it came to her. He pressed his lips to her hair. This was real.

She nestled closer. "Thanks for being here."

As long as he was with her, he wouldn't be anywhere else. "I—"

His pager went off. Shaking his head at the timing, he unclipped it from his belt.

Every muscle in his body constricted with the heat of panic.

"What is it?" She lifted off him. "Ethan, what's wrong?"

He forced his jaw to move. "That's Nonna's address."

CHAPTER TWENTY-ONE

Burned

The same red lights from the other night circled across the treetops. Cass gripped the dashboard as Ethan whipped her Passat up to Nonna's house. She pinned her cell to her ear with her shoulder and reached for the seatbelt buckle.

"Is everything all right?" Ti asked from the other end of the line.

"I don't know. We just pulled up." Cass wrenched the seatbelt free while staring at the ambulance in the driveway. At least there were no flames. *Please let Nonna be okay.*

"Should Sanders and I come? Maybe we can help."

Ethan flipped the unlocked button and zipped out of the car.

In the dark, Cass fumbled around for the door handle. "I don't know, Ti. Let me call you back."

Ethan had reached the porch before she ever got her door open. Two men in blue station uniforms coming out of the house passed a firefighter in full gear who'd stopped to talk to Ethan.

Cass weaved through the vehicles. The diesel engine's steady hum overpowered the voices all around her. At Ethan's side, she slid one hand into his and wrapped the other around his arm.

He craned his neck back, closed his eyes, and exhaled. "Thank God."

"What? What happened?" Cass looked from him to the firefighter, standing in front of the door.

The man took off his helmet and wiped his brow. "She fell. Gave her hip a pretty good bruise, but it looks like she'll be fine."

Fell? They sent the fire department out for that?

A burnt stench billowed from inside the house as a young medic came through the door. So, there'd been a fire, too?

Face taut, the medic flashed Ethan a cautious glance. "I wouldn't go in there unless you want your head bitten off."

Cass pinched her lips. Nonna was probably being as mischievous as she'd been the other night.

Ethan smiled for the first time in two and half hours. "I'm used to it." Still holding Cass's hand, he led her inside.

A charred smell rushed over them with a cool breeze blowing through the kitchen. At least someone'd thought to open the back door to air out the place. But if the haze still lingering around the ceiling were any indication, it'd probably take days to neutralize the odor.

Lady scurried from under a kitchen chair and practically climbed up Ethan's leg. Poor girl had to be scared with all these people around. Cass knelt to pet her, but she seemed to want only Ethan.

He scooped her up, and she trembled against his chest as they followed the voices coming from a back bedroom. Even with Ethan rubbing her head to calm her, she growled at another medic passing them in the hall.

Cass glanced at a fire detector dangling from the ceiling. "Maybe we should shut her in that other bedroom for now."

He shook his head, lips tipped to the side. "I'm not going near Nonna without some kind of backup."

Cass nudged him forward. Was he kidding? All he'd have to do was flash those unfairly disarming blue eyes, and Nonna'd soften in a second. Shoot, anyone would. She might be tough, but she adored her grandson. No mistake about it.

Around the doorway, a short, white haired woman standing beside the dresser fidgeted with her purse. "Ethan." She rushed over and rested an aged hand on his arm. "I didn't know if anyone else would come. I need to get home to check on my husband, but I didn't want to leave Elena alone."

"Go on and get. I don't need a babysitter," Nonna grumbled from her bed toward the woman who must've been a friend. She nodded at a medic, unwrapping a blood pressure cuff from her bicep. "That goes for you, too, Tiffany. I don't want to have to call your mother."

A wry smile lifted the young woman's cheeks. "Now, now, Mrs. DeLuca. That's no way to be treating folks trying to take care of you." She rolled up the cuff and secured it in her bag while Nonna mumbled something in Italian.

Cass inched behind Ethan's shoulder to shield her grin.

"What are you smiling at?"

Gulping, Cass crept out, but Nonna had her gaze locked on Ethan.

She propped herself up a little higher against the headboard. "Come here, young man. And don't try using my Lady as a barrier, either."

Busted.

"Keep an eye on her every few hours," the medic whispered on her way past him. "Good luck," she mouthed before circling through the doorway.

He lowered Lady onto the mattress. As soon as her paws hit the blankets, she scampered up to his grandma's side and wedged her face under Nonna's arm.

Ethan sat on the edge of the bed. "You want to tell me what happened?"

Her tight-lipped expression eliminated the need for an answer.

"Nonna."

"Nothing. I got caught up in a movie and forgot about the lasagna in the oven. That's all." Dodging his gaze, she rubbed Lady's ears.

"What about the fall?"

A huff sent her eyes circling toward the ceiling. "When the smoke started, I lost my balance reaching for the fan's chain. It's no reason for everyone to get all worked up." She blasted a sharp glance at the white haired woman still beside Cass. "If Maureen hadn't called the entire rescue squad, my house wouldn't be Grand Central right now."

"And you'd still be on the floor." Her friend stepped forward. "You better be thankful I came by when I did."

Nonna waved her off until she met Ethan's stern look. She released a pent-up breath and faced Maureen. "Thanks for checking on me." She bunched the sheets under her fingers. "Now, go on home to Winston."

Maureen shuffled over to the bed and kissed her cheek. "You old grump. I'll call you tomorrow."

Except for some stirring out front, a stillness settled over the place after Maureen left. Nonna stroked Lady's back and stared at the bedspread, brow furrowed. Her tension-filled movement constricted Cass's muscles. What now? Had something else happened?

She lifted pensive eyes toward Ethan. "You look so much like your Nonno. Sometimes, I almost think he's here again." She blinked away honest emotion, adjusted the pillow behind her, and winced as she moved her hip.

The same fatigue that'd lined Ethan's face on the drive here reemerged and almost pulled Cass to him. But as much as she wanted to comfort him the way he always did for her, she sensed whatever Nonna wanted to say was between them. She glanced at the door. What were the chances she could slip out without them noticing?

Nonna squeezed Ethan's hand. "We both know I won't be around forever. Stubborn or not."

"Nonna—"

"No use fussing over part of life, dear." She nuzzled Lady closer to her side. "When Nonno died, so did my world. But I had this home to take care of, grandbabies to look after. And even friendship to enjoy." Her gaze wandered across the comforter toward Cass, a distant smile finding her lips. "Which eventually blossomed into more."

The glisten in her eyes sent Cass back to her comment the night they'd met. *"Sweet child, you have your grandpa's smile."* The realization climbed up her throat. "You and Grandpa?"

Nonna's expression held enough memories to answer for her.

Cass's grandma had died decades ago. Grandpa never re-married, but she always assumed he'd found contentment in his work at the camp. How did she not know he fell in love again?

Cass shook her head. "He never said anything."

"No. I suppose he didn't." With her attention back on Lady, Nonna ran her fingers down one of the dog's long, fluffy ears. "Not that he was happy about that."

Ethan hadn't moved. Back flexed, he stared at her. "I don't understand."

"We kept it a secret."

A mix of curiosity and confusion drew Cass to the end of the bed. "Why?"

"Mom. She found out, didn't she?" Ethan pushed off the mattress, face taut with perception. *"That's* why she cut me off from going to the camp as a kid? Because she didn't want you to move on?"

"There's more to it, Ethan. You didn't know your mama before Nonno died." Her focus roamed the patched comforter again as if drifting from one memory to another. "So loyal, she was a daddy's girl like you've never seen. Loved that man something fierce." Her smile saddened. "Losing him shattered her heart."

From what Ethan had told Cass about his mom, it was hard to picture her having a heart at all. Conviction slammed into her as quickly as the thought came. Who was she to talk? She'd spent most of her life hardening her own heart.

Until she met Ethan.

The tendon on his neck twitched. What was he thinking right now? She glided toward him, threaded her fingers through his, and kissed the back of his shoulder.

"In your mama's eyes, my relationship with Colin dishonored Nonno's memory."

Ethan's muscles tightened against Cass's arm. "She had no right to tell you who you could and couldn't be with."

Nonna's shoulders crept a little higher up the headboard. "Now, listen, I'm not telling you all this so you can have another reason to be angry at her."

"As if I need any."

"Ethan James." Her scold merged into a look of urgency. She took his free hand in hers. "I'm telling you because it's time to stop letting pride ruin our family." She reached for Cass's free hand, too, and nodded. "Both our families."

Ethan studied her for a quiet moment. The slightest grin climbed his cheek. "This connection with her grandpa . . . You wanted Cass and me together, didn't you?"

She let go and slid a nonchalant stroke down Lady's back. "Destiny needs a little hand every now and then."

"Or a shove." He laughed.

Footsteps stirred down the hall. Lady's head perked up, teeth baring.

"Cass?" Ti rounded the corner with Sanders right behind her. In a cute sundress, jean jacket, and a cowboy hat and boots, she stopped inside the doorway and looked at all three of them. "We wanted to make sure everything was okay."

Nonna's blank stare turned into an eye roll. "First they send the fire squad, now they send in the cavalry."

Cass barely refrained from laughing. "Everything's fine, Ti. Give us a minute."

With a quick tip of her head, she and Sanders backed out of the room. Lady settled her chin over her paws but didn't release her glare from the doorway. Couldn't blame her. It'd probably been a revolving door all evening.

Cass squeezed Nonna's hand. "I'm glad you're all right."

"God has his plans." She drew them both down into a hug. "Even when we don't understand them."

Ethan kissed her cheek. "Must be part of his sense of humor."

"I knew you'd catch on eventually." Smiling, she patted his hand. "Now, cut that light on your way out, will ya?"

He nodded.

"And if that fire truck is still out there, tell them they better get those huge tires off my grass," she called as they reached the door.

Shaking his head, he hit the light switch on the way through the doorway. They shuffled into the living room toward Ti and Sanders. "Sorry, guys," he said.

Beside the fireplace mantle, Ti flinched and almost dropped a picture frame. She scrambled to put it back in place. "No worries. Everything good?"

He rubbed his temples. "It'll take a lot more than a fall to knock the stubbornness out of her."

Ti flaunted a knowing grin. "Italians."

They all laughed, but the strain left on Ethan's face bore the imprint of a long day. Actually, more like a long *week*. How could so much happen in such a short time?

He clasped Sanders's hand and leaned in for a hug. "Thanks for coming today, bro. Would you be up for crashing in my room tonight? I'm gonna stay here." His attention flitted to Cass. "If you don't mind."

Was he serious? "Of course not." She moved toward him and brushed back the flattened hair that'd fallen over his forehead. "As long as you promise you'll actually get some sleep." He'd been so strong. For her. For the camp. Nonna. He needed to rest and recharge.

Her hand trailed down to his neck, the other to his chest. Holding his gaze made not kissing him almost unbearable.

"Alrighty, then." Ti snagged Sanders's arm and pulled him toward the front door. "We'll be outside when you two are done here."

The screen shut, its echo colliding with Ethan's laugh. His eyes held hers as though reading every yearning she didn't say. He curled his arms around her. "Hold that thought for another time." His grin gave way to an abbreviated version of the real kiss she wanted.

He pulled back. Exhaustion must've made him delirious if he thought she was anywhere near ready to let go. He laughed at her expression, kissed her once more, and wove his fingers through hers. "Believe me. I know."

He kept her close on the way out the door. "You mind riding home with Sanders? I'll be back in the mor . . ."

A gray sedan in the driveway stole his focus. His fingers tightened over Cass's as a woman strode around the front bumper in three-inch heels. Seemed a little late for a business call. She didn't look like a doctor. A lawyer, maybe? She certainly carried herself with stature.

The woman stopped in front of the porch with a stare fixed on Ethan. "Do I need a password to get by?"

This time, Cass squeezed Ethan's hand. She'd been around enough blunt people in the city to roll with it, but something about this lady's arrogance got to her. If she loosened that clip holding her sleek hair back, maybe her chin would drop a notch or two.

"What are you doing here, Mom?"

Mom? Cass shrank behind his shoulder and glanced at Ti, debating whether to take cover with her and Sanders.

Ethan's curt tone didn't seem to throw her. "Same as you. I'm checking on Nonna."

"More like double-checking she didn't burn the house down. We wouldn't want any bad press for the city council."

She started up the steps. "Not now, Ethan. If you want to cast accusations, call Mary and take a number." Her determined strides jerked to a stop. Under the porch light, her eyes constricted at Cass as if just noticing her. Everything Nonna'd confided in them a few moments ago burned in his mom's expression.

Ethan guarded Cass behind him. "This needs to end."

His mom huffed. "Took you long enough to figure that out."

"That's not what I meant. I . . . Wait a minute."

Cass inched beside him and curled her hand around his arm.

His chin sagged to his chest. Eyes closed, he kneaded the back of his neck. "I can't believe I didn't see this before now."

His mom tried to shove past him. "I don't have time for—"

"Being exposed?" He pinned a glare on her.

"What?"

Tall and confident, he blocked the door. "Does your hate run so deep that you'd resort to attacking the McAdams camp?"

She pulled her suit jacket down by the hem. "Attacking? Do you realize what you're saying? That's ridiculous."

"Is it?" He backed her to the stairs. "Deputy Harris. The inspector. You said the word, and they upped the pressure."

Cass's stomach dropped right along with his mom's heels, clinking onto each step. The property taxes. She would've had influence on those, too. It all made so much sense. Was this whole thing some kind of revenge plan to shut down the camp because of Grandpa and Nonna?

He kept advancing. "It must really burn you to know I'm in love with Colin's granddaughter. Another DeLuca tied to a McAdams."

Surprise flashed across her wide eyes, followed by a deep-seated fury.

Cass glanced again at Ti and Sanders off in the corner of the porch. She would've moved toward them if shock didn't have a hold over her feet.

Ethan's mom bumped into the sedan's door panel, but he didn't back down. "You can't stand the thought of Colin's legacy continuing, can you?"

Face reddened, she started to shake. "My father was ten times the man he'll ever be." She grabbed his shirt and gritted her teeth. "His legacy's over, Ethan. You hear me? That camp is over."

No one moved. A car drove past and swept its headlights across the yard. His mom released her hold at the same time the porch released Cass's feet.

Cass stumbled to the end of the stairs, not wanting to believe it. "*You* started the fire?"

A scathing glance soared over her. "And open an investigation?" She brushed off the accusation along with the wrinkles in her jacket. "Please."

Ethan adjusted his shirt. "So, which pawn did you use, then? Whose dirty laundry did you have to flaunt?"

Her jaw flexed. "I had nothing to do with that."

"But you knew about it."

Without answering, she stared into the shadows as though looking backward in time. She shook her head. "That orphan kid hasn't stopped begging for a way to prove himself ever since my first campaign." She scoffed. "The screw-up couldn't even handle a simple task. All he had to do was lure the McAdams girl away from you. That's it."

Orphan? Her words crashed into fragmented memories from the day at the florist's when she'd met Nick. *"My uncle took me in after my parents died in a car wreck ... This town isn't a complete dead end. As long as you know the right people."*

The right people. Like a prominent city council woman? Cass gripped the banister. Nick hadn't accidentally bumped into her that day. Every interaction. Every word. All set up. How could she have been so stupid? When he'd said he called from Manhattan, he was here, playing her the whole time. Her stomach knotted with waves of nausea.

Ethan turned from her to his mom. "Nick." A tendon on his neck twitched. "He's the one who got hold of my phone and keys, isn't he?" He balled his fists. "That little—"

"Really, Ethan." His mom rolled her eyes. "This whole thing is over. Let it go."

"The heck I am."

Her chin shot up. Eyes tightening, she raised a finger. "Now, you listen to me. That vengeful kid's need for attention left a mess I have to clean up. Don't make the same mistake."

"You're talking to *me* about mistakes and vengeance?" He turned her own smirk on her. "How long have you been waiting for Colin to die so you could finally destroy what he built?"

Her eyes darkened again, and he squared his shoulders. "I hate to be more of a disappointment to you, Mom, but I'm not letting you close the camp."

"You're not going to let me? *Let* me?" She charged forward, face a dangerous flood of emotions. "Look at you, standing guard in front of Nonna's house. Where were you when she had her heart attack? Where were you the last five years?"

She edged him backward. "Always ready to take control. So quick to be the protector. Where were you when Isabella was trapped in that car?" She swung at him. "Where were you, Ethan?"

He took each shove, not fighting back.

"I will not stand by another year, watching kids fill this town every summer when my baby girl never will. You hear me?" Composure completely lost, she shrieked through a torrent of tears.

He caught her by the wrists. Same as he'd done for Cass, he wouldn't let her push him away. He held her arms down until she gave in and wrapped them around him.

And in his embrace, a woman as hard as stone crumbled. "I should've been there. I shouldn't have let her go."

All this time, she'd been consumed by loss, driven by it. The ache of it all came through every sob. First her father, then her little girl. It'd been easier to bury it under bitterness. Easier to blame Colin and Ethan. Just like it'd been easier for Cass to pin her pain on Jesse and Dad. The hardest person to face was always yourself.

"It's no one's fault." Ethan held her tight.

Did he finally believe that? That his sister's death wasn't his fault, either? Cass dabbed the skin under her bottom lashes.

"I'm sorry." His mom clung to him, tears still flowing.

Whether she deserved forgiveness wasn't really the question. Where they went from here would be the hard part.

Truth was, they couldn't restore years of damage over night. Some of it may never fully heal. And despite her grief, his mom's actions held significant consequences. But Cass still sensed they needed time alone right now.

She motioned Ti and Sanders over. On her way across the lawn, she met Ethan's gaze. Nodding, he returned her smile, and she slipped into Sanders's car.

Was this really the same day they'd gone to the city? That seemed like a world ago already. The night couldn't possibly have felt any later. But with the darkness in the car blanketed around her, she slumped against the door panel and gave in to her exhaustion.

The tires rumbled over the gravel driveway and jolted her eyes back open. Around the curve in front of the main building, a green Mazda came into view under the flood light. That was the same kind of car . . . Her stomach knotted all over again.

Ti pulled her seatbelt off. "Oh my God."

Cass padded for the door handle.

"Cass, no." Ti twisted in her seat, but Cass climbed out before she could stop her.

Beside Sandy next to the porch, someone rose to his feet and turned. His smile burned through the shadows and latched on to her lungs. No air. No words. Except one.

"Jesse."

CHAPTER TWENTY-TWO

Pummeled

Ethan hung up with Ti, dropped his cell in his lap, and thrust Cass's Passat into drive. He gripped the steering wheel, clenching back the thought of her ex-boyfriend being anywhere near her. If the creep so much as touched her before he got there . . .

He skidded onto the main road, fishtailed for a second, and kept going. Taillights glowed ahead. He rolled down all four windows as he came up behind a service truck. "Come on. Get out of the way."

A car coming from the opposite direction flew by in the lane beside them. After a quick glance out the window, Ethan pushed the gas and whipped around the truck.

The night's cold air flooded the inside of the car. With his blood pumping this fast, he had enough trouble staying in his seat. Forget observing the speed limit.

He gunned up the camp's driveway and screeched to a stop without bothering to turn into a parking spot. He hustled out toward Ti and Sanders. She held an arm up to stop him, same as she'd done in the bar when Cass was dancing with that lumberjack. "Give her a minute."

Was she serious? Forcing his breath to slow, he released his fists. Cass could take care of herself. She'd proven that a dozen times already. Still, if the punk made a single move, Ethan wasn't going to stand down.

Cass straightened her already-rigid spine. "You need to leave, Jesse."

The light behind the loser kept his face in the shadows, but Ethan didn't need a clear shot to see the arrogance rolling off him. His stance alone sneered at him.

"Oh, c'mon. At least show a little appreciation for my coming all the way up here. We can argue later," he slurred.

You gotta be kidding. Was he drunk?

Jesse lurched forward and reached for her hair. "I always liked it when you were feisty."

This time, Sanders had to hold Ethan back.

Cass slapped Jesse's hand away from her and backed up. "How'd you know where to find me?"

"Gomez and Sanchez said you came home."

Ethan clenched his jaw. So much for the sumo wrestler punks keeping their mouths shut.

Jesse leaned a hand on Sandy's head to steady his balance. "You shouldn't have left. Your mom might still be good for information, but she's not looking too hot these days."

Cass's eyes constricted. "You stay away from my mom."

"Relax, doll. You know I don't go for damaged merchandise." He shuffled toward her again. "Only the untainted kind."

She shoved him back. "Get off my property."

Sandy barked as Jesse tottered on unsteady feet. "You kidding? My pleasure. Ten minutes in Timbuktu is long enough." He splayed his arm out. "C'mon, Cass, look at this place. What are you doing, hiding out here? It's time to go home. You belong in Astoria."

She paused so long, Ethan's pulse hammered again. Did she believe that?

She lifted her chin and crossed her arms, assurance teeming in every movement. "Not anymore."

Jesse's mouth twitched. He grabbed her wrist, and something about the image twisted in the pit of Ethan's stomach with a strange sense of recognition. "You're coming with me."

Ethan'd stayed back long enough. He advanced and broke Jesse's hold on her. "Back off, bro."

"Easy, DeLuca," Sanders yelled.

"DeLuca?" Jesse stared at him, wide eyes latching on to his.

A pang of unease clipped into Ethan's gut. Did he know him?

Jesse's look of shock slowly morphed into a devilish smirk and unleashed a booze-scented breath into Ethan's face. "Wait, *this* is the guy you're with now?" He folded in half, laughing without any sound. "Oh, this is too good."

Patience lost, Ethan grabbed his shirt. "You've got thirty seconds to leave before . . ."

At this angle, the light finally lit his face and exposed a tiny scar above Jesse's mouth. A scar left from a busted lip, like one he'd seen before. The sinking feeling in his stomach deepened.

No. The scene from the night Izzy died collided with the one right in front of him. The guy who'd stumbled into him, running away from the fire . . . Those dark eyes . . . The cut on his lip.

His shirt slipped from Ethan's hands. "*You.*" He backed up. It couldn't be.

Jesse's smirk drifted toward Cass and back to Ethan. "How does it feel, knowing you're in love with the girl responsible for your sister's death?"

Cass's arms came undone. "What?"

"You don't remember hearing about this in the news? I followed that junk for weeks, making sure they didn't trace anything to us." Jesse moved closer to her the farther Ethan backed away.

She trembled. "What are you talking about?"

"Jeez, Cass. You knocked the cigarette from my mouth when you hit me. How do you think that fire started?"

Ethan's heartbeat thundered in his ears. All other sound died. The heat from the flames that night compressed around him from every angle. Sweat soaked into his collar. It couldn't be true. Not Cassidy. Anyone but her.

She blinked, tears already streaming. He couldn't face her. He gripped Jesse by the shirt, dragged him to his Mazda, and hurled him against the car. He turned toward Sanders. "Call the cops."

Still laughing, Jesse dropped his keys and stumbled to the ground right after.

Ethan glared at him. "Don't even think about it." He stalked around the bumper and texted Harris Jesse's license plate number. Drunk driving should be enough to lock him up for the night.

The car door slammed. Ethan shot his head up in time to see the car swerving toward him. He jumped back before it clipped his legs. The Mazda squealed in a half circle and careened down the driveway.

Jesse's taillights illuminated the cloud of dust left behind until the engine's throttle finally faded.

An electric stillness settled around them. Ethan's chest rose and fell, but he couldn't get air to his lungs. Sandy looked between him and Cass and yelped.

She reached for him. "Ethan . . . ?"

He slinked away from her touch. "I can't." He handed Ti Cass's keys, climbed into the Jeep, and cranked the engine.

"DeLuca," Sanders called after him while Sandy chased his truck, barking.

Down the driveway, Ethan fought to see his way through the darkness and the hazy visions of the couple fighting on the street that night in the Bronx.

Jesse's haunting laugh pummeled him again and again, but nothing compared to the image of the redheaded girl who'd started the one fire that never went out.

Cass ran after him to the top of the bend. Hand on her head, she begged his brake lights to cut through the shadows like last time. She hadn't deserved it then, either, but he'd come back. Despite everything, he hadn't left. *Please.*

His Jeep reached the end of the driveway and disappeared around the corner without ever slowing. Sandy bounded up the slope toward her. Whimpering, he burrowed his nose under her hand and leaned his warm body against her thigh.

She couldn't speak. Couldn't move. Jesse had to be wrong. She'd run all the way to the subway after punching him that night. No turning back. She'd just wanted to get out of there, to get away from it all. How could one cigarette start a fire? No one else was even around. There had to be a mistake.

Ti came up beside her. "Cass, I'm so sorry."

Sorry wasn't enough. She swiped the keys from Ti. "I have to talk to him." At the door to her Passat, she rifled through the keys for the right one but couldn't steady the tremor in her hands. The key shook against the lock and fell to the gravel.

Ti scooped them up. "You can't drive right now. Not like this."

"Then drive me. I can't just let him leave." Cass raked her fingers through her hair.

Ti rested a hand on her arm and turned Cass around. "He's gonna need some time."

Time to hate her more? "No." Cass pushed back. "I have to explain. I have to make it right." Emotions spiraled. Panic, confusion, fear. They clawed through her muscles and raced for her eyes. She fought back the tears, fought to pull away, but Ti wouldn't let her.

She grabbed Cass's hands. "It's gonna be okay."

The moment Ti closed her arms around her, Cass broke. Remorse took over and buckled her knees. Tears pouring, she balled Ti's jacket in her fingers to keep from falling. "I didn't know . . ."

Ti rubbed her back. "It's not your fault."

Didn't she hear what Jesse'd told them? The hurt on Ethan's face . . . She pressed her lashes together to shut it out.

Beside them, Sanders's keys clinked together. "I'll go check on him."

Ti kept her arms around Cass and nodded toward him. "You're coming back, though, right? If Jesse tries anything . . ."

Sanders stood tall and erect like a soldier. "He's not gonna get anywhere near here again. Not on my watch or Ethan's." He looked down the driveway. "Knowing Ethan, he's probably tailing him right now, but I'll make sure." He set a hand on Ti's shoulder. "I'll be back in a little bit."

His engine started in the background, the rumble of tires soon following. While his car drifted out of view, Ti cupped Cass's shoulder and led her inside and down the hall.

It wouldn't matter if Sanders were able to talk to Ethan. How could he face her now without seeing anything but pain? He was just beginning to heal. All night, he'd been so brave, so forgiving. But this was too much. It ran too deep. She couldn't expect him ever to look at her the same.

In her room, she crumbled onto the mattress and cradled her legs to her stomach. As many times as she'd slept alone, her bed had never felt emptier.

Jax jumped on the bed, pranced right up to her face, and rubbed his head under her chin. She nuzzled him back, smiling through another round of tears. "How do you always know when I need you?"

He pawed over her side and curled up against the crook of her legs as he'd done with Ethan last night. She buried a pillow in her arms and held on to the memory, knowing she might have to let go of hope for anything more.

CHAPTER TWENTY-THREE

Blank Pages

The afternoon heat rolled down Ethan's chest the same way it'd done the last eight days that he'd been working in Nonna's backyard.

He sat on his heels and dragged his collar over his face. At least sweat meant progress. If he pushed hard enough, he'd get these stairs mended before the sun went down today.

He did a double take at his shirt. Shoulders sinking, he brushed off a splinter of wood. For a second, he'd thought it was a strand of Cass's hair.

A high-pitched buzz swarmed around his ear. He swatted the bug away. Stupid mosquitoes. Hadn't they sucked enough life out of him already?

Nonna came through the back door, carrying two glasses of ice water. Though her shuffle seemed a little slower than it had before her fall, she'd worked out most of the stiffness over the last week. He couldn't fault her stubborn genes for some things. Without them, she might not have gotten out of bed at all.

She handed him a glass and set hers on the deck railing. Her stare practically drilled a hole into the top of his head. He didn't even have to look up. He'd sat under her weighted silence enough times to know the exact look she was brandishing above him.

He moved the glass aside and shoved his hammer's claw under a nail. "I already know."

"Know what?"

"Whatever it is you're not saying." He pried the nail free and tossed it into a jar on the grass.

She unfolded her arms from the rail. "Oh, I doubt that, sweetie, or you wouldn't still be here."

Not again. Releasing a hard breath, he grabbed the corners of the wooden board and yanked it up. He didn't want to talk. He wanted to work. The wood chafed against his palms and crumbled where it'd rotted.

He chucked it onto the pile with the others to clean up later. If life were as easy to deal with, then maybe they'd have something to talk about.

Ice-cold water splashed over his head, followed by ice cubes hitting the steps. He lurched to his feet, jumped backward, and shook out his wet hair. An impish grin beamed at him through the streaks running down his eyes.

"That ought to cool you off a bit." She set her empty glass down. "Now, maybe you can screw your head on straight."

He wrung out the bottom of his soaked T-shirt and waited for his gut response to drain with the water.

She eased down the stairs to the last one before the drop-off. "You've been slaving around here all week. Mowing, trimming, fixing everything in sight. Except what really matters."

He snagged a new two-by-four propped against the deck and dropped to his knees in front of the steps again. "I have to finish."

"You're darn right you do. You're not a quitter, Ethan James. Don't you run away just 'cause things get hard."

Blood pressure rising, he clamped his hand around the hammer. "You don't understand."

"Hogwash." She leaned far enough to grab his collar and lugged him to his feet. "Just 'cause we weren't there when Isabella died doesn't mean you're the only one who feels her loss." She cupped his cheeks. "If you hold on to your grief, you'll never leave that car."

He pulled back.

Her arms drifted to her sides. "Did you hear anything I told you the night I fell?"

He drew a nail from the pouch on his tool belt, grabbed his hammer, and knelt to the wood. He didn't want to replay that night over again. Not after reliving it all week.

Without saying anything, she hung her head and plodded up the stairs. At the back door, she turned one last time. "You're quick to judge your mama for letting pride blind her. Yet here you are, being ruled by your own. So much so, you're behind bars, too, and don't even know it."

He swung the hammer and drove the nail's head all the way to the wood. Water dripped off his hair onto the grains, but he didn't look up until the door shut behind her.

Something pricked his skin. He slapped the back of his neck and flicked away the dead mosquito. He didn't have anything left to give. Didn't they get that? Didn't *she* get it? What did she want him to do? Pretend he and Cass both weren't responsible for Izzy's death?

The door creaked open again. "I'm not in the mood."

"Never thought I'd hear those words come out of a guy's mouth."

Ethan glanced up toward Ti, standing on the deck with some type of book in her hands. Great. Just what he needed. A tag team. He positioned a nail over the next mark. "You need something?"

"Not as badly as you do."

Yeah, like a little peace and quiet. If she only knew. He hammered the nail into place and reached for the next one.

"You know, if you came home, you'd actually get to use a razor. Or are you purposely going for the Chewbacca look?" She sauntered down the stairs in the most normal looking outfit he'd ever seen her in, sat in his way, and cradled the book in her lap.

He sighed. Apparently, peace and quiet were out of the question.

She waved a hand over his workstation. "So, how's this working out for you?"

He trudged to the garbage pile and loaded the torn-up beams into his arms. "Just fine when I don't have any distractions."

She flitted over. "Well, that's kind of ironic, coming from the guy who's been hiding behind distractions all week."

He dumped the heap into the trashcan and glowered at her. Like she, of all people, could talk. He winced at the inward jab. What was his problem? He faced the sky and exhaled. "I'm sorry, Ti. I'm really not the best company right now."

"What do you think I'm doing here, Sherlock?" She tapped his arm with her book. "Come here. I want to show you something."

She pulled him by the shirt back to the stairs and sat him down. Beside him, she leaned a shoulder into his. "When we were here the night Nonna fell, I noticed a picture on the mantle of you as a kid." She placed the book in his lap. "The same boy who's in a picture Cass's grandpa has in his office."

A photo of a group of campers looked up at him from what must've been a scrapbook she'd put together.

She pointed to his five-year-old reflection. "You didn't just meet Cass this month." Her finger moved to a redheaded girl with curly pigtails directly beside him. "You've always been connected, Ethan. Even when you didn't know it."

While everyone else's attention was on the camera, his was on Cass, as if he'd been drawn to her even then. How did he not remember this? They'd been connected this whole time. Through the camp, their grandparents, even the fire.

"You can't change the past. Only the future." That was what they'd both thought. But what if he couldn't separate one from the other?

Ti opened the book to page after page filled with photos and inscriptions of moments she'd captured this summer.

Memories that were a part of him—a part he didn't want to lose.

She towed herself up by the rail. "Love's enough to heal wounds, Ethan. But only if you let it."

He caught her hand before she turned. "How is she?"

"As work-driven as you are." She laughed. "The poor girl hasn't stopped moving since you left."

That sounded about right. She likely had her hair swept up in that silly bandana with dirt marks smudged over her freckles, turned into a workhorse like she always did when she was brooding.

The thought tightened his stomach. She was probably going crazy with questions. Or worse, guilt. And he was the source.

He'd walked out without giving her the chance to argue. No chance to explain. And instead of pushing, she'd given him time and space. Way more than he deserved.

He let go of Ti's hand and pinched the bridge of his nose. She and Nonna were right. He'd been hiding. From Cass, from regrets. But more than anything, from himself.

Ti climbed up the steps. "You at least gotta come by to get Sandy. I'm not taking him with me."

"With you?" He sprang to his feet. "You're leaving?"

"You didn't think I'd actually make it in the sticks, did you?" She tilted her head. "No offense."

Of course not.

"You're going back to London?"

She shrugged a shoulder. "I never liked the modeling life."

"So, where to, then?"

"The last place I ever thought I'd go." She pointed to a tear in one of her fluorescent orange New Balances. "When the soles of your sneakers start to wear through, it's probably a good sign you need to stop running." Her laugh faded into a pensive expression. "I've run away my whole life. It's time to go home."

"To Queens?"

"Yeah." Her smile held a sense of purpose. "I'm gonna open an art studio for kids in our old neighborhood. Make it sort of an outlet for them. Lord knows they need one."

Ethan held the scrapbook to his side and returned her smile. "It sounds perfect."

"I think so, too." She backed up one more step. "I leave in two weeks, so don't forget about Sandy."

Two weeks? If Sandy couldn't stay at the camp, did that mean . . . ? His hands turned clammy. He didn't want to ask, but the question trekked up his throat. "Did Cass find a buyer?"

She shook her head. "Didn't need to. Her mom finally found the courage to call her dad and fill him in on everything. He's paying off both liens."

Thank God. His shoulders sank with relief. "That's great."

"Yeah. It's kinda crazy how things turned around so quickly. The city even pushed the inspection back to November. She just has to have it done before taking any registrations for next summer."

She swept her long hair over her shoulder. "Oh, and something about some kind of tax cancelation. I didn't get the details, but Cass was floored."

She wasn't the only one. The city must've already decided to take its own action in rectifying some of Mom's mistakes. Regardless of how her trial played out, hopefully she'd find the courage to take responsibility for the rest.

Could he say the same about himself? He grimaced at the pine boards at his feet. What a world-class jerk he'd been.

Ti strolled across the deck and peered behind her once she reached the door. "And Ethan?" She jutted her chin at the scrapbook in his hand. "There are lots of empty pages in the back. Make sure you don't leave them that way." With a telling grin to match her charge, she nodded and slipped inside.

In the quiet, Ethan studied the photo from his and Cass's childhood. Side by side, two lives intersected from the very beginning. He didn't understand the way God worked. He still had more questions than he wanted to admit. But maybe one answer was all he needed.

He flipped through the pages again, conviction building with each turn. The memory of Cass telling him about the journal her dad had given her flooded back as he ran his hand along a blank page at the end.

"I opened it every day the year he left us, but I never wrote in it. Not once. I kept thinking, if I could just figure out how to rewrite my story, it'd be good enough that he'd come back."

Was that how she felt about him, too? The thought burned in his chest and propelled him up the stairs. He couldn't leave the pages empty even if he tried. They'd been writing him home all along.

CHAPTER TWENTY-FOUR

Promises

Showered and trimmed, Ethan threw on a thermal Henley, shook his hair into place, and gripped either side of the sink.

If he stared in the mirror long enough, maybe his reflection would eventually convince him he was more confident than he felt. His nerves hadn't stopped building since Ti left almost four hours ago.

He tapped both his cheeks. "Time to man up."

On his way out, he stopped beside Nonna's chair in the living room to kiss the top of her head.

She whistled. "Now, there's my good-looking grandson."

He waved behind him.

"Ethan?"

With his hand on the doorknob, he turned and met a smile that'd pulled him through a ridiculous number of trials throughout his life.

Nonna stroked Lady's ears and nodded, saying enough through her eyes alone. "*Ti amo.*"

He dipped his chin and opened the door. "Love you, too." More than he could say. "*Ciao.*"

He hustled to his Jeep and swerved out of the driveway. Jeez, his heart could've outraced the engine. What was his deal? This wasn't the first time he'd had to apologize.

His stomach squeezed as he rounded the corner onto the main road. Apologizing he could handle. Her response was what worried him. Would she forgive him? Was it fair to ask?

He shifted into third gear and flicked the air freshener dangling from the rearview mirror. Why did he have to be such a hothead and stay away this long?

The wind rolling off the mountainside curved around the windshield and poured down his collar. Good thing he'd thrown on a thermal. The temperature was dropping faster than the sunset. Then again, if his pulse kept picking up, maybe that was a good thing. *Relax, already.*

A glimpse of the food mart sign passed behind him. He slammed on the brakes, backed up, and pulled into the parking lot for one quick thing. Reinforcements couldn't hurt.

Back on the road, he rotated his neck and shoulders. What was he gonna say to her once he got there? Sorry for being Schmuck of the Year? She had every right to tell him to pack his things. Or not to talk to him at all. He'd certainly played that card well enough himself.

He turned at the sign and released a slow breath. The driveway had never felt longer. Parked between the Passat and smart car, he scanned the quiet property. Someone must've come in to clear out the wreckage left from the fire.

Was the insurance company taking care of it? He could kick himself for missing this last week.

As soon as Ethan shut his door, Sandy's head popped up from the cement slab left where the canteen had been. He scratched his ear with his hind leg and panted.

Ethan crouched and patted his leg. Sandy sprinted over, mounted his front paws on Ethan's thighs, and licked his chin and neck.

"I know, boy. I missed you, too." Ethan lowered Sandy's paws to the ground and pushed up to his feet. "What do you think my chances are that Cass will forgive me as easily?"

Sandy curled his foot over his nose and folded his ears.

Grinning, Ethan rubbed his shaggy head. "Yeah, that's what I'm thinking, too." He looked for any movement inside the mess hall. "You know where she is?"

Sandy stopped panting and tilted his head as if trying to decipher what Ethan asked.

He couldn't help laughing. He gave Sandy's ears another good ruffle and jogged up to the deck.

Inside, he peeked in the office on his way past the stairs. Light from the kitchen trickled down the hall toward Cass's dark bedroom.

A mixed aroma of coffee and pasta slowed his steps. He better not be walking in on them eating dinner. That'd be real classy. He clutched the shopping bag in his hand and poked his head around the doorway.

"Took you long enough." Ti leaned a hip against the counter while scooping up a forkful of pasta from a pan on the stovetop.

He slinked in, still holding his breath until the empty breakfast table came into view. His gaze rebounded toward the pan of lasagna. "You made dinner?"

"Ha. Do I look like I could've made this?" She traded her fork for a coffee mug. "Cass said it was your recipe. Well, minus the meat."

No meat? What was the point? He leaned over the pan. Still smelled delicious, though. No arguing that. He looked from the pan to Ti, her comment finally registering. "Wait, Cass made this? She never cooks."

"Never say never." She poured him a cup of coffee.

He savored the sip. "Now, *that's* perfect."

"It ought to be. The girl's brewed enough of that Italian blend to turn this place into Little Italy." She laughed. "I think the smell reminds her of you."

"Does that mean she doesn't hate me?"

Ti rolled her eyes. "I'm not even gonna answer that."

Fair enough. "Where is she?"

She cast a glance toward the mess hall and back. "Actually, I'm not sure. She was buzzing around the kitchen like a half hour ago. I don't know where she ran off to."

Knowing Cass, she was probably back to work.

Tiny claws landed above his calves. He turned toward expectant eyes looking up at him from a split-colored face. Jax dropped his paws to the floor, rubbed against Ethan's shin, and meowed. Okay, if Jax didn't hate him either, maybe he was luckier than he thought.

"Are we calling it a truce, big guy?" Ethan bent halfway over to pet him, stiffened, and sneezed. "Or, maybe not." He backed up toward the side door. Puffy eyes and a welted neck wasn't the look he was going for right now.

"Try the boathouse," Ti said as he opened the screen.

Good call. Outside, a hazy glow covered the deck from a sky caught between day and night. He stopped above the stairs, looked across the quiet field, and breathed. After almost thirty years of smelling pine and hay, you'd think it would've lost some of its effect.

He shook his head and smiled at the reminder of Ti's words. *"You can travel the world, chasing after something that's missing. But sometimes it takes coming home to remember who you are."*

And who you wanted to be with. He wrapped the excess of the shopping bag around the box inside it and jogged down the stairs to search for the best part of what made this place home.

Taking the long way around, he swung by the softball field, just in case. Two deer lifted their heads from the grass along the far tree line. They had to have some keen ears to hear his movement over the crickets chirping up a storm in the gully.

He crept toward the white bases until a fox's shrill bark stopped him short. The deer darted into the woods, leaving him alone in the empty field.

He laughed. What was he thinking? Cass wouldn't be out here at night by herself. The memory of her latching on to him the day she'd heard a fox for the first time rushed over him. Her soft hands on his arm, the petrified look in her eyes, the panic when she'd realized she'd shown any hint of fear. His laugh faded into an ache. Man, he missed her.

Across the property, he approached the dark boatshed. He tugged on the new lock and peered through the window. The insurance adjuster must've been by already. Either she'd hired someone to clean up the place, or she'd done it herself. He tapped his forehead on the glass. He should've been here.

He flipped around and hunched against the door. Maybe she left when she saw his Jeep pull up. But her car was still here. Did she go for a run? Wouldn't be the first time she went off by herself this late.

The thought clipped into his side. If something happened to her because she was trying to avoid seeing him, he'd . . .

The hill where they'd stretched out under the stars stole his focus. The night replayed in his mind. Their talk, the way she'd let him hold her, their walk to . . . Cassidy's voice hit him between the eyes. *"The camp's been a safe haven for me. This cabin especially."*

He batted himself in the face with the bag and pushed off the door. "Way to be slow on the uptake, DeLuca." Without a flashlight this time, he kept his gaze on the trail, dodging overgrown roots as he went. There better not be any bats swooping above him right now.

In front of the cabin, he hopped over the three steps leading to the porch and stalled at the door. No matter how she reacted to seeing him, he'd say what he'd come to say. He breathed a quick prayer while turning the knob.

The dim overhead light streaked across the bunks lined against both sides of the room. Cass rose from one in the middle, guitar sliding down her side to the floor. Barefoot, she barely stood taller than the top bunk, and everything in him wanted to lift her into his arms.

His heart rate picked up and turned his mouth dry. He fidgeted with the shopping bag as he edged toward her.

Instead of the bandana he'd expected, a white band held her hair back in a loose ponytail above a turquoise sweater that put her hazel eyes in a whole new category of captivating.

His mouth might as well have been swabbed with a dozen cotton balls. He forced down a swallow as his gaze drifted from the stray curls along her neck to her eyes. "Hi."

Really? After all the time you had to think of what to say, you chose "hi"?

"Hey." She ran her hands down her arms and clasped her elbows, probably wondering what the heck he was doing here.

If he could make his mouth work, maybe he could explain. He thrust the bag at her before he crushed the box inside it. "I thought you might need these." That didn't come out right. Wow, he was really batting a thousand, wasn't he?

A slow smile climbed her cheek as she pulled the box of Swedish Fish out. Okay, maybe he wasn't completely striking out.

"I turned the mart upside down, looking for the oldest expiration date. Turns out people only stock fresh candy. Weird, right?" He nudged her with his arm.

Her lips hitched to the left. "They're missing out."

How had he gone a week without seeing that impish grin every day?

Her arm sagged to her side, her smile following.

He gripped the bedpost to keep from reaching for her. Garnering a smile from her was one thing. Getting her to take him back was another thing entirely.

A deep breath expanded across her shoulders. She lowered her head and toyed with the corner of the box. "I haven't stopped thinking of how to apologize if you came back. And now that you're here . . ."

He smoothed his fingers over her cheek, wanting to take away any guilt he'd caused her. What he'd do to rewind time and never leave.

She set her hand over his. "I'm so sorry, Ethan. For all of it. I had no idea. I . . . I honestly don't know what to say."

"Maybe that's because I'm the one who needs to apologize." He inched closer, breath coming hard and fast as his fingers wove into her hair. He brushed his thumb over her soft cheek. God help him. If he stayed this close to her, he'd never get the words out.

Praying again for strength, he backed up and turned. "It's not your fault."

"How can you say that? You heard what Jesse said."

The turmoil in her voice resonated across the floorboards and held his insides in a vice grip. "The condemnation part? Yeah, I did. And like an idiot, I latched on to it."

He circled to face her. "I'm sorry for giving into anger. For directing it at you, at myself. At anyone. Truth is, no one knows for sure how the fire started. Even if it was from that cigarette, it was an accident, Cass."

She tossed the box of candy onto the mattress. "An accident that cost your sister her life."

"And one that connected your life to mine." He started for her but stopped and craned his head toward the rafters. "I can't tell you the number of times I've tried to rewrite the past. Or worse, pretend it never happened. But we can't. You know that as much as I do. The past is a part of us. It always will be." He lowered his gaze to her tear-filled eyes. "But it's just *one* part."

Slow strides brought him near her again. "I'm not saying we can make it through life without regrets. But I'd rather stumble through a hundred mistakes with you than walk alone, pretending my world makes sense without you."

He lifted his hand to her curls. "I've missed you, Cass. I've missed finding random strands of your hair on all my shirts."

Her mouth pursed beneath her freckled nose.

Laughing, he traced her cheekbone and glided his thumb over the corner of her tight lips. "I've missed facing this headstrong expression every day. I've missed fighting with you, hearing you laugh, watching you work with such drive and commitment."

He unfolded her arms and ran his fingers down to hers. "I've spent so long running from home, from myself. And after only one week with you, I found both."

Her lashes pressed together. Tears coursed off her chin onto her sweater.

He let go of her hand and cupped her cheek. "I can't promise I won't ever disappoint you. Or that I won't always want to try to fix things when I shouldn't." Heart racing, he waited for her eyes to find his. "But I promise not to leave you again. No matter how hard it gets."

A smile caught her tears. "Even when I'm scared and push you away?"

"As long as you don't sick bats on me."

She slapped his shoulder and slid her arms around his neck.

He leaned back just far enough to see the sassy grin that'd hooked him from the beginning. "*Sono innamorato di te.*" He searched her eyes. "I'm in love with you, Cassidy McAdams. I think I always have been."

Breathing in everything that made her *her*, he sank into the place he belonged. Her lips moved against his, soft and slow. Sensations traveled down his body, but it was more than attraction. More than the pull to comfort her or the need to protect her. It ran deeper. To a place inside him he could finally draw from.

Her fingers drifted from his neck and trailed down his chest. Her lashes swept toward him, hazel eyes more vulnerable than ever. His stomach knotted. What was she thinking?

She picked up her guitar and set it on the bed beside them. "My dad forwarded an email from his contact at Cornell." A torn smile pulled at her lips. "You're in. You can start this fall."

He'd gotten the same email, but it still seemed surreal. Did she think he'd go without her? Was that what she was worried about? "Ithaca's close enough to make trips home on the weekends to check on the camp and Nonna. We can both find apartments there. Take Sandy with us." He circled around the bunk and swayed his head. "And Jax."

A grin hiked up her cheek. "Can't forget Jax."

"Never." He curled the tips of his fingers under hers, sincerity taking hold. "Come with me."

"And leave all this?" Her laugh petered as she took in the rustic cabin. "I can't."

She moved to the window and rested her arms on the sill. "Now that they're holding Nick on arson charges, it should be a little less dramatic around here. The insurance company's covering most of the damage, and my dad's helping me brainstorm ways to generate capital during the off seasons, so . . ." She turned and raised her shoulders. "I think we're gonna be okay."

"You asked your dad for help?" He pitched a brow.

She slanted one right back. "This really obnoxious person once told me it's okay to accept help every now and then."

"Oh, really." He edged closer. "Sounds like a pretty wise guy."

"He has his moments."

Ethan tipped his head back. "Not nearly as many as you."

"Glad we agree on something."

Still laughing, he curved an arm around her waist. "I'm proud of you, Cass. I know calling your dad wasn't easy."

She shrugged. "It's kind of hard to deny someone forgiveness when you need it as much as they do."

He couldn't look away from her—this incredible girl who had no idea how brave she was. Through everything, he'd thought he was here to show her how to open her heart, but she'd been the one opening his the whole time.

Her forehead creased. "What?"

He laced his fingers behind her back. "I was just thinking I have no idea what happens after today. I don't have any answers. Except that we'll figure it out together."

She wrapped her arms around him. "Promise?"

"With all I am." Pressing a hand to her lower back, he brought her to him. He might not be able to vow he'd never hold her too tightly, but there was one promise he'd cling to the rest of his life. He'd never let her go.

Home

One Year Later

Cass closed her pen inside her journal, laid it beside a planter filled with dahlias, and leafed through the day's mail until a letter from Ti tipped out.

Smiling, she tore into it. Hearing the primary week campers playing in the background made her miss her childhood best friend all the more.

Ethan came through the screen door in low-hanging jeans and a long-sleeved white shirt against his tan skin, possibly looking more attractive than he did in his navy blue T-shirts. It wasn't fair for him to make her heart race with just one glance.

He crossed the deck, grin hitching sideways as though he heard her thoughts. "Something caught your eye?"

She fought a grin and shrugged. "Nothing special."

"Oh, really?" In front of her, he set his coffee on the rail and leaned in until his lips brushed her neck. "Nothing at all?" His warm breath and whiskers hummed against her skin.

Forcing her pulse to slow, she pressed him back. "Well, I did get a letter from Ti."

"Who can compete with that?" He laughed and picked his coffee up again. "How's the art studio going?"

"Great. She has two other employees now, so she's free to come up next weekend and paint the mural on the canteen like we talked about."

He looked across the field to the newly built structure surrounded by campers bouncing around on sugar rushes. "Think it's big enough?"

Cass rested her chin against his shoulder and followed his gaze. "Considering this *incredibly talented* soon-to-be architect designed and built it, I'd say it's perfect."

Another laugh slipped around his coffee mug. "You might be slightly biased."

"Maybe, but I hear the professors at Cornell aren't. They didn't give you an A on the project for no reason."

He returned his coffee to the rail and draped her arms around his waist. "And you thought *I* was the one who saw other's potential."

He ran his hand through her curls, eyes a bottomless blue. "Thanks for believing in me. But if it's okay with you, I think I'll finish the rest of my degree online."

"You don't like the classroom?"

"I don't like being apart from you." His dimples sank even deeper. "As much as I love long motorcycle rides, only getting to see each other on the weekends doesn't really fit into my plans."

She slid her hands up his solid chest and laced them around his neck. "Since when did you start living by plans?"

"Since my OCD fiancée started rubbing off on me."

She tugged the back of his hair. "Sounds like she's a keeper."

"For life." His lips found hers. Tender, reassuring.

His promise blended with the sensation of his touch and stoked the sense of awe she hadn't stopped feeling since he'd proposed. The love that'd carried them through everything and led them to where they were now overwhelmed her at times.

Still cupping her face, he rested his forehead to hers. "Next month can't get here fast enough."

No kidding. Just the thought of waiting four more weeks to get married was torturous.

"By the way," he said. "Nonna said we better stop checking on her as much, or she's going to return the wedding gift she got us."

She laughed. "Oh, yeah? What's the gift?"

His dimples curved. "An espresso machine."

"Oooh. Guess we better back off, then." Laughter and thoughts mingled as the first time she met Nonna replayed in her mind. So much had happened since then.

He leaned back and studied her eyes. "You okay?"

"Yeah. Just thinking." She toyed with the hem of her shirt. "Do you have any regrets about giving up fire fighting full-time?"

He tilted his head. "Cass . . ."

A little brown-haired girl flew up the stairs and bounded into his legs. "Mr. Ethan. Mr. Ethan. Are you gonna build us a campfire tonight?"

He scooped her up and shifted her onto his hip. "I don't know. You think I should?"

"You're the bestest at making fires. Pleeeease!"

Cass bit her shirt cuff to stifle a laugh. She couldn't be any cuter. The little girl slid the end of her long ponytail between her lips, hopeful eyes looking up at him.

Based on the pictures Cass had seen, she could've been a younger version of Ethan's sister. Her heart squeezed at the image. Seeing the way he interacted with the campers always left her undone.

Ethan scrunched his face into a look of deliberation. "Okay, I'll do it." He winked and set her down. "Just for you."

Beaming, she scurried back down the stairs. "Cynthia, he'll do it," she called to a friend.

He watched the girls skip off to the boxball court, his smile almost as wide as theirs.

He inched toward Cass again. His fingertips curled under hers, and oceans of promise met her gaze. He lifted her hand to his lips and kissed the skin around her engagement ring. "Cass, a second doesn't go by without my knowing I'm *exactly* where I belong."

So was she. Smack in the middle of the one thing she finally understood was enough.

Grace.

Ethan brought their joined hands to his side and bobbed his brows. "Speaking of which. The creek's calling. How about a little canoe ride?"

She looked over to the boxball game underway. "There's—
"

"No more work to be done."

Her focus darted back to him. He was right. They'd finished all the renovations, passed the inspection, and brought the books into balance. They had an amazing staff of counselors and enough camp registrations this summer to carry them through the offseason. It was time to enjoy it all.

She let go of his hand and tried to keep a straight face. "I should probably stay with the campers."

"One . . ."

She folded her arms. "Don't start, Ethan. I—"

"Two . . ."

"I'm telling you. You don't want to race me."

He flaunted her sassy grin right back. "Thr—"

Launching off a giant shove to his chest, she soared down the stairs and across the gravel toward the boatshed.

"You're still a cheater, Cassidy McAdams," he called while chasing after her.

"And you're still an instigator."

He caught her around the waist and swept her up from behind. They twirled in a circle before he returned her feet to the grass. "Guess that makes us a good team."

She traced her fingers over his scruffy cheek. "For life." The one she never thought she'd be living.

Sunshine and laughter curled around her with the sights and sounds that filled the blank pages of her journal every day. And as she sank into Ethan's arms, she settled further into the joy of finding where she was always meant to be.

Home.

ACKNOWLEDGEMENTS

Dave, thanks for giving me a home I can curl into no matter what outside circumstances shake our walls.

Erynn, you have some superpowers of your own, girl. Thanks for the countless ways you helped me polish this story and for reminding me it'd be okay when I possibly might have wanted to freak out. I'm beyond blessed to get to partner with such a stellar editor and friend.

Melanie, years back, I prayed for God to connect me with the right critique partner. As with most things, I'm amazed at His faithfulness. I would've been one hot mess working through this manuscript and launch without our deluge of phone-anxiety-free emails and much-needed long-distance hugs. Thanks for all the brainstorming, processing, and laughs along the way.

Victorine, thanks for working with me through all the nit-picky tweaks that resulted in a gorgeous cover I can't stop admiring with starry eyes.

Franky, Rachel, Victorine, and Melanie, thanks for the many ways your insights, feedback, and encouragement have helped to fine-tune this story. Our critique group has been a joy to work with.

Mom and Rachel, your support alone have kept me afloat numerous times throughout this journey. Thank you for sowing into this book with your sharp proofing skills as well. Grammar Nazis unite!

Jacqui, thanks for ensuring my Spanish was accurate.

To readers who've taken the time to leave a review or send an email to share how much you've enjoyed a character or story, you've encouraged my heart more than I can say. Thanks for sharing in this beautiful, messy, compelling thing we all love, called art.

Proof

Made in the USA
Charleston, SC
28 January 2016